Gabriel's heart was racing. Nothing was going the way they had planned.

Or was it?

He looked over at Hollis, whose head was thrown back, his mouth open in awe. His expression showed nothing less than rapture. In that moment Gabriel understood the truth, knew even before Alec turned toward him, draping his arm over Gabriel's shoulder, knew even before Alec said, "She's gonna get just what she deserves, man." Knew at last, with chilling terror, that this had been the real plan all along.

Gem had reached the side of the building now and was running toward the dirt road that separated them. Her face shimmered with the glow of fire. The smoke seemed to lift her boyish hair—fine and wispy as spider threads—into the night air. Her darks eyes, flaming like coals, locked onto Gabriel's, and she did not look away.

Gabriel doubled over as if he'd taken a blow to the stomach. Somewhere in his mind a voice was screaming over and over, *This can't be happening. This isn't real.*

But there was Gem, only a few yards from the propane tank, and the fire was closing in.

SHADOW PEOPLE

Joyce McDonald

LAUREL-LEAF BOOKS

Published by
Dell Laurel-Leaf
an imprint of
Random House Children's Books
a division of Random House, Inc.
1540 Broadway,
New York, New York 10036

Visit us on the Web! www.randomhouse.com/teens
Educators and librarians, for a variety of teaching tools, visit us at
www.randomhouse.com/teachers

ISBN 0-440-22807-7

Reprinted by arrangement with Delacorte Press

Printed in the United States of America

March 2002

10 9 8 7 6 5 4 3 2 1

OPM

To the RiverStone Writers:

Pat Brisson, Denise Brunkus, Sally Keehn,
Trinka Hakes Noble, Pamela Curtis Swallow,
and Elvira Woodruff,
for all the special moments we have shared

one

They couldn't rip things apart fast enough. They over-turned the soda machine. They slashed the cushions for the lawn furniture that were stacked beneath the over-hang in front of the camp store. They pulled fistfuls of white polyester filler from the gashes. Two of them hurled a metal lawn chair through one of the front windows. Glass shattered, spraying in all directions.

Alec Stryker smashed the sole of his boot against the front door. It sprang open without protest. Gabriel and Lydia stumbled past him, followed by Hollis, who moved with slow determination, seeming to savor each moment.

The store was only one small room at the front of a larger building. A few feet inside an old-fashioned cash register, its empty drawer half open, sat on the rustic pine counter. Gabriel Hart stared at it. The drawer made him

1

think of a tongue hanging from a thirsty mouth. He looked away, glad no one was around to hear them break in. Kate Hennessey, who owned the place, and her niece, Gem, were in Virginia at a funeral. Alec had sworn to it. For the moment, anyway, Gabriel forced himself not to think about Gem. If he did, he would bolt for the woods and never stop running.

While the others smashed a display case filled with silver and turquoise jewelry, Gabriel halfheartedly looked around for something to break, finally grabbing the glass pot from the Mr. Coffee machine and smacking it hard against the counter until it shattered. He had to at least try to make it look like he was into the trashing.

Lydia Misurella stood on the other side of the room watching him intently. One by one she pulled postcards of the camp from the card rack and tore them into pieces. The look she gave Gabriel was knowing and intimate. But he turned away, searching for something else to destroy.

Across the room a refrigerator with a glass door stood almost empty except for a few bottles of Snapple and a six-pack of Coke. Gabriel looked around for something heavy. Something to smash into the door. But then a row of T-shirts and sweatshirts, each with the name Stony Brook Campgrounds emblazoned across the front, caught his attention. With one sweep of his arm they were on the floor. He wiped his muddy hiking boots on the shirts, grinding his heels into them, pretending it was Alec

Stryker's face. His jaw was so tight it felt as if his teeth might crack.

A few minutes ago Alec Stryker and Hollis Feeney had been like dark shadows darting about the room, pulling shelves from the walls, letting their contents crash to the floor. But when Gabriel looked up from the muddy mess of torn and tangled shirts, Hollis was no longer there.

Gabriel stepped outside, pretending to look for him. It was an excuse not to have to watch Alec and Lydia as they continued to trash the store, and he knew it. He leaned against the front of the building. A heavy white frost had begun to settle over everything. Gabriel's nose and fingers were almost numb. Clouds of his breath circled his head.

Inside the building Alec was laughing. Gabriel heard the shatter of glass and knew Alec had broken the door of the refrigerator. Other sounds—the crunch of metal, the thud of heavy wood—he was not so sure about and was surprised to discover he did not want to turn around to look.

The woods across the dirt road beckoned him. He had a sudden urge to make a run for it, but he shoved aside any thoughts of deserting the others. In a few minutes they would realize he wasn't in the store and call him. And he would go. He always did. For a brief moment he squeezed his eyes closed, as if he could shut out everything that was happening.

When he opened them, he saw the tops of the trees, the bare black branches spread across an almost moonless sky, looking like dark exposed veins. Tonight was not like those other times. The rush—the blood pumping so fast through his veins it threatened to burst through his skin—wasn't there. Only one thing was the same. None of what was happening seemed real. If it hadn't been for the sting of the cold on his hands and face, he might have made himself believe he was dreaming. And that would have been fine with him.

Gabriel was still leaning against the front of the store when Alec and Lydia came through the door. Alec headed straight for the woods. A silver and turquoise necklace dangled from his bulging back pocket, and Gabriel knew, despite Hollis's warning not to take anything, that Alec had been helping himself to the jewelry from the smashed display case.

Lydia, who had been right behind Alec, stopped when she saw Gabriel and leaned into him, squinting in the dim, icy moonlight. Her face was so close to his he could smell the lavender soap she always used. Lydia ran her cold finger along his jaw. "Let's get out of here," she whispered.

Gabriel shivered at her touch just as something crashed through the side window. A bright light flashed from somewhere behind him. He whipped around to see flames licking at the pine counter, streaking across the floor toward the windows, lapping at the sills as if trying to get out.

The smell of gasoline stung his nose. Lydia, in a panic, began pulling at his arm. From the edge of the woods

Alec shouted for them to get the hell away from the building.

Lydia began to run. Gabriel followed her just as the other front window—the one they hadn't broken—exploded from the heat.

The three of them stood across the road, watching, transfixed. Then Hollis appeared, seemingly out of nowhere. He stood a few feet apart from the others.

Alec came up behind Gabriel. He could smell the beer on Alec's breath. "When it reaches that propane tank, all hell's gonna break loose." Alec pointed to the large tank that stood about twenty feet from the left side of the building.

Gabriel stared at him as if Alec had lost his mind. No one had said anything about setting the place on fire. That was not part of the plan.

He looked over at Lydia, whose expression was as stunned as his own.

The wind picked up, sweeping through the branches. The fire leaped from the building, tearing through the dry winter grass, swallowing everything in sight.

From the nearby wolf preserve came frantic howls. The wolves smelled the smoke. Gabriel could almost feel their panic, could imagine them tearing at the fencing in desperation, digging frantically to escape beneath it. In a single, chilling moment he realized that more than the camp store might be destroyed that night.

Lydia yanked his arm, shouting something about the wolves. But he couldn't seem to move. He watched in horror as hungry tongues of flame licked the bases of ancient oaks. For one confused and terrifying second, he thought he saw Gem's face through the smoke. That was impossible. She was in Virginia with her aunt. But no. It *was* her. She was holding something over her nose and mouth, a towel maybe, or a sweater, as she ran through the smoke toward the camp store.

Gabriel's heart was racing. Nothing was going the way they had planned.

Or was it?

He looked over at Hollis, whose head was thrown back, his mouth open in awe. His expression showed nothing less than rapture. In that moment Gabriel understood the truth, knew even before Alec turned toward him, draping his arm over Gabriel's shoulder, knew even before Alec said, "She's gonna get just what she deserves, man." Knew at last, with chilling terror, that this had been the real plan all along.

Gem had reached the side of the building now and was running toward the dirt road that separated them. Her face shimmered with the glow of fire. The smoke seemed to lift her boyish hair—fine and wispy as spider threads—into the night air. Her darks eyes, flaming like coals, locked onto Gabriel's, and she did not look away.

Gabriel doubled over as if he'd taken a blow to the stomach. Somewhere in his mind a voice was screaming over and over, *This can't be happening. This isn't real.*

But there was Gem, only a few yards from the propane tank, and the fire was closing in.

two

Cold water sliced across Gabriel Hart's back like
shards of ice. The pain forced his eyes open as he
turned the knob in the shower from cold to hot. Each
morning he did this to make sure he was still breathing,
to convince his body it wanted to face another day. He
had done this every day since his brother, Ben, had been
murdered.

He watched thick white suds slide from his chest.
According to his psychologist, Angela Cortes, if he could
ground himself in the present, focus on the task at hand,
it would keep the other images, images of what those last
few minutes of his brother's life must have been like, from
sucking him into that dark place that was his rage.

Whenever that happened, he began to plot what he
would do when the police finally caught the thugs who

7

were responsible for Ben's death. He liked to imagine how he would sneak into the prison dressed as a guard, how he would gain access to their cells, one by one; how he would tie them with thick rope, letting it cut into their wrists; how he would tape their mouths with silver duct tape so they couldn't scream for help. Then he would whisper barely an inch from their ears what he planned to do to them, so that in those minutes before he finally let them die, they would feel the same unspeakable terror his brother had felt.

Whenever Dr. Cortes tried to get Gabriel to talk about what it was he planned to do to these murderers, his eyes glazed over and he grew silent. He liked Dr. Cortes well enough, but there were some places he did not allow her to go.

It had been almost four months and so far the police had few leads. Gabriel's parents had been putting up a good front, but he could see they had lost hope. They didn't expect the police to find Ben's murderers. Neither did Gabriel, but it didn't matter. He was determined that one day he would find them, even if the police didn't. Because someone had to pay for this.

At his weekly sessions with Dr. Cortes, they sat on the floor, their backs against chairs. Sometimes she had food, which they shared. At their last session they had polished off a whole supersized bag of barbecue potato chips before his hour was up.

Sometimes she sat across from him dressed in jeans, sometimes in a fleece sweat suit, watching him draw pictures on the rug with his finger. He wondered if she was trying to make something out of the lines he left in the carpet pile.

Gabriel's sister, Shelby, and his mother and father met with Dr. Cortes too. But they had never talked to her as a family. Not yet, anyway. And now it seemed they never would. It was too far to travel from their new home to the city. According to his father, they would find another psychologist. But so far that hadn't happened.

Two weeks ago, the day before the movers had shown up, Gabriel had seen Dr. Cortes for his last visit. He tried to convince himself it didn't make any difference. No one, not Dr. Cortes, or his father, or anyone else, could sway him from his mission. The need for revenge was so powerful it filled every cell in his body. It turned his insides bright red. He could see it when he closed his eyes, a fiery glare behind his eyelids.

Someone was pounding on the bathroom door. He knew it was Shelby. Neither his father nor his mother ever made a fist.

"I need to get in there."

A moment of silence. Shelby was waiting for his response. When it didn't come, she pounded again. "I'm going to miss the school bus."

Gabriel turned off the water, reached for a towel, and secured it around his waist like a sarong. The steam was so thick, he couldn't see his face in the mirror to shave. Wiping off the glass was pointless. The steam sneaked back even before he could change the blade in his razor.

Shelby had stopped pounding and was attempting to

reason with him. This amused him, so he let her go on even though he wasn't ready to open the door. "Can I just get my toothbrush? I'll use the powder room. Just let me get my toothbrush and the toothpaste, okay?"

Shelby was five years younger than he was and would be starting seventh grade that morning. Her battles with Gabriel were futile. She rarely won. So over the years she had devised methods of working around him. Usually they involved bartering with information he'd just as soon didn't reach his father, or some other annoying threat.

He waited to see what the price would be this time.

"Dad says you have to drive me to school if I miss the bus."

"In your dreams," he shouted through the door.

When they had lived on the Upper West Side, they had never owned a car or needed one. If they had someplace to go, they took the subway, or a bus, or a cab. Now they had two cars because they were miles from civilization— at least five miles from the nearest town. A town so small you could walk from one end of Main Street to the other in less than two minutes.

The day his father bought the secondhand Explorer— a dark green SUV with creamy beige seats so soft you didn't even struggle when they swallowed you up— Gabriel knew they were moving to a place so foreign, so desolate, that they might never return. A place where they could end up dinner for coyotes or wild dogs. Or reduced to writhing masses of pain by the poisonous bites of timber rattlers. Or mauled by four-hundred-pound black bears who hated human intruders. No doubt about it. His parents had lost their minds.

For Gabriel they had bought a dull silver Toyota Corolla almost ten years old. His mother said it was good enough to get him to and from school. Gabriel agreed. He didn't care one way or the other what he drove.

He had hated leaving the city. That September was the start of his senior year. All his friends were at his old school. He wanted to graduate with them, not with a bunch of strangers. For his dad to uproot them now was a treacherous betrayal. And the only way Gabriel had been able to cope with his double-crossing father was to hate him. He had barely spoken to him for three months, the length of time it had taken his father to secure the mortgage for the house on Thorn Hill Road, somewhere in the desolate mountains of northwestern New Jersey.

Shelby was kicking the lower part of the door. Gabriel turned the lock, holding his hand steadily over the doorknob, waiting for just the right moment. When he yanked open the door, Shelby's kick propelled her through the doorway onto the floor. She grabbed the toilet seat to break her fall just as a rush of steam escaped into the hall.

Gabriel laughed, pleased with his timing.

"You're a stupid *jerk*," she shouted up at him.

He knew this was true, but that didn't keep him from laughing even louder.

The mirror had begun to clear. Gabriel squirted a small mountain of shaving cream into the palm of his hand and smoothed it along his jaw.

Shelby untangled herself from the floor. She was all arms and legs, tall and gangly, with no figure yet to speak of. Her straight brown hair was pulled back into a pony-tail with a purple scrunchie.

When she reached for her toothbrush, a flash of bright blue startled Gabriel. Shelby's nails were thick and long, and heavy with several coats of nail polish. His sister was a nail-biter from way back. Gabriel could still detect the rough red skin around her cuticles, and that was when he realized the nails were fake. But that wasn't what bothered him. What he found unsettling was the scrawny twelve-year-old standing next to him, who had never shown an interest in anything "feminine," who had been a tomboy from the time she could crawl, suddenly flaunting these grown-up fingernails.

Gabriel rested the hand holding the razor on the edge of the sink. He tried to think of a snide remark, but Shelby had already grabbed her toothbrush and the toothpaste and was halfway down the hall.

A half hour later he was heading down Thorn Hill Road in the old Toyota on his way to school, driving be-neath branches cocooned in cotton-candy–like sacks filled with webworms that had stripped them of their leaves. The bare limbs formed a bony canopy overhead. There was no doubt about it. This place gave him the creeps.

Lydia Misurella barely caught a glimpse of the silver Toyota as it passed by the end of her driveway a few hundred yards away. She was too busy flailing her arms, trying to shoo away the swarm of grackles that had gathered in the sycamore outside her bedroom window. But she knew the car belonged to the new boy up the road. She had seen the family move in a few weeks ago, had seen the boy from a distance as she rode by on Millie, her family's dappled mare, hoping to get a closer look.

The grackles' screeching only grew defiantly louder when she tried to scare them off.

"Stupid birds," Lydia screamed at them. Their annoying cackles set her on edge. Every nerve buzzed like a bee beneath her skin.

She slammed the window shut even though it was already eighty degrees outside. She slipped on a short, dark purple print skirt, a navy T-shirt, and black sandals, then swept up her backpack and headed down to the kitchen, spoiling for a fight.

Her brothers, Jacob and Steven, sat at the kitchen table listening to their father lay out the morning's assignments. Both boys were home-schooled. It amazed her that neither seemed to mind.

Lydia, however, had threatened to run away from home if her parents wouldn't let her go to the local high school. After two aborted attempts—one of which resulted in an overnight stay at the Jersey shore—her parents finally agreed to let her go to the regional school. It was a battle Lydia had been prepared to wage again and again if she had to, until she turned eighteen in a few months. It was bad enough she was isolated from the rest of civilization

13

in this stupid log cabin—a large two-story log house, really, but to Lydia, it might as well have been a one-room mud shack. Being trapped night and day with her parents, like poor Jacob and Steven, would be unbearable. She couldn't imagine how the boys stood it.

Jacob, who was three years younger than Lydia and would have been a freshman this year, didn't seem to care one way or the other. He sat at the round oak table in his olive green T-shirt and camouflage army fatigue pants, firing dry Cheerios off a spoon, watching them hit the wall across the room, and occasionally Steven's head, until his father snatched the spoon from his hand and slammed it into the sink with a loud clatter.

Steven, who was two years younger than his brother, sat patiently waiting for his father to calm down. Lydia thought the two of them didn't even look like brothers. Not even close. Steven's soft blond hair was so long it covered his ears and rested on the tops of his glasses. He wore only a T-shirt and a pair of baggy cargo shorts. Jacob, who was tall for his age, and big, had no hair at all. He shaved his head almost every day, although right now a dark stubble sprouted in protest.

Lydia set her backpack on the counter and grabbed a slice of bread from the open loaf of Wonder bread on the table.

Her father looked up from Steven's math book. "You're going to be late."

Arthur Misurella was a small, nervous man with wire-rimmed glasses like Steven's, and a receding hairline.

Lydia stared at him for a minute, then shrugged. She stripped a piece of crust from the bread and popped it into her mouth. As far as she was concerned, this man wasn't even her father. What he said or didn't say was irrelevant to her. Ever since he'd given up a perfectly respectable job as managing editor of a newspaper and dragged his family from their comfortable colonial house in Rolling Hills four years ago to begin what Lydia thought of as a totally insane career—if you could even call it a career—she had more or less mentally divorced herself from the family. She had been thirteen at the time.

Now they lived in the wilderness—by Lydia's standards, practically on the moon—and the ex–managing editor had carved out a new career writing popular books on the art of survival, had his own Web site, and published a monthly newsletter, which he sent to other paranoid survivalists.

In the course of four years he had built the log house, a barn, two sheds, three hydroponic greenhouses, and a bomb shelter on fifteen wooded acres at the top of a ridge in the Kittatinny Mountains. The family shared this land with two cows, chickens, a rooster, four goats, and a half dozen sheep. Her father had recently fenced off a section of open field for three horses, convinced that one day there would be no gasoline available to run their Pathfinder or the pickup. He reasoned that they would need the horses for transportation.

In the basement were two freezers. One held food. The other—an old secondhand freezer—was unplugged. This was where Arthur Misurella stockpiled his ammunition. Hundreds of rounds and clips for his rifles and handguns. The rest of the basement was taken up with shelves crammed with canned goods, medical supplies, and gas masks.

He had trained his sons to hunt, trap, and even poach late at night. They had learned to shear sheep and tan the hides of the deer they'd shot. Lydia and her mother had learned to milk the cows and goats.

But worst of all, her father had forbidden his family to make friends with any of the neighbors. They weren't to so much as wave to any of them as they drove by. Because according to her father, when things started to fall apart—whatever that meant (Lydia was never sure)—the people in the surrounding area would try to break into the Misurellas' house and take what they needed to survive. It would be much easier, her father had explained, to shoot a stranger than a friend and neighbor.

Four years they had lived on the mountain, and Lydia did not know the name of a single one of her neighbors, except for the Steens, whose name was hand-painted in calligraphy on their mailbox. The rule also applied to the people she knew from school. Her father had forbidden her to talk about her family or their survival plans to anyone. She was never to bring anyone to the house. All these years Lydia hadn't had a single close friend. But she didn't much like the kids at Mountain View Regional anyway. They kept their distance. She kept hers. Until now. Lydia smiled and thought of the new boy and his family. Maybe it was time to test her father's stupid rule.

She fingered the nose ring in the pocket of her skirt. As soon as she was out the door, she would put it on. Her father had almost lost it when she came home one Saturday afternoon with a pierced nose. That didn't surprise her. There was little about her that her father liked, including her waist-length, honey-colored hair, which she wore parted in the middle, and which more often than not hung over half her face. He was always asking her who she was hiding from. *If he only knew,* Lydia thought.

She grabbed her backpack and headed for the door, still smiling about the nose ring. She had yet to tell him about the tattoos. She was saving that for the right time. She had had the tattoos since last May. They were of her chosen totems: a tiny head of a timber wolf on her left hip and a small red-tailed hawk below her right shoulder, just where she would sprout wings if she were a bird, or if humans could fly.

three

Gem Hennessey made it to homeroom just as the last bell rang. She slid into her chair and ran her fingers through her short dark hair while taking a quick survey of the familiar faces, many of which she had been looking at every school day since she was a freshman.

She stretched her long legs under the desk, hung her thumbs on the pockets of her khakis, and slouched down in her seat. The khakis were a mistake. It was much too hot to wear long pants. She should have worn a short skirt or shorts.

Over by the window three guys squabbled loudly over whether Wayne Gretzky should have retired from the Rangers or put in a few more years on the ice, which led to an even louder argument about Michael Jordan's retirement from the Bulls. Across the aisle from Gem, Pru

Zimmerman was putting what must have been the fiftieth coat of black polish on her nails. In the seat ahead of her Marcy Hatcher was attempting to comb her hair without removing the earphones of her Discman, while signaling to Gem to check out Brian Steadman and Zoe Pratt, who were huddled in a corner at the back of the room, making out. No one paid any attention to Ms. Kessler, who was making a valiant attempt to get through the attendance roster.

Ms. Kessler, who was also the chemistry teacher, finally raised her voice to a near-earsplitting level, busting her way through the noise. Within seconds the room was totally silent. No other teacher at Mountain View Regional could do that. But Anita Kessler, who barely stood five foot three inches, had the gift. "Matthew Abrams!"

From the back of the room came a forceful "Yo!"

"Erin Atwell."

Just as Erin Atwell was about to acknowledge her presence, a boy Gem didn't recognize showed up at the door. He stood half in, half out of the room, one hand clamped around the strap of his backpack, holding it so it wouldn't slip off his shoulder. Gem thought she had never seen anyone quite so beautiful. Not handsome, really. Not by conventional standards. But there was something about him. She felt drawn to him with such force that she was surprised to look down and see that she was still in her seat.

Marcy Hatcher turned around and grinned at Gem. "Oooo. Fresh meat."

Gem gave her a poke in the shoulder. "Sexist."

Ms. Kessler, who was only two years out of graduate school and wearing a very short flowered dress, actually blinked twice, then lowered her head, keeping her eyes on the list of names in front of her. "May I help you?"

The boy took a few steps toward her desk, then let the backpack slide from his shoulder and land by his feet, as if he needed a rest from the heavy load.

Outwardly, there didn't seem to be anything exceptional about him. He wore jeans, a light blue T-shirt with a cotton plaid shirt unbuttoned over it, and sneakers. His hair was an ashy dark blond, slightly wavy and a little on the shaggy, unkempt side. He kept brushing it away, unsuccessfully, from his forehead. He was tall and thin, with hands that had long tapered fingers. It was the hands that caught Gem's attention. They had a grace, an ease, that the rest of the boy's body lacked.

The boy handed a bunch of papers to Ms. Kessler, who glanced through them, then looked up at the class.

"Everyone—" Again Ms. Kessler's voice swelled to squelch out the laughing and talking. "This is Gabriel Hart. He'll be joining us for his senior year."

An awkward silence fell over the room as all eyes turned to stare at the new boy standing by Ms. Kessler's desk.

"Would you like to tell us a little about yourself?" Ms. Kessler asked him.

"Not especially."

Gem smiled. Kids weren't usually that direct with Ms. Kessler.

Ms. Kessler gave him a curt nod. "Well, take your seat then." She pointed to an empty desk two rows behind Gem.

Gabriel picked up his backpack and maneuvered his way between the desks to the empty one at the end of the row.

He gave Gem a brief nod as he walked by, and she saw that his eyes were hazel, not quite brown, not quite green. She could imagine them changing color depending on what he wore.

It turned out that Gabriel Hart was also in her English class. So when Gem walked into the room and saw him sitting in the last row by the window, she walked right over to the empty seat beside him, dropped her backpack on the floor, and held out her hand. "Gem Hennessey," she said.

Gabriel stared at the open hand, then gently slipped his hand into hers. Gem thought her legs might go right out from under her. She hadn't given any thought to his touch, what it would be like. Now she couldn't seem to get it out of her mind, even after she'd let go of his hand and taken her seat. The feel of his skin against hers lingered on her palm where she wanted to hold on to it forever.

At the front of the room their English teacher, Mr. Sorensen, rambled on about what he expected from them this semester. Gem couldn't seem to hold on to a single word he said. But she did notice that Lydia Misurella, Mountain View Regional's resident recluse, who sat two seats in front of her, had been glancing over her shoulder at Gabriel almost the entire period.

Gem parked the red Toyota pickup in the lot by the main building of her aunt's campgrounds. Her great-aunt, Kate Hennessey, owned two trucks and a jeep, and let her use the Toyota for traveling back and forth to school and for running errands.

From the front the fieldstone building appeared small, not more than twenty feet wide at most, with two large glass windows on either side of the door. But from the side you could see it was much larger, at least fifty feet long, housing rest rooms and showers, one side for men, the other for women. The main desk and camp store were in the front room.

Gem stopped to pull old notices from the community bulletin board on the side of the building, crumpling them into a ball and tossing them in the outdoor trash can. Then she paused at the soda machine, which sat on the concrete slab in front of the building, an area sheltered by an overhang supported by roughly hewn log posts. She studied the selection, put her coins in the machine, and waited for the can of Coke to thump into the tray below.

From inside the store the soothing sounds of Native American flute music emanated from her aunt's portable CD player. Gem tapped on the window, waved, and smiled. Her aunt was behind a large pine structure, which served as the camp check-in desk, the store checkout counter, and a place to sit the Mr. Coffee machine. Aunt Kate welcomed everyone with a free cup of coffee.

Kate Hennessey looked up from the stack of mail she was sorting and smiled at her grandniece. She was a large-boned woman in her mid-sixties, whose short, dark blond hair was only just starting to streak with gray. She had on a denim skirt, sneakers but no socks, and a large T-shirt emblazoned with a picture of a wolf and the name Stony Brook Campgrounds on it. She signaled for her niece to come in.

Gem poked her head in the front door. "Need some help?"

"They're bringing in a new wolf this afternoon. I told them I'd meet them down at the preserve as soon as you got home from school."

Two years ago Kate Hennessey had taken it into her head to fence in twenty acres of her nearly two-hundred-acre camp to use as a wildlife preserve for wolves. It had become a popular attraction and netted her a tidy profit in admission fees.

Kate poured herself a cup of coffee and came around to the front of the counter where Gem stood sipping her Coke. "You mind watching things for a while?"

"No problem," Gem told her.

Kate grabbed a floppy wide-brimmed hat off the counter and plopped it on her head. "I appreciate it," she said, heading for the door, coffee mug still in hand.

Gem set her can of Coke on the counter and looked around the small room for something to do. All the T-shirts and sweatshirts were neatly hung on their rack. The postcards that had been scattered all over the countertop and floor over Labor Day weekend had been tucked back in place. The Native American jewelry in the glass case by one of the front windows was laid out in even rows. Insect repellents, sunblocks and sunscreens, sunglasses, everything was in its place. Her aunt must have had a quiet morning.

Bored, Gem opened the case of Native American jewelry and began trying on earrings, something she did when there wasn't much else to do. And that was usually the case once Labor Day had passed. Her aunt would keep the store open through September, then only on weekends in October. And finally she would close it entirely from November through April. Anyone who needed a campsite during those months could still call and make a reservation. But they were told the main building was closed.

Gem leaned into the small oval mirror that sat on top of the case, tossing her head back and forth to make the dangling silver earrings dance. She was so busy admiring herself that at first she didn't notice a large black GM truck coming up the dirt road, not until it rolled into the parking lot with a loud rumble. She froze, her fingers wrapped around one earring. She knew who it was without looking. Alec Stryker. He'd been driving around with that hole in his exhaust pipe for two weeks.

Alec swung open the door of the truck, hopped down, and with his usual swagger headed for the store.

Gem slipped the earrings off and put them back in the case. If she hadn't promised her aunt she'd watch the desk, she would have locked the door and slipped out the back way.

As it was, she barely made it behind the counter before Alec came through the front door. He gave her a sly grin, then headed over to the freezer chest where her aunt kept a stock of Popsicles and ice cream sandwiches for campers.

What was it that always unnerved her so much about Alec Stryker? Gem couldn't figure it out. He wasn't much older than she was, barely nineteen maybe. The broad shoulders and full biceps stretching against his black T-shirt made him look bigger and more threatening than he probably was. In fact, he wasn't all that much taller than she was, maybe two inches at most. And his face was deceptively innocent, almost boyish, with that light dusting of freckles and those deep dimples in his cheeks. Soft light-brown curls tumbled over his forehead.

But Gem knew better. Alec Stryker had been in and out of juvenile detention through most of high school, mainly for theft, including the stealing of a brand-new Lexus right out of the dealer's parking lot on Route 36. He was a loser, and everyone in these parts knew it. She couldn't for the life of her figure out why he bothered to hang around this place. Why didn't he just leave the state and start over?

Instead, because Alec's grandfather, Walter Stryker, was an old friend of Kate Hennessey's, they had worked it out that Alec could keep a trailer at the campgrounds year-round. In exchange Alec did odd jobs around the camp, a kind of handyman, when he wasn't working part-time laying bricks for Roy Steigler, a local contractor.

Alec had been living at the camp since early May. And not a day had gone by that Gem didn't wish he'd pack up and hit the road. She knew she was probably being unfair. Alec had a right to make a new life, to prove he wasn't the all-time loser everyone thought he was. But she couldn't help imagining that something ugly lurked beneath the surface of his skin, the same way sewage traveled unseen beneath city streets. Maybe that was why everything in her recoiled whenever he came near her.

Alec held up a Fudgsicle and began ripping the paper from it. "Put it on my tab," he said.

There was no "tab."

Gem wondered what her aunt would do under these circumstances. first of all, she doubted Alec would have said such a thing to Kate Hennessey. And chances were even if Alec tried to pay her, Kate would have told him to forget about it.

Exasperated, Gem pulled a notepad from under the counter and wrote down the amount and Alec's name. She couldn't think of what else to do. "Fine," she said. "Here's your mail." She tossed a small pile of envelopes, catalogs, and magazines on the counter.

Alec grinned and strutted across the room, stuffed his

mail in his back pocket, then leaned on the counter across from her. He held the Fudgsicle inches from her mouth. "Want some?"

The tiny hairs on the back of her neck bristled. Her first instinct was to tell him where he could put his stupid Fudgsicle. But she knew he'd only find that funny. Probably twist her words around to make it sound like she was hot for him, something he did a lot. God, what a creep. It was better to ignore him.

Behind the counter was a stack of unopened boxes, canned goods to be shelved. She picked up a knife and slit open the top box. "Kate said if I saw you to tell you she could use some help over at the preserve. They're bringing in a new wolf." This was a lie. Kate had never asked her to deliver any such message. But Gem was desperate to get rid of Alec. She kept her eyes on the cans of chili she held in her hands. She could feel Alec watching her. He was always watching her.

When he finally headed out the door, Gem was annoyed to see that the labels on the cans of chili were damp with her sweat.

Alec Stryker slammed the door of his cramped trailer and flopped down on a dirty yellow beanbag chair. The chair took up most of the room. Silver strips of duct tape held together seams that threatened to burst from years of abuse. Stacks of gun magazines occupied the rest of his free space—precariously unstable piles of *Guns & Ammo*, *Soldier of Fortune,* and *Handguns.*

He hadn't bothered to find Kate Hennessey. She didn't need him to settle in a new wolf. He knew Gem had been trying to get rid of him. She was nervous around him, scared even. He liked that. He never missed a chance to get a rise out of her if he could. She might be one snotty bitch, but she was hot. He could wait.

He pulled the mail from his back pocket and shuffled through it. Junk, as usual. He grinned down at the un-opened Visa bill. Who in their right mind would give someone like him credit? He laughed out loud and flung the bill toward the Formica-top table. It missed by inches, landing on the floor.

Sooner or later these jerks would figure out he wasn't planning to pay them. But in the meantime, the credit card applications kept coming and he had no problem filling them out and sending them back. He could be damn obliging when he wanted to be.

There was also a note from his counselor, Amos Stark. That was what the county bureaucrats called old Amos. A counselor. Parole officer was more like it. Alec tossed the envelope aside unopened.

Why didn't they just leave him the hell alone? That was all he wanted. To be left alone in his trailer, a six-pack of ice-cold beer, good music, his magazines. It wasn't like he was asking for much.

The only other mail was his latest issue of *Guns* magazine. He flipped through it for a while, but it seemed pointless. With his record he'd never be able to legally buy any of these guns, not even if he had a hundred new credit cards.

After a few minutes he grew restless. There was only one thing, short of rolling a joint, that calmed him down when he got edgy like this. His guns.

He pulled a long wooden box from beneath the bed and lifted the lid. Gently he glided his fingers along the smooth, well-oiled barrel of a shotgun. Goose bumps danced along his arm. He slid his fingers over the polished stock of his .30-caliber Remington. His father had given him both the rifle and the shotgun when Alec was eight. Back when they used to go hunting together. Before Alec's mother died. Before his old man took to calling him Colonel Shitforbrains. Before he started saying things like no way in hell was Alec his real son. Before Alec's sister, Jeannie, who was almost ten years older, stuffed her backpack with an extra pair of jeans, a few favorite tapes for her Walkman, and a frayed copy of Kerouac's *On the Road,* headed west, and never looked back.

He ran his hand over the black leather case that held his .357 Magnum. This and the other guns—a second shotgun, a .22-caliber rifle, and three handguns, including a .22 semiautomatic—were his, not his father's. All of them stolen.

He grinned down at the contents of the box. Amos Stark would have a heart attack if he knew about these guns. The thought gave Alec intense pleasure.

He pulled a soft rag from the box and began to polish the already gleaming barrel of the shotgun. Hollis Feeney would be over later. He always showed up sometime after dark. He'd been hanging around Alec ever since last June when Old Lady Hennessey had hired Hollis to design a Web site for the campgrounds and wolf preserve. Alec had accompanied him to the preserve so Hollis could photograph the wolves and scan the pictures into the Web site. After that, for reasons Alec still couldn't figure out, Hollis had taken to following him around, especially when Alec went out hunting at night.

At first Alec had been annoyed. He must have told the kid to get lost at least a thousand times. Hollis wouldn't. But after a while Alec hardly noticed Hollis anymore. It was like having an extra shadow. A shadow who admired him, although Alec hadn't yet figured out why. Still, he had to admit, he'd started to like it.

 four

They had been living in the mountains of New Jersey since the third week of August, so far west they were practically in Pennsylvania, the last exit before the bridge over the Delaware River. Gabriel could see it was already getting to his mother. The commute to her job in the city took almost three hours one way if she drove to Dover to catch the train and two hours or more if she drove all the way to the city, which according to her wasn't worth a daily migraine.

At the moment his mother, Margaret Lowell-Hart, was popping a Lean Cuisine into the microwave. Gabriel stood in the doorway of the kitchen watching her. His mother had her back to him, facing the microwave, arms folded, one foot frantically tapping the linoleum, as if she could somehow will the food to cook faster.

From the back she didn't look much taller or olde
than Shelby. Her short curly hair was currently a dark mahogany. Gabriel wasn't sure of the color. In fact, he'c
never actually seen hair that color on anyone before. Las'
week his mother's hair had been a soft reddish blond, a
shade he'd liked. Since he began taking notice, Gabrie
had counted at least four times that his mother had
changed her hair color since Ben had died.

It was after nine o'clock. She had only been home fo
ten minutes and was still wearing a dark gray business
suit. Sometimes his mother wore long printed skirts and
loose tunic tops, flowing scarves that clung to her slender
neck, and enormous earrings that reached almost to her
shoulders. Other times, like today, she wore dark, sharply
angled suits. It was as if she wasn't sure who she was. This
was something Gabriel could understand, maybe the only
thing they had in common.

The buzzer went off, and his mother lifted the tray
from the microwave. She peeled back the film cover.
Gabriel wasn't sure she even knew he was there. But then,
as she sat down at the kitchen table, she suddenly announced, "I'm getting an apartment in the city."

Gabriel slumped against the doorjamb, folding his
arms. "Why?"

"The commute is hell. I knew it would be. I told your
father."

"So, what's this mean?"

"Mean?" His mother looked up at him, her fork poised
midway between the plate and her mouth.

32

Gabriel shrugged, trying not to show his alarm. The first thought that had come to mind was that his parents were calling it quits, which wouldn't have surprised him. "Are you moving out for good?"

His mother blinked a few times. Apparently she hadn't been expecting that response. "No, of course not. It's so I have a place to stay during the week." She took a bite of food, chewing slowly.

Gabriel waited. He knew there was more.

Margaret Lowell-Hart was editorial director at a major publishing house. She had begun as an editorial assistant, eventually working her way up to her present position. She was not about to give up her career. Gabriel knew this. So did the rest of his family.

His mother had fought a long, hard battle with his father about the move. They all had. But his father wouldn't listen. Not then, not now. Robert Hart was convinced he had done the best thing for all of them. He had moved them to someplace safe.

"I'll stay in the city during the week and come home on weekends," his mother said.

She made it sound so reasonable.

"Your father's here all day, in his studio. It's not like I'm leaving you kids alone."

Gabriel's father was a painter. Right that moment he had a show going on at a gallery in New York, although he'd never even showed up for the reception. From the way Gabriel's father acted these days, you'd have thought they'd never even lived in the city. It was as if he was

33

trying to wipe out everything that had ever happened be
fore they moved to Knollwood Township.

Something in Gabriel's expression must have commu
nicated itself to his mother. She laid her fork aside an
raised her hands, touching just the tips of her fingers to
gether beneath her chin. "I'm not ready to give up my ca
reer, Gabe," she said. "I'm sorry. I was hoping you of a
people would understand."

"Why me?"

"Because I know how much you didn't want to leav
the city."

"Then let me live there with you during the week.
can go to my old school."

His mother shook her head, looking sympathetic. "Th
place I'm renting is a tiny studio apartment, not much
bigger than the master bedroom upstairs. It's all we can af
ford right now, with the mortgage and all. There won't b
enough room."

Gabriel nodded, as if he'd anticipated her answer. So
was a done deal. She wasn't going to *look* for an apart
ment. She already *had* one.

He left her there, eating her soggy dinner, which wa
probably cold by now—anyway, he hoped it was—an
headed out the front door.

The long gravel driveway crunched beneath his sneak
ers. He had no idea where he was going and didn't much
care. And that felt about right. Nobody in his family cared
about much of anything these days. His father didn't seem
to care about his artistic reputation anymore, his mother

dn't care about the family, and Shelby—he had no idea
hat Shelby cared or didn't care about. If his family had
coat of arms, the motto would probably read *Like we
ve a shit*. And the crest? Gabriel pictured some sad-
oking knight emblazoned on it with a bony horse be-
ath him, a broken lance and rusty armor, hands out,
lms up, shrugging. Yeah. He liked that image. It fit.

When Gabriel reached the end of the driveway, he
opped. If he went right, he'd end up at the bottom of the
eep hill. Nothing down there but a few scattered houses.
e'd never been the other way before. As far as he could
ll, nothing but woods flanked both sides of the road. It
as hard to judge since there were no streetlights. And his
yes were just beginning to grow accustomed to the dark.

Strange sounds assaulted his ears. Night sounds. The
ournful hooting of owls, the buzz-sawing of cicadas,
e crackle of crickets—foreign sounds. Where were the
orns and sirens? Where was the clash of TV shows,
ereos, and human voices that used to come from the
ther windows opening onto the air shaft outside his old
edroom window?

Even the air here felt different. Emptier. It had no taste.
Jo substance. It made him light-headed to breathe it. He
linked, still trying to adjust to the dark. And it was into
his black void that Gabriel moved as he stepped onto the
oad.

Gem Hennessey reached the pond across the road from
he abandoned Boy Scout camp just as the moon was

peeking over the treetops. The tall grass shimmered in th
moonlight. She laid an old wool blanket on the groun
flattening the weeds.

With quick, easy movements she slid out of her shor
and tank top as if she was shedding an unwanted layer
skin. The water was warm, but cooler than the humi
night air. It skimmed across her body in silky waves as sh
glided from one side of the pond to the other.

It had been an unusually wet summer and the pon
had swelled, spilling over its banks. The roots of ol
cedars, sycamores, and wild rhododendron bushes su
rounding the edges were hidden beneath the water.

The moonlight created a path for Gem on the surfac
of the water. She swam back and forth on the strip o
light until she was exhausted. Then she climbed out of th
pond and lay on the blanket to dry off. She loved thes
late-night swims. They were hers in a way nothing els
was. Although she knew they would be ending soo
when the autumn chill settled in.

The manmade lake at her aunt's campgrounds was dif
ferent. It was open and exposed. No trees or shrubs hov
ered protectively over the water. Small rowboats an
plastic paddleboats were tied to a dock. Sometime
campers took them out at night. You wouldn't dare t
swim without a bathing suit. Not at Stony Broo
Campgrounds.

On nights like this, Gem could think of no place els
she'd rather be. It wasn't a bad life. Far from perfect
though. In a perfect world her parents would still be

married and she'd be living with them. But at least she had Aunt Kate. For now, anyway, she was not alone.

And it wasn't as if she didn't have other choices. When her parents had gotten divorced five years ago, they had both offered her a home. She'd gone first to live with her mother in California, which had been fine until her mother's new boyfriend moved in with his five-year-old twin boys and her mother got a job in an herbal cosmetics shop. After that, she'd expected Gem to keep house and take care of the boys every day when she got home from school. Living with her father hadn't been much of an improvement. He was a stock-car racer and followed the circuit. Gem had spent a lot of time watching TV in motel rooms, dingy rooms with rust stains in the tub, large questionable spots in the carpeting, and water rings and cigarette burns on most of the furniture. She'd gone to four different schools in one year.

So when she came to spend two weeks with her father's aunt Kate one summer, the summer she turned fourteen, Gem decided this was where she wanted to be. It was the only place she felt truly at home. And she wasn't all that surprised when neither of her parents gave her much of an argument, although it would have been nice if they had put up more of a protest.

She hadn't seen her father in two years, although he sometimes sent postcards from places like Daytona Beach, Florida; Charlotte, North Carolina; and Dover, Delaware. From her mother she always got Christmas and birthday cards. Although the birthday cards sometimes came a few days late. And at least once a year she forced herself to spend two weeks in California, even though it meant being stuck with the twins.

True, Aunt Kate got on her nerves at times, especially when she got on some kick about what things were like when she was in school. As if she actually thought there was a comparison. Gem thought her aunt just might keel over in a dead faint if she knew how it really was in high school these days. Still, being here was a lot better than being stuck with the twins every day after school.

Gem breathed in the heavy night air. It would be nice if life could always be a silky swim in a warm pond. But past experience had taught her otherwise.

The mosquitoes were hungry tonight. She rolled over, reached into the pocket of her shorts, and pulled out a concoction she had made from citrus oil, wood alcohol, and water, and sprayed it over her body. Then she lay down and stared up at the sky, enjoying the tingling coolness as the mist evaporated.

She closed her eyes and thought about the new boy who had walked into her homeroom the day before, who had taken her hand in English class, sending a rush of warmth and pleasure, unlike anything she'd ever known, through her whole body. Gabriel Hart. She wondered where he'd moved here from. What he was like. What it would be like to have him lying there next to her, his arms circling her body. Dreamily, she let him float in and out of her imagination.

After a while she stretched her arms overhead and sat

p, trying to decide whether or not to take another swim before heading back to the campgrounds. It was late, probably close to ten. Ordinarily she would have stood up to put her clothes on. But the strangest feeling had suddenly come over her. As if someone was close by, watching. Still sitting, she slipped on her shorts and tank top, then stood to fold the blanket, all the while keeping her eyes on the surrounding woods.

Silver light poured over the smooth contours of the girl's back. The scene was a contrast of light and shadow. Gabriel stepped off the road and stood knee-deep in weeds, not daring to breathe, not daring to move. He had never seen anything quite so beautiful. He was unaware that his fingers had curved as if they held a paintbrush.

The girl moved to the edge of the pond, then dove in. Gabriel watched as she swam back and forth, watched the shimmering arc of water in the moonlight as she raised her graceful arms. There was something familiar about her. But it was difficult to distinguish her features from this distance.

If he hadn't been afraid of sending her into fits of screaming hysteria, he would have taken off his own clothes and slipped into the water beside her. Instead he remained where he was, watching, although it seemed as if his body were actually in the water. He could almost feel the warm, fluid motion of each stroke.

Did the girl sense his presence? Did she know how dangerous it was, skinny-dipping in the open where anyone could see her? Where some rapist or psychopath could move in on her, as silent as a cat, waiting for her to come out of the water before he pounced?

An image of his brother, Ben, waiting by the door of the C train, ready to step out on the platform when it came to his stop, flooded into Gabriel's mind. This was how he always imagined that night. Ben. Vulnerable, but unaware of it. *Vulnerable.* You could feel your tongue swell with the pressure of saying the word out loud. What made you vulnerable, anyway? The girl's nakedness should have made her vulnerable. Yet for some reason, Gabriel didn't see her that way. Her nakedness didn't make her a victim—at least not here in this place. But Ben's new leather jacket had made him one, had made him someone's target.

Gabriel pictured the killers yanking off Ben's jacket— so they wouldn't ruin the leather—before they knifed him—seventeen times. It had been three-thirty in the morning, and Ben was slightly drunk, coming back from a party in SoHo. He was alone in the subway car. At least until *they* showed up. No one had been sure how many there were. A few passengers in the other cars claimed to have seen four teens roaming from car to car around that time.

One witness, a man who had been waiting for the train and had almost been knocked to the ground by four teens barreling out of the doors as they made a dash for the stairs, had told the police one of them was swinging a ather jacket over his head like a lasso. The man had almost missed the train but had managed to slam his hand against the closing doors and squeeze through. That was when he found Ben, bleeding and barely conscious. Unfortunately the witness hadn't gotten a good look at the thugs and couldn't identify them.

By the time the paramedics arrived, Ben's assailants were long gone, taking their leather trophy with them. He had been rushed to an emergency room but died before anyone from the family made it to the hospital. Gabriel, who had been leaning against the wall, since there were no available chairs, heard his mother's piercing sob from behind the white curtain and knew.

For one long, excruciating moment, everyone in the ward froze—the technician wheeling the electrocardiograph behind another closed curtain; the nurse clasping the rubber bulb in midsqueeze as she took someone's blood pressure; the woman at the front desk shoving insurance forms at distraught relatives. All of them, dozens of people, held their breath when Margaret Lowell-Hart's mournful cry, from somewhere deep inside her, cut like a chain saw through the general hum of noise in the emergency room. A sound so terrible it had almost brought Gabriel to his knees.

Even now, months later, he felt his legs tremble as he recalled that night. He stepped back and leaned against a large oak. The familiar rage swept over him with a fury. A rage so powerful it shook his whole body. If he hadn't

been worried about the girl hearing him, he would hav
slammed his fists into the tree, pounded it until h
knuckles bled.

Instead he rested his palms and forehead against th
coarse bark, taking deep breaths. After a while he couldn
be sure whether the pulse he felt was his own, or whethe
it came from the oak.

He might have stood there, unmoving, until dawn if h
hadn't turned his head and noticed that the girl was no
fully dressed and shaking out a blanket, obviously gettin
ready to leave.

He hid behind the tree and listened, straining to hea
the rustle of grass above the incessant chatter of crickets
Was she coming toward him?

He thought of heading back toward the house but wa
afraid she might hear his footsteps on the road, or the sna
of a twig if he tried to walk in the weeds along the shoulder. A few minutes later he heard the crunch of stone. H
looked from behind the tree and saw the girl, now on a
bike, heading away from him. He breathed easier, relieve
that she wasn't going in the direction of his house. Still
he couldn't help wondering what, if anything, could b
farther down that dark wooded road.

five

Lydia finished putting the last plate in the plastic dish rack, let the water out of the sink, and rinsed the soap from her hands. Every night she cursed her father for refusing to buy a dishwasher. It was pointless, he told her, to get used to something they wouldn't be able to use when they no longer had the electrical power to run it. Whenever that would be. She had argued that they had the backup generator. "For the pump," her father said, "and refrigeration. The absolute necessities. When there's no more gasoline, we won't even have the generator." Lydia thought he was just plain nuts.

She undid the tortoiseshell clip and let her hair fall to her waist. The day, like the past week, had been hot and humid. And there had been little relief since the sun went down. She ripped a paper towel from its roll, held it under cold water, and circled her sweating face with it as she slid the glass door open and stepped out on the deck.

The sky was thick with stars, the moon a huge white lopsided hole in the sky. When Lydia was little, her mother had told her once that if you went through that hole in the sky, you'd find yourself in a completely new world, the way Alice in Wonderland had when she fell down the rabbit hole.

Remembering, Lydia closed her eyes and willed whatever was on the other side of the hole to beam her up. Any place, even the other side of the moon, would be better than where she was.

At least it was cooler outside. Maybe she would go down to her special sanctuary for a while.

She'd already done her homework. Not that she had much choice. Her father insisted she sit down at the kitchen table the moment she got home and not get up until it was done. Even worse, he usually checked everything, and if he didn't like what he saw, he made her do it over. He had been known to rip up an entire essay, right in her face, for finding a single misspelled word.

This afternoon had been different. Her father had been out putting up new electric wire fencing at the farthest end of their property. Only her mother was there when Lydia came home. There and not there. As usual.

Her mother had been on her knees digging out weeds from the flower beds by the front porch and planting fall chrysanthemums.

"So what classes are you taking this year?" she asked when Lydia came up behind her.

"The usual stuff," Lydia said. "Senior English, calculus—" She felt the familiar knot in her stomach. Her mother was doing it again. Staring at Lydia's lips, silently mouthing every word her daughter said a split second after it left her mouth, as if she was trying hard to understand what was being said, as if Lydia was speaking to her in a foreign language.

Lydia looked away, leaving her sentence unfinished. Her mother had developed this strange habit a few months ago. But no one, not even her husband, would mention it to her. They all pretended nothing was wrong.

"I always hated math," her mother said, swishing her hand back and forth in front of her face, shooing away gnats. "Good thing your father does the household accounts."

Lydia started up the front porch steps. In the old days she might have told her mother about the new boy in her English class, Gabriel Hart, who, it turned out, happened to be the same boy who had moved in right up the street. But today it never occurred to her to even mention him. Because the woman bending over the weeds, her fingernails broken and black with soil, wasn't the same mother she'd had when they'd lived in Rolling Hills.

Debra Misurella, the mother who used to be involved in so many community projects she'd almost had a nervous breakdown—a happy nervous breakdown. Debra

Misurella, the president of the Cultural Arts Committee, who almost always played the lead roles in the community theater, who learned her lines while she sorted laundry and beat egg whites to make angel food cakes for school bake sales, who worked out at the gym three days a week and had the firmest butt in Rolling Hills. Had.

The woman kneeling in the dirt below was someone else. Someone who wore gray sweat shorts and wrinkled, soil-smudged T-shirts. Someone whose shoulder-length blond hair had dulled and darkened over these last four years and showed streaks of gray. Someone who silently mimicked every word you said and didn't even know she was doing it. And it was all because of *him*. The nut. The basket case.

Lydia sighed. It was better not to think about the past. By the time she went back into the house, the clock on the stove read 9:30. She listened at the doorway of the hall that led to the living room. Silence. Usually everyone was in bed by nine, since there was no television to watch. Only Lydia stayed up all hours, sometimes reading, sometimes writing poems, sometimes daydreaming. But most of the time she sneaked out to spend a few hours in her private refuge.

Tonight she slipped into the family room off the kitchen, opened the doors beneath the pine hutch, took out a bottle of vodka, and filled a small silver flask. Putting the flask in the pocket of her shorts, she quietly headed out the door.

Every night since he had first seen the girl swimming in the moonlight, Gabriel walked down to the pond and waited. But the girl didn't come. After going back to the pond for six evenings in a row, he had grown discouraged. He wondered if maybe he'd dreamed everything. But then, on a night that was even warmer and more humid than it had been a week ago, a night when he thought he heard gunshots coming from the woods as he came within a few yards of the pond, he caught a glimpse of the girl's back as she walked her bike out to the road, got on, and pedaled into the night. He'd missed her again, but at least now he knew he hadn't been dreaming. She really did exist.

It wasn't until the girl was out of sight that Gabriel noticed a thin strip of light, about three feet long, across the road in the woods, maybe fifty yards away. Again he heard shots in the distance and thought of heading back home. But his curiosity held him back. As he drew closer to the strip of light, a large building with a porch, set back from the road and nestled in overgrown shrubs and tall grass, seemed to emerge from the shadows. The windows were boarded over. The white paint had all but peeled away, leaving weathered gray clapboards. It was obvious the building was abandoned, and yet, there beneath the front door, drawing him forward, was the faint strip of light.

The scent of vanilla spiraled upward from the smoke of the fat, milky-white candle. Lydia, slumped in an old Adirondack chair that was missing one arm, stared into the flame. The flask of vodka lay in her lap, still almost full. She thought of Gabriel Hart. Earlier she had passed his house on her way to her refuge, slowing her steps as she walked by the end of his driveway, hoping to get a glimpse of him through the lighted windows. Looking up the long gravel driveway, she had seen the silver Toyota parked next to an SUV and knew he was home. If it hadn't been so late, she might have walked right up to the front door, introduced herself, and welcomed him to the neighborhood. Although her father would probably kill her outright if she ever did such a thing.

From somewhere close by came the sound of a shotgun. Lydia bolted upright. Her first thought was that Jacob was probably out poaching again, which meant her father might be with him. He had taught both his sons to hunt at night, even though it was illegal. When it came to her father's survival tactics, there was only one true law: the law of the jungle.

Lydia's first instinct was to blow out the candle and head home. Fast. Instead she took another swallow of vodka and continued to listen.

It was unbearably hot inside the boarded-up building, but she didn't dare open the front door. Someone might notice the light, someone passing by, although travelers on this road were rare. Still, the shots were a warning. Someone was in the area.

The last thing she needed was her father or anyone else discovering her here, in this place—an old abandoned Boy Scout camp—where she came to be alone, to get away from her crazy family. This was her sanctuary, her refuge. She had discovered it the first summer they moved to the mountains, noticed the boarded-up windows, and knew no one lived there.

For weeks she had walked by the abandoned house, testing the situation. She never saw a parked car, never saw anyone mowing the grass or sweeping the dead leaves from the front porch. And so Lydia declared squatter's rights. It had taken her almost an hour to pick the padlock with one of her mother's bobby pins, having never before attempted such a feat. But it was worth it.

Inside, after her eyes had adjusted to the gloomy dark, she saw that she was in one big room. Probably a meeting room for the campers. A large stone fireplace stood at one end. A few pieces of furniture had been left behind, broken but not unsalvageable: a pine trestle table, a sagging couch with lumpy springs that smelled of mildew, an Adirondack chair with a missing arm, two aluminum chairs with part of the webbing ripped away, and a blue plastic milk crate. Lydia had no idea what the crate was for, but it made a nice footstool when she sat in the Adirondack chair.

Staircases at both ends of the building led to six rooms upstairs, some still with mattresses, the stuffing torn out probably by squirrels or raccoons. Next to the main room was a kitchen, painted an ugly battleship gray.

Two days later she bought a broom, a dustpan, and a scented candle. She swept away all the mice nests, the powdery dried leaves, the tumbleweeds of dust. She dusted the windowsills and the battered furniture with one of her father's old T-shirts. It never occurred to her to pry the thick planks of plywood from the windows. The boarded-up windows kept her secret.

She came to this sanctuary mostly at night, as she had now, usually after she was sure everyone was asleep. If she was ever caught sneaking back into her room—and so far that had never happened—there was no telling what her father would do. It was better not to think about it.

A moth fluttered around the candle flame. A stupid moth, bent on its own destruction. Didn't it know it would die in the fire, or was it drawn by such a powerful force that it didn't care what happened? She leaned forward, softly blowing on the moth to shoo it away. As if in defiance, the insect flew straight into the flame.

Fascinated, Lydia watched as, in a split second, the fragile wings first became translucent, then turned to ashes floating in the pool of melted wax around the wick. She would have continued her vigil—half expecting the moth to rise up out of its ashes like the mythical phoenix—if a knock at the door hadn't shaken her out of her trance.

Her first thought was to blow out the candle, but this seemed pointless. Whoever was outside must have already seen the light and known someone was inside, or they wouldn't have knocked.

Lydia slipped the flask behind a stack of wood near the fireplace, praying that whoever was at the door wasn't her father. The last thing she needed was to have him catch her with his vodka. It was bad enough she wasn't home in bed where she was supposed to be.

Barely able to breathe and hoping that her legs

wouldn't give out on her, Lydia eased the door open a few inches and stared into the darkness with one eye. She could make out the face of a young man and realized with relief that it wasn't her father. She squeezed her eyes closed and took a deep breath.

The boy stepped closer to the door. Lydia moved back, opening it a bit farther. Even in the dim candlelight she recognized Gabriel Hart. At first she couldn't believe he was real. It had to be the vodka. She'd heard about how people who drank too much sometimes hallucinated.

Head lowered, hands in his pockets, the boy said, almost in a whisper—as if he too couldn't quite believe any of this was real—"I saw this light coming from under the door . . . but the windows were boarded up." He paused and looked over at the candle. "I don't know why I . . . It's just—" He stopped midsentence.

Lydia nodded as if she understood. And in a way she did. She would have been curious too, if she'd seen a light coming from an abandoned building. "You're that new boy, Gabriel Hart."

He nodded.

"You're in my English class." It suddenly occurred to her that she was standing there with the door wide open, light pouring out into the night for the whole world to see. She had to get the door closed. "So are you coming in or what?" She stepped back to give him plenty of room.

Gabriel hesitated. He could tell by the condition of the place that no one actually lived there. But here was this person, this girl from his English class, standing before him. And she seemed right at home.

The front view of her was in shadow, and he could barely make out the features on her face, except for the tiny nose ring on the side of one nostril. The candlelight behind her shimmered on her hair, which fell to her waist in fine spidery waves. She was wearing khaki shorts and a red tank top. In the candlelight, her skin was as soft and honey-colored as her hair.

He was about to step inside when he heard the crunch of footsteps on what remained of the weed-infested gravel driveway. He saw the alarmed expression on the girl's face and turned to where she was looking. Two shadowy figures, one of medium height, the other shorter and considerably heavier, were coming toward them. And there was something else, something far more disturbing. One of the figures, the taller of the two, was carrying a shotgun.

Gabriel's mind went completely blank. He had no idea what to do next. Everything that had been happening, from the moment he had seen the girl riding away on her bike a short time earlier, to finding this abandoned building in the woods, seemed almost dreamlike. But the dream had suddenly become a nightmare.

Lydia's hand jerked instinctively to her throat. At first she thought the two figures coming up the driveway were her father and Jacob. What was she going to tell them? That she'd met this boy while she was out walking?

That he was a runaway who had been living in the abandoned meeting house? Because she certainly couldn't let them know she was the one who had been hanging out in this place.

When the figures were only a few yards from the door, Lydia saw with relief that they weren't her family. And like Gabriel, she also saw that one of them had a gun. But before she could panic, she realized that both faces belonged to people she knew. Not personally. But familiar faces nonetheless. One of the boys, the one with the shotgun, was Alec Stryker, who had been two years ahead of her in high school, a total loser who'd been suspended for a week in his senior year and had never bothered to come back.

The other boy was Hollis Feeney. A wormy little geek who was only fifteen but had skipped two grades and was in Lydia's honors calculus class. He was wearing a T-shirt with a picture of Darth Vader on it. Lydia looked away, stifling a laugh. She thought it funny that these two creepy loners had somehow found each other.

Alec Stryker came right up on the porch, planting himself only a few feet from Gabriel. Hollis Feeney held back, as if he wanted to size up the situation first.

Alec looked Lydia up and down, grinning. Then he glanced over at Gabriel. But it was to Lydia he said, "You know you're trespassing, don't you?" When Lydia didn't respond, he added, "This is Kate Hennessey's property."

"What's it to you?" Lydia knew she didn't sound nearly

as tough as she'd hoped. She was aware that Kate Hennessey owned Stony Brook Campgrounds. And the wolf preserve. Almost everyone in these parts knew that. But this was the first she'd heard about Kate Hennessey owning the Boy Scout camp. Well, so what? It had been abandoned for years. And now it had become *her* place—Lydia's. She threw her head back, thrust her sharp chin forward, and folded her arms. "It's an old Boy Scout camp. It hasn't been used in ages."

"Well, it so happens I work for Kate Hennessey. She owns this land and all the buildings. She used to rent it to the Boy Scouts. I'm just here looking out for my boss's interests."

"You were out poaching," Lydia said. "So don't give me that crap about your boss's interests."

Alec threw back his head and laughed, not in the least put off. Then he glanced around her at the candle. "So, me and Hollis here . . . I guess we're interrupting something." He shifted his eyes toward Gabriel, who stared back at him, waiting.

When no one said anything, Alec stepped into the room, brushing his shoulder against Lydia's. She flinched, then put her hand over the place he'd touched, as if covering a wound.

"So is this an open party or what?" Alec stood in the middle of the room, legs wide apart, holding the shotgun with both hands as if he, not Kate Hennessey, owned the place.

"It's not a party." Lydia said this with her back to him.

She had her eyes locked on Gabriel, as if she was willing him to do something.

"Well, maybe it should be," Alec said. He was standing right behind her now, his face only inches from hers. He sniffed. "The hell it's not a party. Somebody's been partying. You think I can't smell that?" He looked around the room. "Where is it?"

Lydia stood stock-still. "Where's what?"

"The booze, babe. The vodka." He leaned in close to her again, his nose only a few inches from her mouth. "Yep. That's vodka. My old man used to think he was putting one over on my mom, drinking vodka. He thought she couldn't smell it. The hell she couldn't." He laughed. A short, bitter sound.

The minute Alec began checking around the room, Lydia knew he would find the flask. There weren't that many places to hide things. The woodpile was the most obvious place. And as if to prove her right, Alec headed straight for it. Within seconds he had the flask in his hand, shaking it. "Yo, Hollis, get your ass in here. We got almost a full flask here." He unscrewed the top and took a swallow. "Good shit, too."

Hollis Feeney looked at Lydia, his pale, pudgy face expressionless, then stepped past Gabriel and Lydia. Alec tossed the flask at him, laughing as he almost dropped it.

Gabriel leaned toward Lydia. "Maybe we should get out of here."

Lydia, who had already had a few gulps from the flask, wasn't feeling easily intimidated. In fact, she had been growing angrier by the minute. So when she spun around and flat-out demanded Hollis give her the flask back, even Alec's thin lips parted in amused surprise.

Hollis handed her the flask without argument. Alec, however, put his arm around Lydia's shoulder and pulled her farther into the room, lifting the flask out of her hand. "We'll share it. That's what good neighbors do. Right?"

For reasons Gabriel couldn't quite understand, Lydia seemed to accept this compromise.

She turned to Gabriel. "You'd better get in here and shut the door before anyone else shows up."

Gabriel stared at the candle on the table. The flame flickered, making the shadows of the three people in the room seem to dance on the bare walls. He kept his eyes on the light. His instinct was to shut the door, leaving them to their party, or whatever it was, and head home. So no one was more surprised than he was when the next time he looked up from the candle he was standing in the middle of the room with Lydia's silver flask in his hand.

six

By the time the four left for their homes the moon was high above the trees. None of them questioned what they were doing in the abandoned building, or why they stayed until after two in the morning, not saying much of anything.

Hollis Feeney had spent most of the night on the mildewed couch, staring up at the ceiling. He never once took a drink from the flask, even though Alec kept shoving it in his face. After a while, no one paid any attention to Hollis; they just let him be.

The vodka hadn't lasted long, but for some reason no one got up to leave even after the flask was empty. Something about the warm glow of the candle and the scent of vanilla masking the mildew and musty odors of the building held them captive. Perhaps the four were reminded of more innocent times, of crispy marshmallows oozing off the stick and plopping on the tip of your sneaker just as you reached for them, of the smell of wood smoke clinging to your clothes, and of eerie unfamiliar sounds. Or maybe it was something else. Maybe they recognized something of themselves in each other, something they wouldn't dare speak of but were drawn to nonetheless.

Gabriel thought none of these things as he walked up the driveway to his house. He had no idea why he had stayed so long, and he didn't much care. The atmosphere had been seductive. The old building had provided the perfect escape. A place where, for a few hours, you could almost make yourself believe your brother hadn't really been murdered and your father hadn't uprooted the whole family in some quixotic quest for safety.

The house was dark. Not even a porch light. That was how Gabriel knew no one was aware he'd left the house. It figured.

The front door was locked, but he had his own key. Inside, standing in the foyer, he was suddenly stunned by the silence. When you'd lived in the city your whole life, you grew used to the noise; it became a comforting background, the hum of life, a constant assurance that you were not alone.

But here in the woods, even with the night sounds buzzing around him, even with his family asleep upstairs, Gabriel had never felt so alone. The darkness was almost tangible. Something he could touch, something that could leave black smudges on his fingertips.

He slumped on the couch in the great room and looked around. This house was so open and exposed—the cathedral ceiling, the open staircase, the floor-to-ceiling wall of glass at the end of the room, leading to the deck. Why had his father chosen such a vulnerable house? It didn't make sense. Maybe he thought with all these windows he could spot the enemy approaching before the enemy spotted him. Gabriel laughed at the thought.

For a while he sat in the dark, staring at nothing in particular. He was still too awake to go to bed, so he turned on the TV, idly clicking the remote from channel to channel, not paying the least bit of attention to the barrage of images flickering across the screen.

The smooth bark of the sycamore felt cool against her bare arms and legs as Lydia climbed the tree outside her window. The same tree that had harbored the annoying grackles a week earlier. The back door was locked. It locked automatically the second you closed it, and you couldn't get back in without a key. Her father wouldn't allow any of them to have their own keys. He feared someone might steal them and make copies. So for four years Lydia had used the old sycamore as her personal staircase to her bedroom. She always left the window unlocked, blatantly disobeying her father's orders that everything—every door, every window—be secured before they all went to bed at night.

She leaned forward, clamping her legs around a thick branch, slipped her fingers through a small tear at the bottom of the screen, and lifted. The screen slid up, allowing her to open the window.

Without bothering to take off her shorts and tank top, she kicked off her sneakers and flopped on the unmade bed. The motion sent the feathers dancing on the dream catcher that hung on the wall behind her.

She closed her eyes and thought of Gabriel Hart. He was the reason she'd stayed at the camp tonight, had put up with those two morons, Alec and Hollis. She hoped she was Gabriel's reason for not leaving too. He hadn't exactly turned and run when she invited him in. He could have, easily. And that would have been the end of it.

What hadn't worked out quite the way she had hoped was that Gabriel had left before she did. And even though it was after two in the morning, he never offered to walk her home. By then he knew she lived only a quarter mile down the road from him, knew they were neighbors because she'd told him. He could have at least asked. Instead he'd gotten to his feet, headed for the door, glanced at the three others as if he were looking right through them, and said he'd see them around.

Lydia had wanted to run after him but thought better of it. It wasn't a good idea to reveal too much too soon. Disappointed, she had screwed the top back on the empty flask, slipped it into her pocket, looked over at Alec, and said, "Party's over."

Alec snorted a laugh from where he lounged in the Adirondack chair. "The party's over when I say it is." His arm shot out, reaching for her legs. Lydia, who was already on her feet, grabbed the candle and tipped it, spilling hot wax on Alec's hand.

"Son of a bitch!" He tore at the soft hot wax.

Lydia blew out the candle and was out the front door before either of the boys knew what had hit them. She took off up the road, running so fast she thought her heart would burst right out of her chest. Her throat burned from the effort. When she finally dared to look back, she saw that the road was empty. She bent over, trying to catch her breath. Apparently they couldn't be bothered to come after her.

But now, as she stripped off her clothes and let the delicious warm breeze from the window cool her sweaty body, she began to wonder if maybe Alec had decided to wait for another time to get even.

The thought was disturbing. But what she found even more upsetting was that these people knew about her sanctuary. Her secret hiding place. Would Alec tell Kate Hennessey about her trespassing? He might do that just to get even for the hot wax. Fortunately, as far as Alec knew, this was the first and only time she'd trespassed. There was no way he could ever find out that she'd been calling this place home for over four years. Not unless she told him, which she'd never do.

And she wasn't about to give up her sanctuary, either. Not without a fight.

When Gabriel opened his eyes, shortly after dozing off, the first thing he saw was four shadowy forms standing between him and the TV screen. Dark but transparent forms. Like black smoke given human shape.

He blinked, then squeezed his eyes closed. "It's a dream," he whispered. "A stupid-ass dream." But when he opened his eyes again, the shapes were still there.

Shit. Wasn't he ever going to outgrow these nightmares?

By now his shirt was soaked with sweat. His heart was pounding so furiously, he was sure it would explode right out of his chest. He fumbled around between the cushions of the couch looking for the remote. If he could turn off the TV, if there was no light in the room, the shadows would disappear.

But even after he'd found the remote, even as he was ready to hit the power button, he realized he would be plunged into total darkness. And although he would no longer see the dark shapes, he couldn't be sure they weren't still there. So in the end he did what he had always done as a child. He grabbed two of the throw pillows and hid his face beneath them, feeling ridiculous, even childish, but still afraid.

He called them the Shadow People. They had first come to him the night after he'd seen two older boys chasing a stray mutt with long, whiplike sticks, cracking them on the dog's back. They didn't let up until they had run the poor animal right into the path of an oncoming car. Gabriel had been five years old at the time.

That night he had awoken to find two dark figures beside his bed. He could see right through them into the hallway where the night-light burned on a small oak table. When they didn't disappear, he pulled his pillow over his head and waited for them to leave, because he did not know what else to do.

For almost a year after that, his parents or Ben would find him sleeping on the floor under his bed, Ben's baseball bat clutched in one hand, a flashlight in the other. He would leave it on all night, and by morning the batteries were always dead. They had gone through a lot of batteries that year. When he was twelve, the nightmares finally stopped. In all those years he'd never told anyone about the Shadow People. Not even Angela Cortes.

And maybe he should have. Because the truth was, after all this time, the Shadow People were back. Four of them. They had come to him the night after Ben had been murdered. And now it seemed these nighttime specters had tracked him down in the remotest corner of New Jersey, in the new house. The "safe" house.

SEPTEMBER 19

Lydia waited until two nights had gone by, waited as always until everyone in her house was asleep, then climbed out her bedroom window onto the old sycamore.

When she was almost to the Boy Scout camp, she saw the faint crease of light beneath the door. Her heart sank. It had to be Alec, lying in wait. She thought of going back home, but that would be giving in. Somehow she had to

63

find a way to convince him to let her keep using the building. It wasn't like she was hurting anyone.

For the next few minutes she sat on a large rock at the end of the driveway deciding how she was going to handle Alec. Hollis wasn't a problem. She had decided he wasn't anything more than Alec's lackey—his personal yes-man.

If she had to, she would offer Alec money to keep her secret, although she wasn't sure where she would get this money. There was always her mother's secret cash reserve. Years ago Lydia had discovered the places in her mother's wallet where Debra Misurella hid neatly folded twenty-dollar bills: in between school photos of the boys when they were small and still went to public schools, in between her old library card and health insurance card, both of which she no longer used, behind credit cards that had expired and were never renewed but never thrown away either.

Lydia knew each and every place. She also knew that her mother no longer kept track of where she stashed these bills. That was how Lydia, with the help of a boy at school whose brother was a senior at a local university, was able to restock her father's supply of vodka periodically.

She dreaded the day she would sneak into her mother's purse and find no hidden twenty-dollar bills. But so far that hadn't happened.

Money, she thought as she headed up the driveway. She

would offer Alec money. As she put her hand on the doorknob, she whispered a silent prayer that he would accept her offer. She was so immersed in her plan, so sure that it was Alec on the other side of the door, that she wasn't at all prepared to find Gabriel Hart sitting in the Adirondack chair.

Her eyes traveled from him to the lit candle. *Her* candle, left behind three nights ago. There was no sign of Alec or Hollis. When she could trust herself to look at him, she saw that he was smiling. He hadn't said a single word to her in English class these past few days, had acted, in fact, as if he'd never met her, never spent hours with her and the others at the Boy Scout camp. And here he was, smiling.

Lydia closed the door, crossed the room, and slowly lowered herself onto the grungy couch. The coarse upholstery scratched her thighs. She wished she had worn jeans instead of shorts, even though it was a warm night.

Gabriel didn't seem all that surprised to see her. He reached under the Adirondack chair and dragged out a six-pack of Coors. Four were left. He pulled one from the plastic ring and held it out to her. "It's not cold."

Lydia didn't like the taste of beer, but she took it anyway, sorry she hadn't brought her flask of vodka. But she had been afraid Alec would be there and insist on sharing again. The thought of his mouth on her flask made her queasy.

She pulled the tab on the can and took a quick swallow, barely a sip really, trying not to make a face.

Gabriel could see that she didn't want the beer. "Come here often?" He grinned over at her.

Lydia smiled in spite of herself. Not just because he was mocking that lame pickup line, but because she, and only she, knew the truth about just how often she *did* come here. "It's not bad, once you get used to the poor service."

"We need music, though. Don't you think? Maybe I should bring my portable CD player next time."

Next time? Lydia felt the soft fluttering of her heartbeat as it speeded up. "Sound travels through these woods," she told him. "Sometimes on hot nights when the windows are open you can hear the Steens a half mile away fighting like two screeching cats. Playing music could get us in trouble." She rolled the beer can back and forth in her palms. "We're trespassing, you know."

"Alec won't say anything, if that's what you're worried about."

"How do you know that?"

"It's cool. Don't worry about it."

Lydia leaned against the back of the couch and pulled her legs up to her chest, balancing the heels of her feet on the edge of the cushion. "I want to know how you can be so sure."

Gabriel shrugged. "Who do you think supplied this six-pack?" He was amused by the look on her face.

"Not Alec?" Lydia couldn't believe Alec would have given Gabriel free beer. She doubted he did anything that wasn't in his own interest. "He *gave* you that beer?"

"I gave him the money and he bought it for me. He's got fake ID."

"Figures." Lydia sighed, rolling her eyes toward the ceiling. Shadows flickered in the candlelight. "Why would he do that? You don't even know each other."

"Let's just say I tip well."

Lydia shook her head. "He can probably get you more than beer if you want." She wondered if Gabriel knew Alec had spent time in juvenile detention for selling drugs.

"So he said."

She couldn't help smiling at that. Now she had something on Alec. Something big. He was buying alcohol for a minor with fake ID and offering to sell him drugs. This was useful information. Something to bargain with. Lydia tucked it away for future reference. Trespassing was nothing compared to dealing drugs. For the first time in three days she breathed a little easier.

"So Alec's already been here tonight?" Lydia silently prayed that Alec had come and gone. She wanted Gabriel to herself.

Gabriel shook his head. "Not tonight." He held up his beer can. "This is from last night."

Lydia felt as if someone had broken into her house while she'd been away. Had somehow violated her space. She looked away, not wanting Gabriel to see how upset she was. Somehow she managed to say, "You were here last night?"

"We've been here every night since I found this place," he told her.

Then they still might come. Alec and that geek, Hollis. Lydia stared down at the can of beer in her hand and actually thought of leaving.

Gabriel was watching her. "I thought maybe you'd be here too."

"It's not like I hang out here every night," Lydia told him. Although she felt a tiny shiver of pleasure, knowing he had expected her to return.

"So what is it with this place? Is this where kids around here hang out?"

Lydia shook her head. "No! And don't you *dare* tell anyone. Nobody knows about this place. Just us." She squeezed her eyes closed and took a deep breath. "Except now there's Alec and Hollis. But we don't want anyone else to find out."

Gabriel shrugged. It was no skin off his nose. If he were being honest, which he wasn't, he would tell Lydia why he'd really been coming to the camp these past three nights, and to the pond every night the week before. He was hoping to see the girl who had been swimming the first night he'd come here. But he knew that in some way Lydia had laid claim to this place, even though she hadn't said so, knew intuitively she had been here many times before. And if he wanted to keep coming back, he would have to play his cards right. "What about that cinder-block building across the road, and the pond, is that all part of the Boy Scout camp?"

She nodded. "It's a garage, but I think they used it for more than that. There's still an old pool table over there, and a rusted car, and other junk."

"What about the pond? Can we swim in it?"

"If we don't get caught." She twisted a long strand of hair around her finger. "That's what this is about, right? Having a secret place no one knows of. A place where you can do anything you want, as long as nobody catches you." She kept her eyes on his when she said this. He stared back, unsmiling, waiting for her to go on. She could tell he was interested. And for the first time, she saw something in his eyes she hadn't noticed before. Something . . . intense. Maybe even dangerous. She could have sworn she felt the heat from his body, although he was at least five feet away. Her own body grew warm. She could barely swallow because her heart was in the way.

If Alec and Hollis hadn't shown up a few minutes later, Lydia might have climbed right into Gabriel's lap, put her arms around his neck, and kissed him until their lips were purple with bruises.

But the others did show up, bringing two more six-packs of beer with them. And Lydia, feeling unusually light-headed, found herself proposing that they make a pact never to tell anyone about this place.

Hollis, who rarely said anything, suddenly announced, "Then we'll need to seal it in blood if it's going to mean anything."

Gabriel and Lydia exchanged worried looks. Nobody in their right mind mixed their blood with someone else's. Not in this day and age. Not with the threat of AIDS looming over them. Each of them waited to see if the other was going to speak up. But it was Alec who punched Hollis in the shoulder and said, "Man, have you lost it!"

But Hollis surprised them by not backing down. He'd gotten some crazy notion in his head and wouldn't let it go. "You can't seal a pact without blood." That said, he headed out to the porch and came back with a burlap sack.

A slow, snide grin spread across Alec's face. He nodded his approval.

Lydia looked over at Gabriel and rolled her eyes. Gabriel shrugged, as if to say, Okay, yeah, it's stupid, something a kid would think up, but hey, let's humor him.

Hollis reached into the sack and pulled out something furry. Before she could utter a single word of protest, he laid the object on Lydia's lap. Lydia froze. She was as stiff as the cold dead rabbit that lay across her bare thighs. Alec and Hollis had been out poaching again, that much was clear.

She sat, unmoving, with the wooden corpse of the rabbit on her lap—a log with fur. Her instinct tore her in two directions: part of her wanted to shove the thing on the floor and part wanted to stroke it. She had begun to shake, just slightly. But she didn't dare let on how upset she was. Not in front of the others.

Hollis stared at her, his mouth half open in an awkward grin of anticipation, waiting to see what she would do.

One of his upper front teeth slightly overlapped the other. The bottom teeth were all crooked. Lydia had never noticed that before. To be honest, she had never looked that closely at Hollis Feeney, or cared to. He was short and round, with a pasty fat face and bristles of light brown hair. What was there to look at?

Lydia couldn't read the weird expression on his face, and she found that unnerving. She was usually pretty good at gauging people's emotions. Finally she said, "Is there a point to this, Geekoid?"

He pointed to the wound in the rabbit's side. It had crusted over. The wound had been made with a bullet from a rifle. Lydia could tell because there wasn't any sign of buckshot like in the animals her father and brothers killed. Hunting with a rifle in New Jersey was illegal. So was poaching. So was hunting at night. Lydia smiled. She had a few more things on Alec to add to her negotiations list.

"There's our blood," Hollis announced. Then, before anyone had time to protest, he jabbed his finger in the wound, opening it. "With this blood we pledge a vow of secrecy." He smeared a red streak across his forehead. Alec did the same.

Gabriel tried to suppress a laugh. This whole thing was ridiculous. Yet at the same time an uneasy queasiness seeped into his stomach. He didn't want to do this. But he wasn't about to back down, either. If he didn't agree to the pact, they wouldn't let him come here again. And while he didn't much care if he ever saw these three—a bunch of rural losers living in the middle of nowhere—after tonight or for the rest of his life for that matter, he did want to be there when the girl who swam in moonlight came to the door, as he hoped she would one day.

So as he visualized the girl gliding across the shimmering water, he poked his finger into the blood and painted a red gash on his forehead. Lydia, who had been watching him this whole time, did the same. She was sorry she had ever mentioned making a pact. But it was too late to turn back.

Hollis grabbed the rabbit from her lap and held it above his head like a trophy. "We are one in blood," he told them. "This is our sacred meeting place. We will defend it to the death. No one speaks of these things to outsiders. Or there will be grave consequences."

Gabriel wasn't sure whether to laugh out loud or be worried. Mostly he thought that this Hollis character had played one too many games of Dungeons & Dragons. So he let it go.

But later, once he was outside, the first thing he did was head for the pond to wash away the blood.

seven

The early-morning sun had not yet burned off the heavy fog that had swept down from the high ridges, when the sound of a pounding hammer woke Gabriel from a restless sleep. He padded to the window and looked out. There, below, was Shelby, looking like a hooded monk in her gray sweatshirt. Beside her was a stack of mildewed lattice she'd discovered beneath the deck off the great room. She was trying to nail the sections together to form a small rectangular fence. The idea, as she had explained it to all of them as they sat in the kitchen eating Frosted Mini-Wheats for dinner the night before, was to build a protective barrier to keep the local cat population away from two chipmunks who had taken up residence in the backyard.

Gabriel squinted into the mist and shook his head.

Shelby had to be out of her mind, hammering at this hour of the day. The sound echoed like gunshots through the woods. Truckers probably heard it on Route 80.

Watching his sister diligently building her fortress, he thought how much she was like their dad. Anyone could see how futile her efforts were. The lattice might keep the cats out, but it would never keep the chipmunks in. They would run beneath the openings as if the fencing weren't even there. And they'd be fair game for anything waiting outside Shelby's safe haven. But he knew better than to get into an argument over it. When Shelby got an idea in her head, she was like a bulldozer, she stopped for nothing. Better to let her figure out on her own how pointless her fortress was.

Gabriel glanced over at the digital clock on his nightstand. It was barely seven-thirty. And Saturday morning, no less. Usually on weekends he slept until noon. He thought about going back to bed, then decided that with all the hammering outside, he wouldn't be able to sleep anyway.

Instead he grabbed a pair of jeans from the open suitcase on the floor, slipping one leg into them while he dug around in another suitcase for a T-shirt. His mother, when she was home, as she was this weekend, constantly nagged him to unpack the suitcases and the stacks of boxes in his room. But so far he hadn't bothered. He liked the bare walls, the curtainless windows, the empty dresser. He had refused to let his mother put even so much as a throw rug on his wood floor or a comforter on his bed. The only objects that were visible were a lamp on his nightstand, a digital clock, his Discman, and a few CDs.

This was not his room. It was a temporary cell. And he wanted them, especially his father, to know it. He planned to leave everything in boxes and suitcases ready to move out on the day he graduated from high school.

He couldn't remember where he'd left his comb, so he rototilled his tangled hair with his fingers as he headed downstairs. No one else besides Shelby was awake. If he moved fast, he might make a clean getaway before one of his parents showed up and handed him a rake or came up with some other mindless chore for him to do.

He grabbed his hooded sweatshirt jacket and a bagel from the breadbox and headed out to his car, although he had no idea where he'd go. Even the malls weren't open at this hour.

But by the time he reached the end of the driveway, he knew exactly where he was going: Down the road past the Boy Scout camp, the same wooded road the girl on the bike took after her moonlight swims.

What got his attention was the sign. In large black letters painted on natural wood it said Lakota Wolf. And beneath those words: Visit our wolf preserve. Another, larger sign nearby read Stony Brook Campgrounds.

Before he was even aware of what he was doing, Gabriel swerved into the gravel parking lot next to a long building with a fieldstone front and switched off the ignition of the Toyota. He glanced at his watch. It wasn't quite eight o'clock yet. He doubted the place would be open.

But when he peeked in one of the front windows, he saw someone behind the counter pouring water into a coffee machine. He tried the door handle and found it locked.

The person behind the counter must have heard the sound, because she looked up, surprised, then came to open the door. Gabriel recognized her at once. It was the girl who sat across from him in English class, Gem Hennessey. That was when he remembered Alec talking about someone named Kate Hennessey who owned the Boy Scout camp. He wondered if the woman was Gem's mother.

For the first few seconds the girl stood there staring at him as if he'd just stepped out of a spaceship from another planet. He began to feel so awkward that he almost turned around and walked away. Still, he managed to say, "I saw your sign about the wolves."

Gem twisted the doorknob back and forth behind her back. "We don't open until eight. But that's okay." She stepped aside to let him in. "Want some coffee? It'll be ready in a few minutes."

Gabriel followed her into the building, a small store of some sort, probably for the campers. "Do you work here?"

She nodded. "Actually, I live here. Well, not in this building. Back there, up on the hill." She stood by the window, pointing to a large house nestled on the edge of the woods several hundred yards away. "Do you live around here?"

"Yeah, right down the road, about a mile or so."

"You live on Thorn Hill Road?" Gem couldn't believe her luck. For weeks she had been daydreaming about Gabriel Hart. But aside from a nod or an abrupt "Hi" in English class, he hadn't said much of anything to her. Up until now, she'd had no idea how she was going to get to know him. And all this time he was living right on the same road. "How far past the Boy Scout camp?"

At the mention of the camp, Gabriel felt his face grow hot. He wondered what she would think of him and the others trespassing on Hennessey property. He cleared his throat, not trusting his voice. "Not far, about a quarter mile maybe."

Gem poured him coffee in a Styrofoam cup. "It's complimentary," she said, handing it to him. And when he looked confused, she added, "The coffee."

Gem hoped he hadn't noticed her hand trembling when she handed him the cup. She was almost afraid to breathe, afraid she might be dreaming and the slightest motion would wake her. "There's a pond down by the camp. I swim there sometimes."

Gabriel set the cup on the counter, worried he might spill its contents. Because the very moment Gem handed him the coffee and mentioned the pond, he realized that the girl standing in front of him wasn't just Gem Hennessey from his English class. She was the same girl who came to swim in the pond on hot summer nights.

He looked away, embarrassed, as if he was, at that very moment, watching her sleek naked body gliding effortlessly through the water.

"About the wolves," Gem said, breaking into his thoughts. "I'd take you down to see them, but my aunt isn't here right now. In fact, she'll be gone most of the day. So I have to watch the store."

Gabriel wasn't at all sure what he should do next. finish his coffee? Stay and talk for a while? Leave? Set up a time when he could come by to see the wolves? But then Gem said, as if reading his mind, "If you want to come by next Saturday, I can take you to see them then."

"Great." Gabriel took a swallow of coffee. He wasn't ready to leave yet. But he wasn't at all sure what to say to keep the conversation going. That was when he remembered what Gem had said about her aunt. "You said your aunt was going to be gone all day? What about your folks?"

Gem poured herself a cup of coffee. "My parents are divorced. Neither of them lives at the campground. It's just me and my aunt Kate. Great-aunt, actually."

Gabriel didn't know what to say to that. He glanced over at the streak of sunlight that was streaming through the side window. The room was beginning to lose its damp early-morning chill. Outside, the fog melted into the warmer air.

"What about you?" Gem asked. "Where'd you move here from?"

"New York." Gabriel looked around the store for

someplace to sit down. But there wasn't a chair in sight. "So how come your folks named you Gem? I mean, it's a great name, just different."

"It's really Meg. Except when I was little, my mom's dad, Grandpa Torres, told me that Meg spelled backward is Gem. He said that's what I was. He used to call me his precious Gem. It sort of stuck." She shrugged. "Pretty corny, huh?"

"No. It's nice. Different."

"So why'd your family move way out here to the boonies?" Gem leaned across the counter and folded her arms. She was only inches away from him.

Gabriel felt suddenly uncomfortable. The last thing he wanted to do was talk about his family. "Who knows? I guess my dad was tired of living in the city." There didn't seem to be any good reason *not* to tell her the truth, *not* to tell her about Ben, but something stopped him. And that was when he realized he was embarrassed to tell Gem the reason. As far as he was concerned, his family had run away, like a bunch of scared chickens. The move to this place was cowardly. And even though it was all his father's doing, it made them all look gutless, the whole family.

Gabriel wanted to believe that if they had stayed in the city, he might have had a better chance of helping to find Ben's killers. Not for a minute did he believe that the cops were going to find them. Not after all this time. He knew they had more recent crimes to keep them busy.

In June, when he turned eighteen, he would head straight back to the city. Maybe he'd get an apartment with some of his old friends who planned to go to NYU, and he'd begin his own investigation. Nonstop, night and day, until he'd nailed those bastards.

He was suddenly aware that Gem was watching him, her expression both cautious and full of concern. And was it any wonder? His jaw ached with tension. He knew he'd been frowning.

"Is something wrong?" she asked.

Gabriel shook his head. "Not a thing." But he was already halfway to the door. "So I'll see you next Saturday then."

"Actually you'll see me Monday," Gem reminded him. "In homeroom."

"Right. I meant about the wolves." And before she could say another word, before she could ask him any more questions, he was out the door.

From the back window of his trailer, Alec had a clear view of Kate Hennessey's house. Gem was in the yard tossing a Frisbee to her aunt's Irish setters, Sam and Sadie.

Without any forethought, he reached for his leather jacket and headed out the door. The dogs saw him before Gem did. But he was a familiar sight around the campgrounds, so they kept right on chasing the Frisbee, never missing a beat. At least not until Alec jumped in the air and intercepted their catch with one hand.

Gem stuffed her hands in the pockets of her blue fleece jacket and glared at him.

Alec tossed the Frisbee at her, fully expecting her to reach for it. She didn't. He watched it sail right by her. The two dogs almost knocked her over trying to get to it.

"What do you want?" she asked.

Alec cocked his head to one side and frowned at her. "Lighten up. Jeez, I was just playing around." Sam came running up to him with the Frisbee dangling from his drooling mouth. He stood there panting, waiting patiently until Alec took the Frisbee and flung it into the air.

Gem turned to leave. "You can bring them to the back door when you're finished playing with them," she said to Alec, nodding at the two dogs.

Sam returned with the Frisbee. When Alec didn't seem to notice, the dog pushed the top of his head against the palm of Alec's hand. Distracted by Gem's receding figure, Alec stroked the dog's head indifferently.

Jeez, you'd have thought he was radioactive or something, the way Gem acted around him. It was really starting to get on his nerves.

With one swift motion he yanked the Frisbee from Sam's mouth and almost threw it right at Gem's back. He could picture it hitting her neck, maybe taking her head clean off her shoulders. *Shit.* Why did he have to think stuff like that? He hated it when he got like that. Why couldn't he just act normal around her? Whatever the hell that meant. He really had no idea.

After Gem disappeared into the house, Alec stayed awhile longer, tossing the Frisbee for Sam and Sadie. Even when the temperature took an unexpected plunge and his fingers began to ache with the cold, he kept on throwing until the sun finally set behind the trees.

When he brought the dogs to the back door, Kate Hennessey was there, but not Gem. He hadn't really expected her to be, but that hadn't stopped him from hoping.

And at least he had somewhere to go tonight. Somewhere to take his mind off Gem. The others would be there too. Just as they had every weekend since early September. He was sure of it. Because like him, they had nowhere else to go.

By nightfall the temperature had plunged below forty. Lydia bundled into a long-sleeved T-shirt and a light sweater. She pulled on thick wool socks, stuffed her wool gloves in the pocket of her navy blue peacoat, took the half-empty flask of vodka from under her mattress, and slipped out the window onto the sycamore.

It was probably insane, going down to the Boy Scout camp in this weather. There wasn't any heat in the building. But she couldn't seem to stop herself. She hadn't seen Gabriel, except from a distance, all week.

The wind had picked up, stinging her face as she headed down the road toward the camp. She had to be crazy, going out on a night like this, even crazier to think Gabriel was going to show up. But she would completely lose it if she had to sit at home all alone in her room thinking about him. And she wanted to believe Gabriel was feeling the same way.

The building was dark. Lydia pushed the door open slowly, without stepping inside, to make sure nothing was lurking there. Lately she'd been uneasy about coming here. It wasn't like the old days when she'd believed no one knew about this place but her. She'd felt safe here then. But ever since the others had shown up, she had come to realize that anyone could find this place. Anyone could be lurking in the shadows, waiting to grab her. For all she knew someone might be in one of the upstairs rooms, or in the kitchen, or hiding in one of the two enclosed staircases. That was why she had been coming later than she used to, knowing the boys would probably be there and the candle lit. Except for tonight. Tonight she wanted to get there before Gabriel.

She stepped inside and listened. The only sounds were the tapping of brittle branches on the roof and on the windows. The room smelled damp and mildewy.

No sooner had she lit the candle than she reached for the flask of vodka in her pocket. It would help to keep her warm while she waited to see if anyone else came.

In past years she rarely ventured out on cold nights. The sanctuary was for spring and summer, and early fall. Only a few times when the snow was over the tops of her boots and the schools closed had she plodded down here to spend a few peaceful hours away from her family, and only in the daytime. On those days the room had been cold and gray, but the snow muffled all sound, and she could pretend she was the last person on earth, stranded in a world as pure and pristine white as she believed it was intended to be.

Lydia slid into the Adirondack chair. She could feel the cold through her jeans. Fortunately she didn't have to wait long. She had no sooner settled in than the door creaked open. And there he was, looking beautiful through the warm, comforting haze of vodka, his face golden in the flickering light of the candle.

Gabriel stood with his hands in his pockets for a few seconds, watching her, then closed the door behind him. Like Lydia, he wore several layers beneath his jacket.

"I didn't think you'd be here tonight," he said, sitting on the couch across from her. "I mean, it's really cold out."

So far she hadn't said a word. Instead she held out her flask.

Gabriel took it.

At first they didn't say much, taking quiet sips from Lydia's flask, lost deep in their own thoughts.

When Gabriel looked over at her again, he seemed surprised that she was there, as if he'd completely forgotten about her.

"Why do you keep coming here?" Lydia asked.

He shrugged and slumped against the back of the couch. "Where else is there to go?"

"You've got a car. You can go anyplace you want."

"Like where?"

Lydia stared over at the candle in the middle of the table. "If you don't mind driving a ways, you can usually find a rave."

"I'm not into raves."

"Okay, movies. There are a lot of theaters around. And parties. Somebody from school almost always has a party on the weekends. Especially during football season."

He studied her with his hazel eyes, eyes that seemed to shift between brown and green in the candlelight. "Okay, if all that stuff's going on, what are *you* doing here?"

"I don't have a car," Lydia said, a little too quickly. She wasn't about to tell him her father had forbidden her to get a driver's license—just another way for him to control her.

"You've got friends with cars, don't you?"

She wished Gabriel hadn't said that, because she felt compelled to respond, to tell him that no, she didn't. And would he please just shut up about the whole car thing? Instead she said, "Maybe I like coming here." This was more than she had intended to share, but at least it would, she hoped, get him off the subject of cars.

"With parties on weekends? Raves? Movies?" He narrowed his eyes at her, then gazed slowly around the room, taking in all the decay. "Yeah, I can see why you'd prefer this place over all that other stuff." He pointed to her flask. "It's not like they don't have booze at parties. Or do you just like drinking alone?"

His sarcasm annoyed her. She would have liked to tell him how things were, how she didn't really have any friends at school, how her father was a tyrant who kept her from having any social life at all. But she didn't dare. She couldn't let him think she was a complete loser. Somehow she had to make him believe being here was her choice. She racked her brain for something clever to say, but all that came out was, "What I do and why isn't any of your business." It was lame and she knew it. Still, hopefully, it would get him off her case.

Gabriel grinned. "You're right. It isn't."

Lydia was beginning to wish she hadn't come here tonight. This wasn't at all what she'd imagined. She had been hoping to find Gabriel alone, hoping to talk to him, maybe get him to open up a little. Instead they were having this inane conversation about why they had come to the camp, and neither of them was being honest. Well, maybe Gabriel was, a little, she conceded. Maybe he really didn't know where else to spend a Saturday night around here. Yet Lydia knew it was more than that. He could rent videos and watch them all night if he wanted or hang out at the mall. He had a car; he could ride around until sunrise. But he hadn't done any of those things. He had come here. Which meant—she scarcely dared to hope—that maybe, just maybe he had come here to see her.

eight

An early-October moon, a harvest moon, full and bright orange, lit the path as Alec Stryker slipped silently through the woods. It was so crisp and bright out that a thin film of frost shimmered on the leaves. He pulled the knitted wool cap farther down on his head to cover the tips of his ears.

For the past two days the temperature had been bitter cold. Leaves that had only halfheartedly begun to turn now donned brilliant colors almost overnight.

It had been weeks since he had come into the woods alone. And it felt good, just him and his rifle. No Hollis. He had no idea why Hollis hadn't shown up tonight, and he didn't much care.

He couldn't figure Hollis out. Hollis had never asked to

borrow any of Alec's guns, had never asked to shoot one while they were out hunting.

Once, when Alec had offered him one of his shotguns, Hollis had run his hand along the cold metal barrel. Alec could tell he wanted to take it. But in the end he shook his head and pushed it away. It didn't make sense.

Alec climbed a deer stand that belonged to someone else, although he had no idea who, and slid a pint of Jack Daniel's from his pocket. This was how it used to be, before Hollis. And he wished it was that way again. He'd like to tell Hollis to stop hanging around. Except it wasn't that easy. Hollis knew too much. Alec wasn't sure how that had happened.

All he knew was over the past four months Hollis had somehow managed to find out things, things Alec had thought he would never tell anyone. Things so dark he couldn't bear to think of them himself. Stuff he had done when he was a kid, like killing his father's favorite hunting dog, a bloodhound named Boss. To this day his father still believed some hunter had shot the dog by mistake. But Alec knew better. That was how much he hated his old man. His stupid asshole old man, who cared more about his damn dogs than his own son.

There had been other car thefts too, besides the one he had spent time in juvenile detention for, ones he'd gotten away with. And there was the heroin and crack cocaine he sold across the river, down in Easton. Was still selling, when he needed money.

Thinking about the stuff he'd told Hollis, Alec began to

wonder what the hell he'd been thinking. He had to be crazy, telling that fat little geek stuff like that. But Hollis made it so easy. It was like talking to yourself half the time. Talking out loud when nobody was around. Yeah, that was what it was like.

He and Hollis, walking in the woods at night, Hollis a few feet behind. His voice would seem to float up out of nowhere, sort of quiet. You had this feeling you were only half awake. It reminded Alec of his mother's voice, trying to wake him out of a sound sleep when he was small. Only the voice said things like, "What's it feel like to kill something?" And Alec would find himself thinking about that, wanting to put it into words. Because he never had.

He remembered the night Hollis asked him that question. They were out poaching. Hollis had been trudging along behind Alec, like his shadow, only a shorter, heavier version.

Alec had stopped and looked over his shoulder. Hollis was standing with his hands in his pockets. No expression. He had just asked Alec the question about killing, about how it felt.

"What kind of question is that?"

Hollis had looked him straight in the eyes. "Considering what we're doing out here, I'd say it was a fair question, wouldn't you?"

Ordinarily Alec would have turned around and kept on walking. Instead he surprised himself by saying, "Depends on what you're killing and why."

Hollis nodded thoughtfully. "So give me an example."

Alec thought for a minute, then said, "Out here, poaching, it's impersonal. You don't think about it."

"So when's it personal?"

And that was when Alec had told him about his father's old bloodhound, Boss.

By now the moon had reached the tops of the trees. It was so bright, Alec had to look away. He took a swallow of Jack Daniel's. On nights like this he knew he wasn't going to shoot anything. Lately it seemed he'd been doing most of the shooting because Hollis kept pointing things out for him to shoot. But tonight he didn't plan to kill anything. That wasn't why he had come into the woods. He had come here, as he always had, to get his bearings. Thinking about the past always got him all riled up. But sometimes he liked to imagine that maybe he hadn't screwed up so bad that he couldn't start fresh. That was what he was thinking tonight.

Two nights ago, when he and Hollis got to the camp, they'd found Lydia and Gabriel already there, talking. They were so into what they were saying, at first they hadn't even noticed him standing in the doorway. In those few seconds Alec had caught a glimpse of something, something he wanted more than he cared to admit. He wanted whatever was going on between Gabriel and Lydia in that moment. He wanted someone to look at him the way Lydia had been looking at Gabriel. And he knew exactly who he wanted that someone to be—Gem Hennessey.

Most of his life he'd been a loner. But there was something about going down to the old Boy Scout camp, hanging out with Gabriel and Lydia, that had made him think maybe things could change. He had no idea why that should be. All he really knew was that deep in that place where a small kernel of hope refused to die, he continued to dream that one night Gem Hennessey would stumble into their hangout, just like he and Hollis had, and Gabriel.

He wanted her to see he had friends. He wanted her to see he wasn't a total loser. But most of all, he wanted a chance.

OCTOBER 9

When Gabriel got home from school on Friday afternoon, he found Shelby and some boy watching a video of *Titanic* in the great room off the kitchen. They had their hands submerged in a bowl of popcorn wedged between them on the couch.

He didn't know why he should be surprised. Shelby liked hanging out with boys. She liked football and soccer. She'd always had more guys for friends than girls. But this was different, because for the first time he noticed Shelby was wearing lipstick. Not some soft neutral color, but a dark plum—so dark it was almost black.

Ordinarily when his sister had friends over, he wouldn't even bother with them. He'd get a soda from the fridge, grab a bag of pretzels, and head up to his room. But that wasn't going to happen today. Before he realized what he was doing, he had flopped down on the couch next to Shelby.

If she was annoyed at the intrusion, she didn't show it. Her eyes were glued to the TV screen.

"Where's Dad?"

"Studio."

"So who's this?" Gabriel shifted his eyes toward the boy sitting on her other side. The boy, whose left eyebrow was pierced with two gold studs, never even bothered to look his way.

"David. From school."

David, Gabriel figured, was probably in the same grade. He looked harmless enough, slouched down into the cushion with the heels of his black Nikes resting on the coffee table.

Gabriel waited to see if Shelby was going to add anything more. When she didn't, he left them alone to finish their movie and headed upstairs to his room. But he couldn't shake the feeling that he should have said something, or done something, maybe sent the kid home. What was he supposed to do in situations like this? Why wasn't his mother here? Did she know Shelby was wearing lipstick? And fake nails with bright blue polish? Bringing boys into the house to watch videos? And not some campy slasher movie—a love story, for Pete's sake. He wondered if his mother would even care. And with a sickening swell of emptiness he realized the answer was probably *no*.

Ever since she'd taken that studio apartment in the city,

they barely spoke to each other. She came home late on Friday nights and left Sunday afternoons. In between she read manuscripts she brought with her. He wondered why she even bothered coming home. Part of him wished she'd just stay in the city, divorce his father, and get it over with if that was what she had in mind. Anything would be better than this limbo.

His father wasn't much better these days. He'd practically sequestered himself in his studio out back, painting from the time he got up in the morning until late at night. Or at least he gave the impression he was working. Gabriel didn't know for sure what the man did with his time anymore. More often than not he didn't bother to come in for dinner. Not that dinner was much of anything these days. Whatever you could stick in the microwave. They were all pretty much on their own when it came to meals, although once in a while he and Shelby ordered a pizza.

If he'd still been seeing Dr. Cortes, Gabriel would have told her his family was falling apart. His parents barely spoke to each other, or to him or Shelby. They were four people in four separate corners with nothing but a wide, dark pit in the center. They clung to their separate walls, fearing that if they took one step forward they would be swallowed up in all that darkness.

He would tell Angela Cortes this was how it felt, living with these people, and maybe she would know what to do. But no one had mentioned Dr. Cortes since they'd moved to this place. And when Gabriel asked his father if they were going to see a new shrink, his father seemed to drift off somewhere, a place where Gabriel couldn't reach him. He never gave Gabriel a direct answer. The closest he'd gotten was a cryptic "We'll see."

From his mother, he heard, "It's too expensive. Especially if we all go." Sometimes she said things like "We'll have to work through this ourselves."

But they weren't working through it, Gabriel thought. That was the problem. They wouldn't even talk about what happened to Ben, much less mention his name. Sometimes it seemed as if Ben had never existed. No, worse. As if his parents thought Ben was still alive, still away at Princeton, and they were just waiting for December, when he'd be home for break.

It was only three-thirty in the afternoon and already Gabriel found himself anticipating the moment when he could slip out into the night and head for the Boy Scout camp. He realized he had been pacing around his bedroom like a caged animal. There were things he should be doing, his homework for one. But he couldn't seem to focus on anything much these days, least of all math problems.

Hamlet, though—now, that had surprised him. At first he couldn't believe his English teacher had assigned a play Gabriel had already read as a freshman. Back then he'd hated the play. Reading it had been like trying to translate a story written in a foreign language. It had been all he could do just to read the words, forget deciphering the meaning behind them. But this time the story had captured his imagination. He understood Hamlet's need to avenge his father's death, understood Hamlet's passionate outbursts, his rage, his hatred, his single-minded purpose. Gabriel was pulling for him, even though he already knew how the play ended.

He dug into his backpack, which lay on the floor by his bed, and found the play. But even Hamlet's torment couldn't keep his mind focused this afternoon. It actually made things worse. Like Shakespeare's haunted character, Gabriel felt driven to action but unable to act. After three pages, read as many times, he tossed the book on the floor.

If he stayed in this house another minute, he would smash everything in sight. Instead he got in his car and took off. If he had to he'd drive around for the next five hours, until it was time to head for the camp.

The prescription note was tucked in her mother's wallet. Lydia had been searching for hidden twenty-dollar bills but instead had found this. She stared at the note and realized it was from Dr. Abrams's prescription notepad. Dr. Abrams had been their family physician when they'd lived in Rolling Hills. Before they moved, her mom had worked part-time in his office as a receptionist, filling in for a friend who was on maternity leave. The family never went to Dr. Abrams anymore. He was too far away. If they went anywhere, it was to a local medical center in Knollwood.

She tried to make out the writing on the note, but she didn't recognize the words.

Lydia slipped the prescription note back into the wallet, forgetting to look for any more money. Instead she headed straight for the medicine cabinet in the bathroom. There wasn't a single prescription bottle in sight. But she wasn't satisfied and wouldn't be until she'd gone through every drawer in her parents' bedroom.

She had a bad feeling about this, especially since her mother seemed so out of it lately. Mostly Lydia chose not to notice how her mother went about her days almost mechanically, like a sleepwalker, how she silently mouthed other people's words. It was easier to pretend her mother was the same person she'd always been. But now, after finding the prescription note, Lydia needed to know the truth. Maybe the medication her mother was taking was affecting her. And so began her search.

When she didn't find anything in her parents' bedroom, she went through every room in the house except the living room, where her mother was asleep on the couch, an open copy of *Good Housekeeping* draped across her stomach.

Lydia stood in the archway, watching the sleeping form on the couch. So far she had found nothing. Where else could she look? And then it came to her. The one thing her mother was rarely without and never let out of her sight: her knitting bag. There it was, on the floor beside the coffee table.

Without giving it another thought, Lydia slipped silently into the living room, lifted the bag, and headed for the powder room down the hall, locking the door behind her. She began to lift skein after skein of wool yarn from the bag until something slipped from inside one of the skeins. A small amber-colored bottle. A plastic prescription bottle. She recognized the name of the drug. It was Valium. She knew it was a tranquilizer.

She wiggled her fingers inside the centers of the other skeins and found more bottles with names on their labels, some of which Lydia had never heard of, like Alprazolam and Demerol. One prescription was for Percocet. Percocet was a painkiller, wasn't it? A narcotic? So what was her mother doing? Mixing drugs? That would explain why sometimes Lydia had seen her lose her balance, grab for the back of a chair or for the kitchen counter.

On the bottom, beneath the rest of the skeins, Lydia found two prescription pads with Dr. Abrams's name on them.

For a long time she sat on the rag rug in front of the sink, holding the bottles of drugs in her lap, trying to understand why her mother would do such a thing: steal prescription pads from Dr. Abrams and then forge his signature. Because it was perfectly obvious to Lydia that that was exactly what her mother had been doing. And Lydia knew without a doubt that these drugs were the reason for the change in her mother's behavior, knew also why her mother didn't seem to mind living in this godforsaken wilderness anymore. All this time she had been forging Dr. Abrams's signature, writing prescriptions for drugs, drugs to help her tolerate the intolerable.

Lydia had no idea what to do. She began to stuff the prescription bottles back inside the skeins of wool, then buried the prescription pads under the yarn. If her father found out, he would take the drugs away from his wife, and who knew what else he would do to her? Without the drugs, would her mother return to being the same vibrant, interesting woman she had been when they lived in Rolling Hills? Lydia doubted it. It terrified her to think this, but she suspected that the drugs were the only reason her mother could get out of bed in the morning. Without them, she just might decide to never get up again.

Her mother was still asleep when Lydia came back to the living room. Lydia placed the knitting bag on the floor where she'd found it. For a few minutes she stood next to the couch watching her mother. Then she went to the front hall closet and pulled out her peacoat, feeling the pocket to make sure the flask she'd brought to school earlier that day was still there. How could she blame her mother for doing whatever she could to escape? Wasn't Lydia herself doing the same thing? Wasn't that what the flask in her pocket was for?

It was almost dinnertime. Lydia knew she should stay and help. Her mother would wake up soon. And her dad would be coming down from his attic office, where he'd been working on the next issue of his survivalist newsletter. But really, she didn't much care. All she wanted was to get to the old Boy Scout camp, where she could have some time alone before the others showed up.

There would be hell to pay when she got home. They'd want to know where she'd been. Why she'd just disappeared without telling them. Her father would shove her into a chair and read her the riot act. It was a given.

Lydia sighed, then headed to the kitchen. She pulled a notepad from the drawer and wrote: *Went to a pep rally with some kids from school. Spending the night at Janeane's.* There was no Janeane. And Lydia had purposely not put a last name so her father wouldn't try to call some total stranger's house to talk to a daughter who wasn't there. She taped the note to the kitchen cabinet next to the stove, where her mother would be sure to see it, and read the note again. *Pep rally.* Lydia grinned. Now, *that* was funny.

nine

The mood at the camp was different that night. They all felt it, although no one said anything.

Alec had been working on the chimney. He was on the roof, plunging a brick tied to a rope into it, trying to scrape off the biggest chunks of creosote so they could use the fireplace without risking a chimney fire. If they were going to spend winter nights hanging out there, they would need the heat. They had logs, but so far they'd only used them at the base of the door to keep anyone outside from seeing a crease of light—as Gabriel had—that might give them away.

Lydia had already told them she was worried about the smoke attracting attention. But Alec assured her that since there were only three or four families down the road, two of which were Lydia's and Gabriel's, it was unlikely anyone would be coming by. Besides, the building was set back in the woods. No one would see smoke coming from the chimney in the dark.

But Lydia knew better. When the wind was right, the smell of smoke from the Steens' wood-burning stove filled her bedroom, even though the Steens' house was halfway down the mountain. It was the *smell*, not the *sight* of smoke, that could give them away. And she told them as much. But no one seemed to care.

When the fire was built, they all huddled around it, Hollis sitting in the broken Adirondack chair, the others on the floor. No one had much to say that night. But even though they seemed locked in their own thoughts, they were acutely aware of each other's presence. They were not alone. And that was why they were there.

Hollis was the first to break the silence. "I think it's about time Gabriel and Lydia go through the initiation," he said. The others stared up at him, waiting. His eyes seemed to reflect the dancing flames as he kept his gaze on the fireplace. "We can't have any uninitiated members hanging around here. It's too risky."

The other three exchanged puzzled looks, but Hollis's eyes were on Alec now. He kept them locked on him. Waiting.

Slowly a knowing smile pinched the corners of Alec's mouth, just slightly. Hollis, in his own strange way, had reminded him that he, Alec, held all the cards. Gabriel and Lydia were here only because he hadn't told Old Lady Hennessey about them trespassing. Alec held all their future nights in this place right in his palm. And the feeling that knowledge gave him was intoxicating, better than a whole pint of Jack Daniel's on a cold night in the woods, better than bringing down a twelve-point buck.

"Yeah, Hollis is right." Alec told them. "You want to hang out with us, you gotta prove yourselves."

Lydia hiccuped a nervous giggle. "You're kidding, right?" She looked over at Gabriel for reassurance. But he didn't seem to know how to play this hand any more than she did. "What makes you think we even want to hang out with you?"

"You keep showing up, don't you?" Alec stood to throw another log on the fire. Hot embers burst into the air like miniature fireworks.

"I was coming here long before you guys ever found this place," Lydia told him. Her voice hissed along with the dying embers that had landed on the hearth. She could have bitten her tongue for telling him that. How could she have been so stupid?

"Really?" Alec arched one eyebrow. "Well, I'm sure Old Lady Hennessey would be interested to know that."

Alec shifted his attention to Hollis, who was staring up at the ceiling, hands folded on his large belly. He seemed lost in his own thoughts, but Alec knew he was listening to every word. He also knew the ball was in his court. Hollis wasn't about to help him. On the contrary, he knew Hollis was waiting to see what he would do.

So far Gabriel hadn't said a word. Now he looked up

at Alec, who was leaning against the mantel, and said, "What kind of initiation?"

"We need to know if you're going to be loyal to our gang," Alec told him. "And if you can take orders without whining."

"I hate that word—*gang*," Hollis interrupted. "We're not some clique or posse, or street gang, or some fringe group. We're an intelligent force, an organization."

"I didn't ask *why*," Gabriel said to Alec, ignoring Hollis. "I asked *what*. What kind of initiation?" He licked his lips. They felt cracked and dry, probably from sitting too close to the fire.

"I thought we'd do some shopping." Alec stuck out his hand, palm up, flexing his fingers a few inches from Lydia's face. "Let's have that flask."

Reluctantly she pulled the flask from her coat pocket and handed it to him. The thought of Alec's slimy lips on her flask made her stomach turn. She wished now she had left it home. But lately Alec had been bringing his own booze, mostly beer, so she had brought along her flask of vodka.

He lifted the flask above his head. "We need a little something to get us in the mood." Then he took a long swallow and passed the flask to Gabriel, who hesitated for only a split second, then did the same. When it was Lydia's turn, she tried to remember that Gabriel's lips had been the last to touch the flask. Then, after taking a drink, she started to hand the flask to Hollis.

"I don't drink," he said, flatly.

"Hey, man, it's a gang—group thing," Alec said. "We're—"

"Ever." Hollis said this with such intensity that the other three just shook their heads and looked away, embarrassed.

Alec shrugged and headed for the front door. "Fine, no problem." He looked back over his shoulder at Hollis. "We'll take my pickup."

"Aren't you going to put out the fire?" Lydia was suddenly afraid that without them there to keep an eye on it, the whole building might go up in flames. She didn't want to come back to find a pile of cinders where her sanctuary had once stood.

"Leave it," Alec ordered. "We're coming back."

No one said anything more. They were on a mission of sorts, although except for Alec, they had no idea what that mission was. But they trudged along behind him to the cinder-block garage on the other side of the road, where Alec had hidden his truck next to the frame of a rusted old Volkswagen.

Only three could fit in the cab, so Lydia sat on Gabriel's lap, which was fine with her. She was beginning to like this initiation thing.

Alec slipped a tape into the tape deck and turned it up full blast. "This'll get us in the mood," he said, backing the truck onto the road.

Gabriel had begun to feel ridiculously light. He had no idea what Alec had in mind, and somehow it didn't matter. There was something about speeding down rural back roads, about the persistent throbbing from the bass, the heavy metal music vibrating through his whole body, about the truck blasting fallen leaves in all directions, creating a whirlwind of colorful chaos caught briefly in the reflection of the headlights as the pickup ripped through the night, something dangerous and wild.

A short time later they turned onto the highway that led into the town of Knollwood. No lights were on in the few houses set back from the road. It was almost midnight.

They found Main Street as dark as the rest of the town, except for streetlights and a few dim fluorescent lights inside the stores. On the outskirts of town, where Main Street intersected again with the highway, there was a small strip mall. All the shops were closed, except for a 7-Eleven across the street.

Alec glanced in the rearview mirror. Not a car in sight.

Behind the 7-Eleven were a loading dock and a few parking spaces, presumably for employees. Alec parked the truck, shut off the engine, then turned to the others.

"This is rookie stuff," he told them. "Any kindergartner could pull it off."

"Pull what off?" Lydia asked.

"We need to stock up on some supplies. Stuff to keep at the camp." Alec leaned over the steering wheel. He was talking to Lydia and Gabriel. "Hollis is going to stay outside the door and keep an eye on things. He'll let me know when you're coming out."

"How come it's just me and Lydia?" Gabriel was

suddenly uncomfortable. He knew Alec was sending them in the store to cop stuff, whatever they could get away with. Nobody had said that, it was just understood. He reminded himself that kids did this kind of thing all the time. He'd done it a few times himself. No big deal. He'd known plenty of kids who stole stuff, even Ben.

Except Gabriel couldn't seem to get his dad's face out of his mind. For a moment he actually thought he felt Robert Hart's heavy hand weighing on his shoulder as it had when he was seven. The time Gabriel slipped a small He-Man action figure into his pocket. It had been the week before Christmas and his dad had taken him to FAO Schwarz on Fifth Avenue to see the window displays and roam through the huge toy store.

Later, when they were in the cab going home, Gabriel had made the mistake of easing the action figure halfway out of his pocket, just for a peek. He thought his father wasn't looking. He was wrong. His father had made the cabdriver turn around and head back to FAO Schwarz. He took Gabriel by the arm and marched him right up to the store manager, where the boy handed over the action figure and apologized. It had been one of the most humiliating moments in his life.

Thinking about that now, thinking about his father, Gabriel suddenly found himself smiling. It was perverse, he knew. He sure hadn't been expecting that, but there it was, and the grin was getting broader. If only his old man could see him now.

Alec was eyeing him suspiciously. "You want to know

why just you and Lydia? Because you're the rookies. Me and Hollis, we already know the ropes."

Gabriel doubted Hollis had ever stolen so much as a piece of gum, but for some reason Alec seemed to feel the need to let him off the hook. It was hard to tell whether Hollis was relieved or not. His face was totally devoid of expression.

"You think I've never stolen anything before?" Gabriel said.

"Yeah," Lydia added. "I'm no rookie either." She didn't bother to mention that she'd copped only two, maybe three things in her entire life. Small stuff, a Baby Ruth candy bar, a Chap Stick. She'd felt so guilty about the candy bar she'd given it away to the first little kid she saw coming down the street. And she never did use the Chap Stick, afraid her lips would break out in huge fever blisters, announcing her crime to the whole world.

"There could be video cameras taping you," Hollis said, ignoring their feeble protests. "And there will be parabolic mirrors in all the corners. I didn't see any cars out front, so there probably aren't any customers, which means whoever's behind the counter will be watching you pretty closely. You need to work as a team, one of you blocking what the checkout person can see in the mirror and making sure the video cameras can't pick up what you're stashing up your sleeves and in your pockets."

"So . . ." Lydia shook her head, confused. "What? You want us to stay close together so I can slip stuff into Gabe's pockets and he can put stuff in mine?"

"Exactly," Hollis said.

Alec shifted his weight, leaning his back against the door. "Play it up. Pretend you're on your way home from a date and you can't keep your hands off each other."

Lydia was beginning to think this wasn't going to be all that bad. She liked the idea of having Gabriel put his hands on her. She opened the door and slid from his lap. Gabriel followed with Hollis right on his heels, although before they reached the front door Hollis stopped by the ice machine in the corner. This would be his lookout post.

Only one checkout person was behind the counter, a girl about their own age, maybe a year or two older, with short spiked hair the color of an eggplant and eyes rimmed with heavy smudged eyeliner. The girl was so into reading the latest *National Enquirer,* she didn't even look up when Lydia and Gabriel came through the door. Lydia was relieved to see that the girl wasn't someone she knew, or who would know her.

Lydia slipped her arm possessively through Gabriel's and leaned in closely. He smelled like wood smoke from the fireplace. "Before we leave we should buy something. Even if it's only a can of soda, so she won't get suspicious," she whispered. Gabriel nodded, then put his arm around Lydia's shoulder. She slid her arm around his waist. By now he had scouted out the cameras and the mirrors.

Most of the small items, the ones that fit up sleeves or in pockets, were up front by the checkout counter. They took their time casing the aisles. When they reached the bakery section, Gabriel bent Lydia toward the shelf as if he was going to kiss her. Lydia's heart was pounding like a jackhammer. She couldn't be sure if it was because Gabriel's body was so close to hers or because she was scared they would be caught.

In a panic she wrapped her fingers around a package of Hostess cupcakes and with shaking hands slipped them into the inside pocket of Gabriel's jacket. Then she surprised them both by kissing him. Gabriel almost lost his balance but then found himself kissing her back. "We have to make it look real," she whispered in his ear.

Gabriel's heart had been pumping double-time from the rush of adrenaline ever since they'd gotten out of the truck. Now it began to beat even faster. He bent over to kiss her again and felt her shoving something else into another pocket. He wasn't sure what was causing the wild rush he was feeling—maybe Lydia's mouth on his, or the light scent of lavender emanating from her, maybe the stealing, or maybe it was everything together. But it didn't matter. He was beginning to think he could go on doing this all night. Except now Lydia was leading him over to the refrigerated section, opening the doors and lifting out cans of Coke. Some she slipped into his pockets. Two others they carried up to the counter.

The girl looked up from her tabloid. "That it?"

The two of them nodded in unison. They were a team.

Once outside, out of sight of the clerk, Gabriel lifted Lydia into the air and swung her around. She wanted to tell him that wasn't necessary. She was already flying, had been ever since they'd set foot inside the store. Instead she only laughed louder, louder than she had in a long, long time.

Hollis stood a few feet away, hands stuffed in the pockets of his baggy cargo pants, his head cocked to one side, quietly observing them. He had the look of an entomologist studying two bugs under a microscope.

"You're both acting as if that was real high-risk or something," Hollis said as the three of them climbed back in the truck.

Alec could see right off that Lydia and Gabriel were full of themselves. He knew that feeling. He'd been there. Lots of times.

Lydia was handing out sodas so they could toast their success. She tossed a snack-sized bag of potato chips into Alec's lap and the Hostess cupcakes into Hollis's.

As Alec steered the truck through town, Lydia and Gabriel popped the tabs, held up the cans, and tapped them together. "To teamwork," Gabriel said.

Alec hadn't looked their way since he'd started the engine. Not because of anything Gabriel or Lydia had said or done. This was about Hollis, about the look of disappointment Alec had seen on Hollis's face the minute he opened the door and climbed in the truck. Maybe Hollis thought he'd let him down. Alec knew he shouldn't let that bother him, but it did. Hollis had handed him a golden opportunity. Alec had had the chance to make Lydia and Gabriel do something big-time. Something really dangerous. And what did he do? He sent them on a stupid shoplifting mission.

Alec couldn't even bring himself to look at Hollis, who sat next to him sipping his Coke in silence while Lydia filled them in on every little detail of their petty, ridiculous 7-Eleven adventure. Alec had a crazy urge to stop the car, open the passenger door, and tell her she could either shut up or walk the rest of the way home.

Instead he waited for Lydia to take a breath, then said, "So big fucking deal. You made it past the first step."

"What?" Lydia clamped her hand onto Gabriel's shoulder. She felt his arm tighten around her waist and knew she wasn't the only one taken by surprise.

"The initiation," Alec said. "This is just the first step, babe. Don't tell me you thought that was it? Man, this is just the beginning."

No one said anything. But Alec felt Hollis shift in his seat, sitting taller. He could tell by the way Hollis's shoulder, which was pressed against his, rose three inches higher that he had said the right thing.

Sometime after three in the morning, Lydia climbed the sycamore and slipped into her bedroom. She stepped out of her jeans, leaving them in a pile on the floor, and dropped her peacoat and sweatshirt next to them. She pulled the T-shirt nightgown from under her pillow, tugging it over her head, then slipped between the icy sheets.

Outside the wind blew fiercely. The few leaves still clinging to the sycamore finally let go and were beating against the window like yellow rain. Lydia wondered if her mother had found her note and covered for her, as she had on a few other occasions. Probably. That was, if she wasn't too doped up to know what was going on.

For a long time Lydia lay there waiting to feel the same guilt she had felt as a child when she had stolen the Baby Ruth, or when she was thirteen and took the Chap Stick from the pharmacy only a week after they'd moved here. Would she feel driven to walk all the way back to Knollwood to return the stuff they'd taken? But then that wasn't possible, was it? Because they had already drunk the sodas and eaten most of the food on the ride back.

Maybe she could send the money to the 7-Eleven in an envelope with no return address. But she knew she wouldn't do that, either. Because this time was different. She had no words to describe what it had felt like, with Gabriel's arms around her as she filled his pockets with stolen food. And she knew without any doubt whatsoever that she would do it again in a minute.

ten

They were there, standing at the foot of his bed. The Shadow People. He had left his door open just a crack, and the light from the hallway spilled into the room, giving shape to the dark faceless figures. Gabriel's fingers tightened around the edge of his blanket. Sweat prickled his skin. He closed his eyes and told himself he was only half awake. The smoky forms were part of his unconscious, part of his dream world. They weren't real. They couldn't hurt him.

If he could only bring himself to get up and close the door, they would fade into the night. But his legs would not move. When he finally dared to open his eyes, the shadows were gone. But their chilling presence lingered. It took him hours to fall back to sleep.

Later, in the predawn, while bats nestled beneath the

deck and wrapped their wings about themselves for warmth, Gabriel dreamed he was standing at the edge of the pond across the road from the abandoned Boy Scout camp. Something moved gracefully through the water. White arms lifted sheets of water that shimmered in the moonlight like the wings of angels. He knew the swimmer was Gem Hennessey.

As he took a step closer to the pond, thinking he might join her, a sudden sucking noise rose into the night air. His boots began to sink in soft mud. No matter how hard he tried, he couldn't seem to lift his feet, and he was sinking deeper and deeper. When he looked up, he saw that the pond had grown larger. He could barely make out Gem in the distance. If he didn't hurry she would disappear altogether. But his struggle was futile. By now the mud was up to his knees, and he knew he might never escape.

When he woke the next day, Gabriel's first thought was of Lydia, which surprised him. He thought of her warm mouth on his while she'd filled his pockets with stolen food. His body shuddered with intense pleasure at the memory. Except, when he tried to imagine kissing Lydia someplace else, at the camp, in his car, he felt nothing. He hadn't thought Lydia was his type, although she did bear some resemblance to his ex-girlfriend, Celia, whom he'd broken up with a month after Ben's death. Still, there had been that moment in the 7-Eleven last night. Such moments made you think twice about some things.

So why, he wondered, had he dreamed of Gem?

Maybe, he thought, it had something to do with saying he'd stop by to see the wolves. It was Saturday. The day he was to meet her at the campgrounds.

He glanced over at the digital clock. Despite his mother's annoying taps on his door and her incessant reminders that his father wanted him to rake the front yard, Gabriel had managed to sleep until noon. Robert Hart had some crazy notion that if they raked the leaves every few days, they'd be able to keep on top of things.

"We live in the woods, for God's sake," Gabriel had told him over a week ago. "We're surrounded by a million trees. We'll never be able to keep up."

His father had been standing in the middle of the kitchen with two bamboo rakes, one in each hand, that he'd bought at the local True Value. "If we don't rake, the leaves will kill the grass."

Gabriel had stuffed two Pop-Tarts into the toaster, then slid into a chair. "So, okay. Then we won't have to worry about mowing the lawn anymore." Wadding up the empty Pop-Tart package in his hand, he had looked up at his father and grinned. "It's a win/win situation, Dad. It doesn't get much better than that."

His father had not been amused.

Gabriel thought of how every Tuesday night his father dragged the garbage cans all the way to the end of the driveway for the trash haulers to pick up the next morning. And every Wednesday morning, when he went to retrieve the cans, he found that the bears had been there first, before the haulers. Trash was strewn everywhere.

White plastic bags had been dragged to the edge of the woods or slashed open, leaving garbage exposed on the driveway. Each time, his father picked up the trash and put it back in the can, hoping the bears wouldn't show up the following week. But they always did. It was an exercise in futility, like the fence Shelby had built around the two chipmunks.

So was raking the leaves when you lived in the middle of a forest. Only his father couldn't seem to grasp that, either.

Gabriel's mother was rapping at his door again. He rolled over on his side, facing the wall, listening to her voice on the other side of the door as she droned on about how everybody had to pull their weight around here. And even though she didn't say it, he still heard the unspoken words, "Now that Ben is gone." His mother would never say this out loud. She didn't have to. The words crashed into his eardrums as if they were coming from a Dolby soundtrack playing full blast. And there was no way to block them out because they were coming from inside his head.

He didn't need anyone to tell him the wrong son had been murdered. He was reminded every day. He saw it when his father read the sports pages in the local paper and looked up to ask him for the hundredth time if he thought he might try out for basketball this year. Ben had been the best player on the varsity team in his junior and senior years of high school, leading them to the state championship two years in a row. And he had gone on to play center on the basketball team at Princeton. Robert Hart had followed his son's games religiously, attended them as he would have church, that was if he'd ever decided to join a church. Gabriel found the whole sports fixation thing funny. His dad, the artist, an avid sports nut. Weird.

And Shelby. Shelby had been on the soccer and softball teams in her old school. Only this year she no longer seemed all that interested. Gabriel wondered if that had something to do with Ben's death too. Ben had always been there to encourage her, to help her with her footwork or pitch a few softballs for her.

A week ago Gabriel had told his father he might go out for track, just to get him off his back. Right now he had little interest in sports. Still, he was fast and he knew it. Running. That was what he did best. His father had given him a nod and turned back to the sports page. Gabriel couldn't decide whether the nod was meant as encouragement or a dismissal.

He saw it in his mother's eyes, too—the reminder. Sometimes she would make dumb jokes, puns. His mother loved puns. Ben had loved them too. His mind had been as quick and original as his mother's. Once, on their way to spend a week in Maine, Ben and his mother had traded puns for practically the whole trip. Sometimes Robert Hart joined in. They were making up funny song titles, and his dad had suggested "The When Hell Freezes Overture." Even Shelby got into it. Only her puns were usually pretty lame jokes like What kind of exercises do birds do?

Worm-ups. Dumb stuff like that. But at least she'd come up with *something*. Gabriel, on the other hand, had spent the whole trip feeling as if the battery in his brain had died. He couldn't even jump-start it. He hadn't been able to come up with a single pun. But no one seemed to notice.

He remembered thinking he couldn't wait until they came to the next rest stop. He planned to hop a bus, any bus, when nobody was looking and go wherever it took him. It didn't matter, as long as he didn't have to listen to any more dumb word jokes. But the truth was—when he let himself remember those times—he had felt stupid. Worse, brain-damaged. He would never be as quick and clever as Ben. Not if the two of them lived to be a hundred, which was never going to happen now, not for Ben anyway.

His mother had finally stopped talking to him through the door. She opened it a crack and poked her head in. "It's almost noon, you know. What time did you get home last night?"

That took him by surprise. He didn't think she even knew he'd gone out. Gabriel kept his face to the wall. Why didn't she stay in the city on weekends, too? They were getting along fine without her. All she ever did when she came home was nag them about what a mess the house was. Who needed it?

"Jeez, Mom. I have to get up at six every morning for school. Give me a break." He didn't bother to tell her he hadn't gotten home until almost three.

When he heard the door close, he looked over his

shoulder to make sure she was gone. The last thing he was going to do was waste his weekend raking leaves. He didn't care if the leaves piled up so high they buried the whole first floor of the house.

Today he had other plans. He slipped on a pair of jeans, a T-shirt, and a dark green fleece pullover. He planned to meet Gem that afternoon, maybe around one o'clock. First he'd grab a sandwich, then head straight for his car. Not that he was in any great rush to see Gem—or so he told himself—he just didn't want to get stuck raking leaves.

But as it turned out, his mother nailed him before he ever made it out the front door, and it was almost four o'clock by the time he pulled into the parking lot of the Stony Brook Campgrounds, where he found Gem brushing leaves off the furniture on the patio in front of the store.

This past week at school he'd been friendly enough with Gem. They'd joked around in English class and all. But whenever the image of her swimming naked in the moonlight slipped into his memory, which was more often than he cared to admit, he told himself it was an illusion. The reality sat across from him in class. A girl with short dark hair and eyes the color of rich mahogany, so deep you could lose yourself in them forever. Still, he couldn't seem to make the imaginative leap from this girl to the one who swam in moonlight. Even now, as she brushed the palms of her hands together, walking toward him.

Kate Hennessey, dressed in a loose-fitting corduroy jumper with a bulky sweatshirt pulled over it, was busy

119

reading something on her laptop computer, which sat on the counter in front of her, when Gem and Gabriel came into the store.

"This is Gabriel Hart," Gem told her aunt. "A friend from school."

Kate extended her rough, callused hand and gave Gabriel's a hearty shake. "Come to see the wolves?"

"As a matter of fact, he has. And don't you dare try to charge him admission," Gem said to her aunt.

Kate Hennessey chuckled. Her pale blue eyes crinkled at the corners. "Never even occurred to me."

Gem, who knew that it darn well *had* occurred to her, just grinned back at her aunt. "Come on," she told Gabriel. "Before she changes her mind."

They took the pickup over narrow, rutted roads to a fenced-in area. The barbed wire at the top leaned outward rather than inward. Gabriel suspected it was intended to keep humans out, not the wolves in. He couldn't tell where the high chain-link fence began or ended. "How big is this place?" He was following Gem up the steps to a wooden platform that looked down on a section of the preserve near the main gate.

"About twenty acres." Gem sat cross-legged on the rough boards. "We have seventeen wolves so far; some are timber—you know, gray wolves—a few arctic, and some tundra. Aunt Kate had a new one brought in just last month."

Gabriel sat beside her, facing the fenced-in area. He

saw nothing but trees and shrubs. "It looks like they're not interested in company right now."

"Wait." Gem rested her hand on his arm as if she expected he might suddenly leap up and run off. Then she did something that turned Gabriel's blood ice cold. She threw back her head and began to howl. A deep, throaty howl that seemed to rise up out of her very center. She kept it up, and then the most amazing thing happened. Her howls were joined by other howls, howls going up from all parts of the refuge. And there was Gem, mouth open, eyes shining, her face flushed and glistening.

Gabriel didn't dare speak. He was afraid he might be interfering in some way. And he was right.

Something was moving below, in the brush behind a large sycamore. And suddenly, there it was, large and gray with rust-colored fur behind its ears and on its head. Thick, beautiful fur. Another came behind it, and then another. The wolves' heads reached toward the sky as the eerie sounds leaped from their throats. But they kept their distance. Gabriel had the strangest feeling they had come to pay their respects to Gem.

He looked over at her. She had stopped howling and was smiling down at the wolves below. "The almost black one, the really large one to the right, that's Dark Cloud. And the one over there by the wild rhododendron, that's Crow."

"They have names?" For some reason, Gabriel was surprised by this. The wolves, after all, were wild. Not pets.

Gem shrugged. She pointed to the wolf she called Dark Cloud. "Only he knows who he is. Giving them names helps me distinguish between them, that's all."

"Why were you howling? Don't wolves do that when they're threatening something?"

Gem shifted her weight and stretched her legs out in front of her. "Yeah, that's what most people think. Howling's just the way they communicate. It usually means they're content. People think it's scary, but to the wolves, it's more a feeling of well-being. When they're being hunted, that's when they get quiet and secretive."

Apparently the wolves didn't feel at all threatened. They were lying in the tall dry grass, watching Gem and Gabriel with their yellow eyes, licking their paws. A few circled around the others, stopping to rub against the rough bark of a black birch.

"Where'd you learn to do that? The howling thing?"

"Aunt Kate. She gives lectures on the wolves and runs howling sessions for people who are interested."

For a while neither of them spoke. Gem had told him not to stare the wolves in the eye because they might feel threatened. So Gabriel pretended to look out over the preserve while occasionally glancing at the wolves below.

He'd been thinking Gem seemed pretty happy living here with her aunt—either that, or she was putting on a good act. Still, he couldn't help wondering if she wouldn't rather be with her parents, at least one of them. It was just a matter of time before his own parents got divorced. He was sure of it. What if he had to choose which one he'd live with? How had Gem handled it? It was none of his business; still, he had to ask, "Why did you decide to live here, instead of with your mom or dad?"

Gem didn't answer right away. She was remembering the year she had spent with her father, living in motel rooms in different towns. How lonely she had been.

By the time she returned to San Francisco to live with her mother, she'd lost all interest in school, her grades, her parents, even herself. She flat-out didn't care about much of anything. It had gone on like that all through eighth grade, until the summer after she graduated from middle school, the summer she had come to visit Aunt Kate. She still got angry about those times, but not as much. Now she struggled to find the words to reconnect to that time in her life so she could answer Gabriel's question. But in the end it was too hard. So all she said was, "It was better for everybody."

She looked over at him. "I was an incredibly obnoxious kid after my parents got divorced. I guess because I was angry. I acted out in school a lot, stuff you don't want to hear about."

"That's pretty hard to believe."

"Believe it."

"So how did you get rid of all that anger?"

She looked over at him and shrugged. "I learned to howl with the wolves."

The sun was an orange ball suspended above the treetops, setting the yellow and red leaves on fire. In a few minutes it would drop below the mountains. Dusk came early to this area. In another two weeks they would abandon daylight savings and it would grow dark even earlier. Gabriel looked at his watch. It was almost six.

"I guess I'd better get home."

"You could stay for dinner." Gem kept her eyes on the wolves. She was afraid to look at him, afraid he would say no.

It was Saturday night. Gabriel knew the others would be at the Boy Scout camp later. They would be waiting, expecting him. He knew if he stayed for dinner he wouldn't be able to leave when he wanted. It wouldn't be polite. Gem would expect him to spend the evening with her. And that would only be right.

One of the wolves lifted its head and let out another howl. The others picked up the cries. Gabriel felt his blood quicken. He had the same restless feeling he had had the afternoon before. If Gem hadn't been sitting right next to him, he might have begun pacing back and forth on the platform.

"Maybe another time," he told her.

eleven

Gem sat on the bare hardwood floor of her bedroom and leaned one shoulder against the edge of the pine bookshelves Aunt Kate had made for her. Rocks of all shapes and sizes lined the lip of each shelf in front of the books. Idly she lifted a rock and closed her fingers around it.

She remembered the night she had found it, that first summer she had come to visit Aunt Kate. It had been a sticky, humid night. A squadron of no-see-ums had slipped undetected through the kitchen screen, leaving bites up and down her arms that drove her crazy with their itching. As she stood at the sink washing dishes, a couple in a nearby trailer had begun to argue. The woman, it seemed, had wanted to spend the week at the beach at Seaside Heights, while her husband had insisted they go camping. The argument continued to escalate into a real screaming match until the noise grew so loud that all the children in the camp rose from their sleeping bags and curled into their mothers' laps, seeking comfort.

The voices of the shouting man and woman began to blur in Gem's head, mixing with the voices of her parents, reminding her how they were always fighting before the divorce. The battle between the couple at the camp raged on as Gem continued to wash the dishes, even while salty sweat streamed down her face, stinging her eyes. But the temptation to smash the plates against the sink was overwhelming. Her hand shook as she put each dish in the plastic rack to dry.

If she'd thought they would hear her over their ranting and raving, Gem would have shouted at them through the window to shut up. To stop the fighting right that minute. Instead, unaware of what she was doing, she grabbed the handle of a butcher knife from the soapy water and plunged the blade through the screen at the exact moment Aunt Kate walked into the room.

Aunt Kate lifted the knife out of Gem's hand and plunked it back in the dishwater. Then she opened the cabinet doors beneath the sink and took out a large flashlight. Before Gem knew what was happening her aunt had propelled her outside and the two were heading through the woods down to the stream with only the white circle from the flashlight to guide them.

Later Gem would put a Band-Aid over the gash in the screen to remind herself of how out of control she had gotten. And how terrified and sickened she was when she realized how much rage she had within her.

That was the night Aunt Kate had helped her find her first rock. It had to fit just right in the palm of Gem's hand, and only Gem would know when she had found it. When she came across a smooth rock in the shape of a half moon, she closed her fingers around it. It fit snugly into her palm.

"Close your eyes and wait," her aunt had told her. "Your rock will ground you, give you balance again." And there in the dark by the stream, with the peepers shrieking their shrill greetings, Gem had begun to feel the solidity of the things around her and her place among them.

The rock she now held was the same one she had found that night with her aunt over three years ago. Once again she folded her fingers around it, feeling it settle into her palm. For a moment, with her eyes closed, she felt solid again, grounded, real. The opposite of being with Gabriel, of being in love.

This discovery, that she had fallen in love, had come to her the very second Gabriel Hart told her he couldn't stay for dinner. She had been attracted to him from the moment he had walked into her homeroom over a month ago. And then, for this entire week, ever since he'd walked into the camp store and they'd spent time talking, getting to know each other a little better, she hadn't thought of anything or anyone but Gabriel. Her only desire, after he'd left the store last week, was to be with him again. And it had seemed he might have begun to feel the same way, although all she really had to go on was that he sometimes joked around with her in English class. Still, he was friendly. He seemed to like her company. It was something to build on. Or so she had thought.

They'd been having fun that afternoon, enough for Gem to feel comfortable asking him to dinner. When he declined, his rejection had sent a strange buzzing sensation rippling beneath her skin, like molecules pulling away from each other. She had become filmy, as light as steam.

Maybe this was what happened to you when the person you'd fallen in love with didn't love you back. One minute you were on solid ground, and the next you thought you might just evaporate into thin air, because there was nothing holding you together anymore. All those dreams and hopes that filled your waking hours were suddenly gone, and there you were, left with only the air inside you.

Gem squeezed the rock harder, letting it dig into her palm. A first love was unavoidable. A fact of life. Like losing your first tooth. Like getting your first period. It was bound to happen sooner or later, and there wasn't a thing you could do about it.

She'd had crushes before, but nothing like this. She couldn't even find words to describe what it felt like to be near Gabriel, because for the first time in her life, it wasn't about words. It was about sensations.

She wished now she hadn't been such a complete idiot, putting it all out there to get stomped on. Of course he wouldn't stay for dinner. It was Saturday night. He probably had a date. And her invitation had been so last-minute. Although of course it wasn't. She just wanted it to seem that way—spontaneous. The truth was, it had been part of her plan all along.

The rock grew warm in her palm. For a brief moment Gem thought she felt it pulsating, then realized the gentle throbbing came from her own fingers. With her other hand she lifted a chiseled piece of milky quartz she had found in the Delaware River a few years ago. She liked the roughness, the irregular edges. It felt different every time she held it.

She sat, her back braced against the bookshelves, the fingers of each hand enveloping the rocks, eyes closed, until after a while she began to feel the molecules coming together again, taking solid form.

A few hours after he left Gem, Gabriel was in his room reading the third act of *Hamlet,* waiting for the time when he would head down to the camp. It was after nine, and he figured he could slip out without anyone noticing.

Shelby was just opening the bathroom door as Gabriel walked past. His first thought was that her head looked like a nest of short rat tails. Behind her, on the tile floor, were piles of her long brown hair. A bottle of styling gel and the large scissors with orange handles that his mom usually kept in the kitchen drawer sat on the countertop by the sink.

"What the—"

"One word, just one word and you die," Shelby said, snapping up the scissors and pointing the tip at his chest.

Even with death threats hanging over his head, Gabriel knew some things were just too good to pass up. Yanking Shelby's chain was one of them. "Man, you know you got a bunch of ugly worms crawling around on your head?"

"I told you—" Shelby's outrage ended in a half sob. She sent the scissors flying into the sink. They landed with an angry clatter. "It's not done yet. It has to dry and then I'm going to dye the ends some other color. Magenta, maybe."

What was it with the women in this family and their hair? he wondered. First his mom, then Shelby. That was when he spotted the nose ring. Where had that come from?

Shelby must have noticed he was staring at it because she suddenly announced, "It's not real, so you can forget running to Mom."

"The thought never entered my head." It was the truth. You couldn't go running to a mother who was hardly ever there. Still, he found the nose ring almost as disconcerting as he had the fake fingernails.

Ever since they'd moved to this house, Shelby, the old Shelby, had been disappearing by little bits and pieces that were being replaced by artificial parts. It seemed each time he saw her, there was something new about her. And even though he missed the old Shelby, he could sort of understand some of what was happening. Hadn't he been changing too? Not outwardly, maybe. But he was no longer the person he'd been six months ago. Not even close.

Gabriel lifted one of the short jagged strands of Shelby's hair. It felt stiff and sticky. The gel was still drying. The haircut went way beyond amateur. Spikes of hair, some only a little more than two inches, some longer, jutted up from her scalp, defying gravity.

Shelby jerked her head away and smacked his hand. "It's ugly, right?" Tears sprang to the corners of her eyes. "*I'm* ugly." Her shoulders began to tremble, and she pulled savagely at her ragged hair.

"Whoa, hey, Shel." Gabriel rested his hands on her shoulders and gave her a gentle shake. "It doesn't look half bad." He took a step back and pretended to eye the wormy mess critically. "Really. It looks a lot better than that time you cut your hair in preschool." That actually got a laugh out of her. They both knew nothing could ever top that haircut: a half dozen practically bald spots even a professional hairdresser couldn't hide.

"Mom's going to kill me." Shelby's eyes pleaded for mercy.

He could tell she was practicing, waiting to see if her remorse worked on him before she tried it on anyone else. He tried not to laugh.

"How come you didn't just tell Mom you wanted to get your hair cut?"

Shelby sniffed and wiped her nose on the towel she

had wrapped around her shoulders. When she looked up, the nose ring was gone. Gabriel didn't bother to mention it.

"I did," she told him. "I've been trying to get Mom to take me for weeks. All she ever says is I look fine the way I am. I don't need to change my hair."

"Well, I guess you showed her."

This brought another flood of tears and Shelby retreated to her bedroom, slamming the door behind her. Gabriel stared down at the carnage on the bathroom floor. He was glad he wouldn't be there later when Shelby and their mother collided.

Hollis Feeney was the only one who didn't show up at the camp that night, which sent Alec into a frenzy of pacing.

"That little shit is chickening out. I know he is."

Lydia had brought new scented candles, three of them, one lavender, one strawberry, and one pine. For some reason the combined smells clashed and the odor was nauseating. Gabriel blew out two of the candles and looked over at her. "They don't work together."

"They stink," Alec told her.

"A little edgy tonight, aren't we?" Lydia reached into her pocket and pulled out her flask.

"If he tells anyone about the 7-Eleven last night, he's a dead man."

"Why would he tell anyone?" Gabriel said. "He was in on it."

"Because he has no guts is why. Every time we go hunting, I'm the one doing the shooting." But even as Alec said this, he knew Hollis wasn't the squeamish type. He'd never been able to figure out what it was about that kid, but he was no coward.

Gabriel and Lydia weren't paying much attention to anything he was saying. They seemed preoccupied. Alec didn't like to be ignored. "We don't need him anyway. Not for what we're doing tonight."

Lydia had been staring up at the ceiling, watching the shadows from the candle flickering overhead. "What about tonight?"

"It's Saturday. You want to sit around like a bunch of losers?" Alec had resumed his pacing. He was like some caged animal. The tension in the room was electric.

"Well, Hollis will just have to miss out on the fun," Alec told them. He grabbed a slender log from the wood-pile next to the fireplace and handed it to Gabriel. "Consider yourself armed," he told him, heading for the door.

twelve

They began with mailboxes. At first Gabriel was embarrassed. While roadside mailboxes weren't something you saw in the city, the idea of smashing them just for the hell of it seemed juvenile. He couldn't believe Alec had suggested it. But as he hung out the truck window aiming the log dead center, he found he actually enjoyed the sound of crunching metal, was surprised at how easily it caved in.

Lydia, sitting between the two boys, didn't share Gabriel's rush. "This is stupid kid stuff," she told them.

Alec only laughed, then headed down another dark back road. "We're just getting started, Lydia. Relax." He reached under the seat and pulled out his .22-caliber rifle, balancing it carefully with the end of the gun stock braced against his inner thigh and the barrel hanging out the open window. Something was running along the side of the road. Its eyes flashed yellow in the headlights. Two eyes, floating in darkness. It was hard to tell what it was, a raccoon maybe, an opossum, or even a cat. But that made no difference to Alec, who lifted the rifle, curving his finger around the trigger, while he continued to steer the truck with his other hand.

The shots rang through the cab, followed by a short sharp scream. "Is there a point to this?" Lydia said, not even trying to hide her revulsion, although none of this really surprised her. Alec was a thug, a creep. What did she expect?

"It's a rush. A high." Alec nudged her with his elbow. "Come on Lydia, you need to get in the spirit."

Lydia ignored him.

"Give her the log," Alec told Gabriel, leaning forward and looking over at him. "She needs to bust up something."

Gabriel slid the log onto Lydia's lap.

"Suppose I start with your windshield," she said to Alec, tapping the log against the dashboard.

Alec threw back his head and howled as if this were the funniest thing he'd ever heard. Lydia stared at him in disgust, wishing like crazy she could be alone with Gabriel, that Alec were somewhere else—anywhere but with them.

"Okay," Alec said. "Now, that's what I'm talking about. Now you got the idea." He turned the truck onto the main highway that ran through the outskirts of

Knollwood, driving by the small strip mall, a diner, two gas stations both on the same side of the road, and the 7-Eleven across the street, and turned off onto another road past the park.

Gabriel had no idea where Alec was taking them. But he sensed Lydia's impatience and wondered if maybe she was right, that is, until he closed his eyes and once again felt the metal mailboxes giving way to the force of the log. He couldn't pretend it didn't feel good. "You bring that flask with you?" It was a stupid question. Of course she had the flask. She always had it with her.

Without looking at him, Lydia slipped it from her pocket and handed it to Gabriel just as Alec swung the car down a narrow dead-end road and into an empty parking lot.

Lydia recognized the abandoned train station. No trains had come through Knollwood for over thirty years. But the building had served as headquarters for other businesses, most recently a radio station that had gone under about a year ago. Her first thought was that maybe Alec was thinking of using this place for a new hangout. She was surprised by how much she wanted this to be true. Because if that happened, she would have her sanctuary back again, all to herself.

But even though the station was nestled in an isolated ravine, it wasn't that far from town, and houses were close by, within a few hundred yards. She doubted Alec would think this was a good place for them to meet. It was obvious he had other plans for the building.

She slid across the seat and stretched her legs to the running board. Alec and Gabriel were already at the door of the station. Lydia got out of the truck and followed them. The door was padlocked. Alec pulled out a Swiss Army knife and went to work on it. After a few minutes the lock sprang open. He pointed to it. "I didn't spend all that time in juvie for nothing. At least I managed to get a little practical education."

Inside the station it was pitch dark. No outside streetlights shone through the windows. Gabriel felt the hairs on his neck bristle. Much as he hated to admit it, he knew he'd come to the camp tonight hoping they'd find another 7-Eleven. But now he was having second thoughts.

Ever since Alec had picked open the padlock, Gabriel had been growing more tense. This was breaking and entering, which was more than he had bargained for. If they were caught they'd go to jail for sure. "There's nothing here. The place is totally empty," he said, hoping Alec would just forget the whole thing.

"It's got walls," Alec reminded him, putting his foot through the Sheetrock. Then he punched another hole and another, leaving foot-sized craters in his wake. "Use your imagination, man."

He turned to Lydia. "Get us some rocks. We can smash them through the windows." He spotted an old dial phone sitting on the floor, picked it up, and hurled it at a sliding glass window that separated two rooms. "Oh yeah oh yeah oh yeah," he shouted, arms in the air, bouncing on the balls of his feet as if he'd just made a touchdown.

When Lydia returned with two large rocks, Gabriel lifted one, aimed, and hurled it through a front window. With the shatter of glass, something inside him let go. He grabbed the other rock from Lydia and flung it through another window. The sound sent ripples of pleasure through him. He felt light, almost as light as when he and Lydia had left the 7-Eleven the night before. But he wasn't quite there yet.

Outside, he searched for more rocks. The moon was barely the size of a fingernail clipping. It took a while for his eyes to adjust to the dark. He found a large slab of broken blacktop and hurled it at one of the windows from the outside. His heart was pumping like crazy now, and he raced back inside, kicking holes in places Alec had missed. Neither of the boys noticed Lydia, standing in the doorway leading to another room, her shoulder braced against the doorjamb, her hands in her pockets, her mouth twisted in disgust, watching them.

Alec had his Swiss Army knife out and was tearing huge gashes in the indoor-outdoor carpeting in one of the offices.

Lydia walked up to Gabriel, who was shrieking loud war whoops as he tore an old bulletin board from the wall and threw it on the floor. "I'm going to wait in the truck, keep a lookout in case anybody shows up," she said.

Gabriel, his foot poised squarely on the bulletin board, looked over at her. "What are you worried about? Nobody can see this place from the road." Something about the expression on her face was disturbing. "You got a problem?"

For one brief moment Lydia thought of telling him yes, she did. She had a problem with the two of them acting like total morons. Lunatics. She lived with crazy people. She didn't need to hang out with them too. But she suspected if she said anything, they would only laugh at her. Even Gabriel. Because she could see he was too caught up in the adrenaline rush to be able to stop. And there wasn't a thing she could do about it. Instead she turned and walked outside without saying another word.

It was cold in the truck. Lydia wrapped her arms around herself, shivering. A wind had come up and leaves were blowing everywhere, blocking her view from the windshield. Not that she could see much in the dark anyway. But she wanted to be able to spot anyone coming.

For some reason she thought of Hollis, wondering if this would have been happening if he'd been here. Probably not. Although she had no idea why she should have thought that. Maybe it was the way he had called Alec's bluff the night before, after the 7-Eleven incident. She had watched as Alec floundered around, trying to recover from Hollis's disappointment over their small-time heist, which was when he had suddenly announced this was only the first step in the initiation. That hadn't been lost on Lydia. Hollis, she suspected, had far more interesting things in mind, things Alec couldn't even begin to imagine in that thimble-size thug brain of his. She wondered what Hollis would think of tonight's random destruction. Probably not much.

When Alec and Gabriel finally came through the front door, they were so wound up they kept jumping in the air and high-fiving each other all the way to the truck. Lydia had the sinking feeling they weren't finished yet, that other equally destructive plans were under way.

"I have to get home," she told them. She wasn't at all sure why she was behaving this way, except maybe because she felt resentful and a little angry. Never once did it occur to her she might be feeling left out. It wasn't in her nature to smash her foot through a wall or hurl rocks into windows. If she was honest with herself, she would have to admit she was envious of their exuberance, jealous of their stupid high fives. Because that high was exactly how she had felt the night before when she and Gabriel had come running out of the 7-Eleven. She wanted that feeling back. But trashing a building wasn't going to do that for her. It would have to be something else. That much she understood.

"Oh, come on, Lydia. We're just getting started." Alec reached over and squeezed her knee. She crossed her legs and leaned into Gabriel's side. He put his arm around her and pulled her into his lap. She could tell by the way his hands slipped under her jacket, slid along her back, by the way his mouth opened on hers, as if he were going to suck the very breath out of her, that he was in that same place they had shared the night before. How could she tell him she wasn't there this time, that the passion she had felt when she put her arms around him in the 7-Eleven and kissed him was missing tonight? Yet wasn't it Gabriel's passion, his intensity she was most attracted to? So what was wrong with her?

She turned her face away from Gabriel. "I can't," she told Alec. "You'll have to drop me off first."

Alec looked over at Gabriel. "You chickening out too, Hart Man?"

"No way, man. I'm revved." Gabriel could barely sit still. Lydia could feel his legs twitching beneath her. "Let's go," he told Alec.

"I'm not chickening out," Lydia said. "It's after one. I don't feel like spending the rest of the school year grounded."

Neither Alec nor Gabriel knew what things were like at home for her. They didn't have a clue her family was in bed by nine and the likelihood of her getting caught was slim. So when Gabriel said, "Guess we'd better get her home," Alec merely shrugged and turned the ignition key.

As they pulled up a few yards from the Misurellas' driveway, Alec leaned across the front seat to where Lydia still sat on Gabriel's lap. He put his arm around her shoulder and whispered close to her ear, "It's devil's night, and you're gonna miss it."

Wednesday, when *The Knollwood Press* hit the stands, Hollis Feeney, who hadn't been in school on Monday or Tuesday, bought three copies. He dropped one on Lydia's desk in calculus class and one on Gabriel's lap as he sat on the bench in front of his locker toweling off after gym. Later he left one outside Alec's trailer.

In school the three never hung out together. They had an unspoken understanding. They barely even nodded to each other in the halls.

During the week they were the same kids they'd always been. Hollis, the honor student and computer whiz; Lydia, the loner; Gabriel, the new kid who didn't say much. None of them had decided this course of action in advance. It was intuitively understood. At the camp they were a group. In school they were just three of eight hundred students.

None of them belonged to any clubs—except for Hollis, who belonged to the math club but rarely bothered going to the meetings—or were in sports, or hung out at the diner a few blocks from the school where most of the seniors spent their afternoons. The three, like Alec before them, were not joiners. Even their own group wasn't something they had consciously joined; it had merely happened. Four people converging in the same place on the same night. That was all.

Only, today Hollis broke the code. When he dropped the newspaper in Gabriel's lap he said, pointing to the front-page story, "Some people have the IQ of iceberg lettuce." Then he walked off.

Gabriel stared down at the headline, which read, "Vandals Trash Train Station." A rush of excitement surged through him until he got to the second paragraph. The article called the vandals disorganized and brutal, speculating that the people who trashed the train station might have been the same ones who smashed the mailboxes along Frog Creek Road and in other parts of town, and the windows of cars in the parking lot of Knollwood Village Apartments, which was where Alec and Gabriel had gone after they'd dropped off Lydia.

The reporter referred to the vandals as "probably teenagers of below-average intelligence with nothing better to do on a Saturday night." The hair on Gabriel's arms and neck bristled. He wanted this stupid-ass reporter to know he'd scored 1450 on his PSATs last year.

For the next three nights Gabriel stayed away from the Boy Scout camp. He needed time to think, to clear his head. He wondered how Hollis had figured out they were the ones who had vandalized the train station. He didn't think Lydia had said anything to him. Maybe Alec. But Hollis wasn't even in school until Wednesday. So why had he given Gabriel a copy of the newspaper? Why had he said what he had about the vandals?

Not only that, but he'd made it pretty clear he thought what Gabriel and the others had done was plain stupid. And this bothered Gabriel. Maybe it *was* juvenile. But the way he'd felt afterward—he'd never felt like that before. He was indestructible, ready to take on the world, including the thugs who had killed his brother. That feeling had stayed with him, like electricity buzzing through his veins, for days. It got him through those times when he didn't care if he lived or died. And he had a lot of moments like that.

One thing he knew for certain: This was a violent, unpredictable world. He was learning how to survive in it, that was all. He wasn't any better or worse than the next guy.

By Saturday night he knew he wouldn't be able to stay away from the camp. He needed to be recharged, he needed this fix to get him through the next week. If it was possible to be addicted to destruction, Gabriel knew he was hooked bad. And there didn't seem to be anything he could do about it.

thirteen

Saturday night there was barely a sliver of moon in the sky. Frost coated the grass, branches, stumps, and what leaves remained on the trees with glistening white crystals.

Lydia stood in the doorway of the camp house bundled in several layers beneath her peacoat. The others were already there, hunched over the table, reading something. No one looked up. She closed the door and came over to the table. They had improvised seats out of large, unsplit logs from a pile stacked by the small shed behind the main building. The stools were about a foot in diameter and almost two feet high. A little wobbly but serviceable, better than the aluminum chairs with the torn webbing. Lydia sat on one of the makeshift stools, rocking slightly until she found her balance.

Hollis pointed to the newspaper lying on the table in front of him. "What were you thinking?" He looked straight at Alec when he said this. "We're better than this; we're better than a bunch of losers who have to resort to kids' pranks for a little attention. Frankly, I was ashamed when I read this."

Alec's Adam's apple slid up and down as if he was having a hard time swallowing. His face turned a blotchy pink. Lydia looked away, embarrassed for him. Like Alec, she was caught off-guard by Hollis's comments—Hollis, who usually said so little, who blended in with the wall better than anyone she knew. Bland old pudgy Hollis. Lydia didn't know what to make of him.

"So what's the big deal? Some kids trashed the train station," Gabriel said.

"You think I don't know it was you three?" Hollis gave Gabriel a disgusted look. "Why do you think I gave you copies of the newspaper? To improve your reading skills?" He smacked the headlines with the back of his hand. "This is the kind of stuff that could get us caught. There's no thought behind it. No planning. No covering up possible clues that could expose the group. Just senseless, random behavior."

"This whole initiation thing was your idea," Alec reminded him. His voice was sullen, bordering dangerously on a whine.

"I thought you had more imagination than this." Hollis nodded toward the newspaper. "Obviously I was wrong."

His voice was still cool and removed. He was merely an observer stating a fact.

But Alec didn't see it that way. He lunged across the table and grabbed the front of Hollis's crewneck sweater, twisting it in his angry fist. "You little shit! You wouldn't even be here tonight if it wasn't for me."

Hollis didn't so much as blink. He clamped his hand over Alec's wrist and set his stony gray eyes on him. "The same might be said of you."

Alec pulled Hollis's face close to his, his lip curling in a snarl, even as his heart pounded with the frantic rhythm of a trapped animal. Hollis knew about the guns in his trailer, about the poaching, about selling crack in Easton when he needed money, and that was only for starters. Hollis could turn Alec in to the police whenever he felt like it. All this time Alec had believed Hollis was afraid of him, that he wouldn't dare cross him. Now he knew different. Hollis wasn't scared of him at all. It was Alec who should be afraid, and he was just now figuring that out.

He gave Hollis's sweater one last twist, then let go, flopping back down on his stool stump so hard a piece of dried bark popped off. A bulge remained in the stretched wool right below Hollis's double chin. "Yeah, so where were you Saturday, anyway? Couldn't hack it, right? Probably sitting home shaking in your Star Trek boxers over what'd happened the night before. Am I right?"

Hollis settled his cool eyes on him. He wasn't in the least bit shaken. He had spent the past few weeks listening to the three of them, observing. He had by now figured out their pressure points, if not the reasons behind them. He still lacked most of the details. But he knew what was important. He knew Lydia hated living here and would do just about anything to escape, that Gabriel was seething with rage, was out for blood, and Alec, he was a time bomb just ticking off the seconds. It was all too perfect. No way could Hollis let all that rage and passion go to waste. He had big plans for this group. *Big* plans.

"I had interviews last weekend," he told them. "We were up at M.I.T., then stopped at Yale on the way back. I didn't get home till Tuesday night." His voice was flat and even. He didn't bother to explain who he meant by "we," and no one asked.

The others were staring at him, waiting. No one said anything.

"I'm applying for early acceptance," he said.

Alec let out a loud snort. "The little geek's a genius. He's only fifteen and he's going off to M.I.T."

"While I was away I did a lot of thinking," Hollis said, ignoring Alec's remark. "We have something special here, whether you're aware of it or not. We are a force to be reckoned with. An intelligent and dangerous force." Hollis shoved the newspaper in Alec's face. "Not a bunch of petty vandals."

Gabriel caught the stunned expression on Alec's face and stifled a laugh. It was actually comic. But as Hollis talked on, Gabriel felt a surge of excitement, like an electric current shooting through his body. *Dangerous force*. He liked the sound of that.

"First, we need organization. We all need to understand our place, the roles we're going to play." Slowly he shifted his gaze to each of them, one by one. "And we need a name for our group."

"What kind of name?" Lydia asked. She'd been listening to everything that had been going on and was seriously considering leaving. She loved this old building. It had been her refuge for four years. Without it she doubted she could have continued living up here on this desolate mountain with her family and still have kept her sanity. But listening to the boys, she had begun to wonder if maybe she hadn't already lost this place, her sanctuary. Maybe it was time to let it go.

"There is power in a name," Hollis said, turning to look at her. "A name defines you—defines *us*. And at the same time, it should make us feel indestructible."

"Knights of Chaos," Alec suggested, thinking about the night he and the Hart Man had trashed the train station. He grinned. "Like the Knights of the Round Table."

"Hardly," Hollis said, his lips pressed tightly together.

Gabriel shook his head, agreeing with Hollis. He had liked what Hollis said about power. He remembered the feeling that had kept him charged for almost the entire week. That was when it came to him. "Lords of Destruction," he blurted out. He caught just the slightest movement in Hollis's face and knew he approved.

The three boys looked so solemn that Lydia found herself laughing. It was perverse, she knew. But she couldn't seem to stop herself. Tears were actually streaming down her cheeks.

"*What* is your problem?" Alec snapped at her.

Lydia wiped her eyes with the sleeve of her peacoat. "Nothing. Only, do you guys have any idea how ridiculously serious you all sound?"

The three of them stared at her.

"Well, for God's sake, it all sounds so doomsday melodramatic."

"Are you in or not?" Alec said, ignoring her outburst. "Because if you're not, you can forget about setting foot inside this place again."

Lydia thought of announcing that she could just as easily tell Kate Hennessey on the three of them. Then they'd have to find someplace else to hang out. She might not be able to come back here, but then neither would they. The thing was, she couldn't seem to make a decision one way or the other. So she sat there, silent. And from her silence, the others assumed her answer was yes, that she was in.

Lydia was halfway up the sycamore tree when she heard one of the goats bleating. Afraid something had gotten into the barn, a coyote or bear, she made a beeline for it, flicked on the light, and looked around. Everything appeared to be okay. As she counted the goats to make sure none were missing, two of them got up from their nest of straw, wandered over to her, and nuzzled her hand. They were all there. She was surprised at her relief. She'd never given any of these animals much thought. In her mind they were chores, extra work her father had dumped on her.

For a while she stood there, letting the smallest of the goats lick the palm of her hand while she thought about what had happened at the camp that night. As soon as the others had started making plans, Lydia had known it was too late to back out. She knew too much. If she left now and the slightest thing went wrong, they would blame her, even if she hadn't told anyone. And while she didn't see Gabriel or Hollis as a threat, she wasn't at all sure what Alec might do.

But it was more complicated than that. There was Gabriel. She was starting to fall in love with him. If she dropped out of the group, the only place she would see him was in school. And she knew that wouldn't be enough.

She was so lost in her thoughts, she didn't hear the soft shuffling of footsteps approaching the door. When she turned, she was facing down the barrel of a shotgun. The intake of breath was so sharp and quick it felt as if a rock had hit her in the throat.

Her father lowered the gun. "What the hell are you doing out here? I thought you were some thief."

Lydia's heart was still pounding uncontrollably from the sight of the gun pointed at her. She fought to collect her thoughts. "I thought I heard something in the barn.

A noise. I was afraid a coyote or something might have gotten in."

"So you came out here by yourself, unarmed? Are you out of your mind?"

You're the one pointing a shotgun at your own daughter, Lydia thought. *If anybody's nuts here, it's you.* But she said nothing, only stared back at him as he stood there in his sweat pants and his fleece-lined moccasins, a denim jacket barely covering his undershirt. His thin hair, uncombed, hung in a point over his forehead, exposing the bald patches on either side. "The animals are fine," she told him, walking slowly toward the door.

Her father lowered the shotgun just enough for the barrel to bump against her stomach, like a border guard stopping an illegal immigrant.

Lydia continued to look straight ahead, keeping her eyes on her goal: the back door of the house. She could see her father's breath condensed on the air, hanging like a cloud in front of her face. He was turned toward her. "Just how did you expect to get back in the house?"

"I didn't think of that." She was afraid to swallow, afraid he might notice she was nervous. "I just wanted to check on the animals."

"And then what?"

It was obvious he suspected something, but she couldn't be sure what. Maybe he thought she was just now sneaking out, that she planned to meet someone. It was only a little past midnight.

"If you think I'm sneaking out someplace, then explain

what I'm doing standing in the middle of a lighted barn announcing to the world I'm here." Lydia hoped this would defuse him and any ideas he might be getting.

Arthur Misurella lifted the gun and began walking back to the house. Lydia followed and stood shivering on the back porch while her father fumbled through the cluster of keys he kept on a chain around his neck along with his whistle.

She had barely started up the stairs to her room when the shrill blast of his whistle sounded through the house. One of his impromptu drills. Lydia knew he was doing this to warn her, knew she'd been playing a kind of Russian roulette on the nights she sneaked down to the camp. On any one of those nights her father could have blown his whistle and she wouldn't have been there, wouldn't have come running from her bedroom like the others. For four years she had been waiting for this to happen.

Not that there hadn't been close calls. One time she was halfway down the sycamore when she heard the whistle. She had scooted back up the tree, scraping the inside of her leg, but had managed to come running from her room along with the rest of the family. Once, she had been back home for less than ten minutes, had barely changed into her flannel pajamas when he called a drill. There had been more times like that than she cared to remember. But so far, she had been lucky.

Jacob and Steven were coming down the stairs, Jacob in his camouflage sweat pants and a T-shirt, ready for action, and Steven wearing only boxer shorts, his blond hair sticking out in all directions. He rubbed his sleepy eyes. The boys were followed by their mother, in her plaid flannel robe and heavy wool socks. Her eyes were wide and glassy.

Lydia's father was herding them toward the cellar door, shouting, "Nerve gas. Bombs containing nerve gas are heading straight for this area. Let's *move it!*" They all knew what to do. They'd been drilled so many times they could do it in their sleep. The chemical protective suits and gas masks were in the basement. Her brothers charged through the kitchen to the cellar door. Even sleepy Steven had come awake. Until Arthur Misurella signaled the all clear, none of them would know whether the situation was for real or not. They never knew.

When they first got their chemical protective suits, Lydia's father had made them practice over and over until they could climb into them within ten seconds. Then one morning he blew the warning whistle and herded them into the basement without telling them what they were facing. Lydia heard the door close and noticed right off that her father wasn't with them. Before she had even had time to think why, the door flew open and something the size of a soup can flew down the stairs. Her father's voice had bellowed from overhead: "Gas gas gas." Then the door slammed shut.

They had all watched in horror as the tear-gas grenade landed on the concrete floor; then they'd made a mad dash for their suits, all except their mother, who darted up the stairs two at a time and lunged for the door, pounding with her fists, screaming for her husband to let them out. Lydia, already in her suit, looked up at her mother, who was choking and gasping for breath, tears streaming down her cheeks. This was her father's idea of a simulated attack.

The masks would have been enough in that situation, but Lydia and the others knew Arthur Misurella expected them to be fully protected, to be prepared for the worst. A real bomb could contain anything, not just nerve gas but a biological nightmare: smallpox or anthrax, rare viruses or bacteria that could seep into their pores, like water into sand.

Only, tonight Lydia knew there was no real threat, except maybe for the one standing in the middle of the kitchen holding the shotgun. She knew this was her father's way of letting her know he was the one in control and that she'd better shape up. So she fell in line behind her brothers because, for now anyway, she had no choice.

fourteen

The following Saturday Gabriel spent the morning in the library trying to find research material for a history paper. He was so intent on searching through the computerized catalog that he didn't notice Gem Hennessey standing less than four feet away watching him. Not until she said, "Working on your paper for English?"

He looked up, startled. She was talking about their paper on *Hamlet*. It was due the following Friday. Gabriel had almost forgotten about it, he'd been so worried about his failing grade in history and the paper that was due on Monday. "I've made some notes," he told her. The "notes" consisted of two or three possible ideas for the paper, none of which he considered worth pursuing.

Gem shifted the armload of books she was carrying so they rested on her hip, and looked over her shoulder. Marcy Hatcher stood by the front desk, adjusting her Discman earphones and moving her body to the music while she waited for Gem. She grinned over at them and waved.

Gem held up her index finger to signal she'd only be a minute. "I'm writing about Ophelia," she said, turning back to Gabriel. "You know, about her passion for Hamlet and how his weird behavior contributes to her going off the deep end—sorry, no pun intended—especially after he accidentally kills her father."

It took Gabriel a minute to realize the pun she was referring to had to do with Ophelia drowning. Up until that moment all he'd been thinking about was how beautiful Gem's eyes were. But now he was suddenly reminded of his mother and Ben, both of whom loved puns. And for a brief, uncomfortable moment, that old feeling of stupidity came creeping back. "Good topic." What else could he say?

"What about you?"

"What about me?"

"What's your topic?"

"Oh." Gabriel stared down at the monitor, trying to collect his thoughts. "Revenge," he said out of the blue.

"Revenge?"

"Yeah, you know. How obsessed Hamlet is, wanting to punish his uncle for murdering Hamlet's father." He pulled at his lower lip, looking thoughtful. "Maybe I'll talk about the consequences, you know? How all these other people end up paying for Hamlet's actions in the end."

Gem looked impressed. "Sounds like an A-plus paper."

"Yeah, well, after my last two quiz grades, I could use an A."

For a minute the two stood in silence as people circled around them, making it obvious they were waiting to use the computer. Gabriel ignored them.

Then, just when he thought Gem might be leaving, she said, "I was thinking of renting the video. You know, that really intense version with Mel Gibson playing Hamlet. You could come over if you want and watch it with me." Gem couldn't believe she'd blurted out an invitation like that, invited him to her house, especially after he'd turned her down for dinner two weeks before. What was wrong with her?

At first Gabriel didn't know what to think. He wanted to say yes, but he wasn't sure what he'd be getting himself into. He liked Gem, but he didn't really want to get involved with anyone right now. His life was too screwed up. So he was surprised to hear himself asking, "When?"

Gem could feel the warm flush on her face and looked over at Marcy, trying to collect her thoughts. It was Saturday. She didn't want to make the same mistake she had two weekends before when she had invited him to dinner. "I don't know. Maybe one night next week? Tuesday or Wednesday maybe?"

"Sounds like a plan," he said, relieved she hadn't suggested the weekend. Especially not tonight. He was meeting the others at the Boy Scout camp.

"So, I'll see you in English on Monday and we can decide which night," Gem said, walking backward toward Marcy, who couldn't seem to stop grinning at them.

Gabriel wished he'd been able to come up with an excuse not to go. But he hadn't been fast enough. Maybe he could think up something before he saw Gem on Monday.

"This is our manifesto," Hollis said, passing around copies of a ten-page document. "I spent all last week working on it."

Gabriel stared down at the first page, but he had trouble focusing. Hollis had to be kidding. A manifesto, for God's sake!

Lydia frowned at Hollis. Ordinarily she would have found this manifesto thing hilarious. But this was different. Lately something about Hollis bothered her, although she couldn't have said what it was. He still had that chubby cherubic face, doughy with baby fat. His pale gray eyes, though cold as two stones, looked harmless enough.

"We live in a conformist society," Hollis was saying. "Everyone around us is trying to fit into some mold, some preconceived idea of who they think they should be. But that hasn't happened to us. And you know why?

Because we think for ourselves. And that makes us unique. It's our uniqueness that makes us powerful. Together we're a powerful force."

The others were staring at him. He held out the manifesto, shaking it in each of their faces, one at a time. "This is our campaign against the scum of the world."

The candle flickered in the middle of the table. Gabriel had the strangest sensation. He glanced over his shoulder, half expecting to see a camera rolling and a director sitting in a chair shouting orders. It was as if they were in a movie. Only he wasn't sure of his lines.

Hollis's voice echoed around them in deep dramatic tones as he read. His manifesto was full of puffed-up prose, sometimes swaggering, sometimes theatrical and oozing with self-importance. He ended with a grand gesture, on his feet, pounding his fist on the table. "They must pay for what they've done," he shouted. Then, looking from one to the other, locking his eyes on theirs, he lowered his voice and said softly, "Let the games begin."

Gabriel didn't even have to wonder who "they" were. He knew. Because he'd been planning to make them pay all along. So when Hollis drove home his fist and the unsteady table rocked beneath the blow, Gabriel saw the thugs who had murdered Ben.

Lydia knew who "they" were too. People like her father. People who tried to control her, who thought they were doing what was best for her, when they'd never even taken the time to get to know her.

Alec knew too. He was certain Hollis was talking about

the people who had pushed and shoved Alec through the system, suspended him from school, condemned him in court, sent him off to the Juvenile Detention Center. All of them would pay. Alec would see to it.

"We need to establish a reputation that will strike fear in the minds of the public," Hollis told them. "We aren't a bunch of petty thieves or vandals. We have intelligence, organization, and above all, legitimate motives."

Gabriel, who was only half listening, flipped over the manifesto, and taking a pen from his jacket pocket, began sketching on the blank side while Hollis laid out the group's plans.

"We need to do something big. Something that'll show everyone in this stinking township that we're a force to be reckoned with," Alec said. He had crossed the room and was standing by the fireplace. He tossed a log onto the fire.

"I agree," Hollis said. "What do you have in mind?"

Alec began to pace back and forth across the room. "You want a motive? Okay. How about we start with that asshole Lukowski." Byron Lukowski was the principal at Mountain View Regional.

"Okay, so we know *your* motive," Lydia said dryly. "He got you expelled. Personally, I don't have anything against him."

Gabriel looked up from his drawing. "Taking on Lukowski is asking for trouble. It's too high-profile."

"What's your plan?" Hollis said to Alec, not ready to rule out his idea until he'd heard it all.

"I don't know, burn his house down." Alec was frantically waving his arms around as he continued to pace, making the shadow on the wall behind him look like some monstrous creature with tentacles.

Gabriel had stopped sketching again. He looked over at Lydia, who was chewing on her lower lip, then at Hollis. "That's a little extreme, isn't it?"

"Ah, the voice of reason," Hollis said. But Gabriel didn't miss the sarcasm in this remark and wondered what was going on in Hollis's mind. He could be such a creepy little geek at times. Nerdy maybe, harmless probably, but still creepy.

"Wouldn't it be better to strike where it hurts them, without being obvious?" Lydia said. "I mean, shouldn't we leave them guessing, like they can't be sure whether or not someone has committed the act intentionally?"

"A fire can be made to look like an accident," Alec said, obviously not ready to let them give up on his idea yet.

"One house on fire isn't big enough," Hollis told them. "We want something stupendous. Something that'll really get their attention."

Gabriel had an eerie feeling that Hollis had known all along what the stakes in the first game would be. "Like what?"

"You know that tool and die plant out on Route Forty-eight?"

Lydia and Alec knew. But Gabriel, who hadn't been in the area for more than two months, shook his head.

"It's this huge empty building," Lydia explained to him.

"So big deal. An empty building." Alec let out a snort of disgust.

A slow grin distorted Hollis's thin lips, revealing his crooked teeth. "Not just any empty building. The Knollwood town council has big plans for it. Don't you people read the newspaper?"

Hollis slid his log stool back from the table and moved over to the Adirondack chair, lifting his feet onto the milk crate.

"The town council has been working overtime, oiling the wheels of commerce. They've wined and dined these corporate bozos from Digitech Computers. And wonder of wonders, Digitech's gotten this third-party manufacturer to consider refurbishing the old plant and turning it into a manufacturing facility for making metal components for their computer cases."

"So?" Alec finally sat back down at the table, much to Lydia's relief. His pacing made her nervous.

Hollis smiled over at Alec like an indulgent teacher dealing with a remedial student. "If you want to take your best shot at this whole town, then you begin by destroying their dreams for the future." He linked his fingers together, stretched them, and cracked his knuckles. "The whole town council, nailed in one shot. All these out-of-work people just hanging on till the new plant opens up—*pow*! Got 'em."

Alec finally looked interested. "Yeah, okay. Not bad," he conceded, nodding slowly and squinting as if he was trying to picture the town's reaction. "Okay. So how?" He had a particular fascination with explosions and was hoping that was what Hollis had in mind. He wasn't disappointed.

"We're going to blow up the building," Hollis announced. "When we get through, it'll be a flaming pile of rubble."

Lydia shot a worried look at Gabriel, who had stopped drawing and was staring over at Hollis. "You're going to blow it up?"

"We," Hollis said, leaving no room for insurrection. "Not for a while, though. We can't rush into something this big. I'll need time to work on the plans, then we'll go from there."

"I say we do it next Saturday," Alec said. "It's Halloween. It'll be perfect."

"And it'd be a stupid thing to do," Hollis said.

Alec cringed and a dark flush of red crept up his neck to his face. The tips of his ears looked like burning coals. His father's voice echoed in his head. *Colonel Shitforbrains, Colonel Shitforbrains, Colonel Shitforbrains,* until he thought his head was going to explode. "Shut up, you little geek. You don't know shit. I've got more experience with crime than you could ever dream about."

"And with doing time for it," Hollis said, thinking how much he hated being called a geek. He was destined for great things. He'd known that practically from the day he was born. And someday—very soon—no one, including the people in this room, would ever dare call him a geek again. "I don't plan on getting caught. The cops will be out in full force on Halloween, and the night before, probably every night that whole week, looking to catch kids pulling their mindless pranks. That's not what this is about. What *we're* about. When we perform, we're going to be center stage. I don't share the spotlight with anybody, least of all a lot of barely pubescent middle-schoolers stringing toilet paper from trees."

Alec got up and slammed another log into the fire, even though it was already raging full force. He pretended not to be paying attention.

Gabriel had been sketching the whole time Hollis and Alec had been talking. Now he held up one of the drawings. It was a disembodied hand clutching a sword. The steel blade appeared to be transforming itself into pure fire so that the tip was nothing but shooting flames. A skull with empty dark sockets stared out from the sword's handle. Beneath the skull, neatly printed, was their name: Lords of Destruction. "Our logo," he told them.

Hollis lifted his bulk from the Adirondack chair, came back to the table, and took the drawing from Gabriel's hand. He nodded his approval. "It's good. I'll scan it into my computer. We might be able to use this."

"Oh, right. Let's make up some letterhead and envelopes, why don't we?" Lydia said, unable to keep the sneer off her face. "Maybe some business cards." She looked over at Gabriel. "That'd be *really* cool, wouldn't it? We could hand them out at concerts and raves and stuff. In case anyone's in the market to have something blown up."

Hollis waited with exaggerated patience for her to finish. "Are you through?"

"Okay, if not on Halloween, then when?" Gabriel asked, hoping to break the tension.

"Maybe the night of the next new moon, when it'll be pitch dark. Or maybe sooner." Hollis narrowed his eyes at them and nodded slowly. "It'll be our own personal hell night. We'll meet here next Sunday, the night *after* Halloween, to talk about the plan. I need time to do a little research first. Nobody's to come here next week, understand? Especially not on mischief night or Halloween. The cops will be out in droves. They'll be checking places like this one, expecting trouble."

Hollis returned to the Adirondack chair, lacing his fingers behind his head, and looked up at the ceiling, smiling, his eyes closed as if he could see the whole scenario unfolding right in front of him. "No newspaper will dare use phrases like 'disorganized' and 'below-average intelligence' when they write about us. Not after we pull this off."

Gabriel surprised Lydia by walking her home that night. It was only a little past eleven. The LDs—as they now referred to themselves—had called it an early night. Both of them were unhappy with Hollis's instructions to keep away from the camp for the next week. They knew the group couldn't take the chance of having the cops find them in the abandoned building; still, they both dreaded having no place else to go, no place where they could get away.

The night was thick with stars. As much as she had loved living in Rolling Hills, Lydia had to admit her view of the stars had been limited by ground light. Here the stars seemed to hang in the air right above your head, so close you felt as if you could inhale them with every cold breath.

Gabriel trudged along beside her, his hands stuffed in the pockets of his sweatshirt jacket. They had barely spoken since they'd left the camp. Now Lydia looked over at him, hoping that he was as worried about Hollis's plan as she was. "Blowing up a whole plant," she said, trying to sound as if she were just thinking out loud. "Even an abandoned one—I don't know—I mean, have you ever done something like that?"

"I never had any reason to."

"And so what? Now you do?"

"Maybe." Gabriel knew he was being cryptic. But he didn't know how to explain to Lydia what had begun to happen to him when Hollis first described the plan to destroy the old factory. The whole time Hollis had been talking, Gabriel kept expecting himself to get up, walk through the front door, and never look back. That was what the old Gabriel would have done. That sane, sensible kid from West 86th Street, the honor roll student, the junior-class vice president. But he hadn't done that. Instead he'd stayed put, had kept right on sketching. Not just the logo, which he had shown Hollis, but two other pictures—vivid, detailed pictures—on the blank backs of pages from the manifesto.

While Alec talked of setting fire to Lukowski's house, Gabriel had drawn a house on fire with Lukowski bursting through the front door in terror, flames shooting from the top of his head and his clothes. And when Hollis described the explosion of an entire plant, Gabriel drew sections of rubble from a large building, debris flying in all directions, the building itself nothing more than a burned-out shell.

The pictures had pulled him in, deeper and deeper into the fantasy, right along with Hollis's words. He could see the whole explosion unfolding right before his eyes, like a movie playing inside his head. And it was magnificent. His blood had begun to pump wildly through his veins, his heart raced, his whole body buzzed with an adrenaline high. And this wasn't even a dress rehearsal. They had only been making plans. All he knew was that ever since the night of the shoplifting spree, he had begun to feel alive again. He no longer started his day with ice water cutting across his back in the shower.

They had come to the end of Lydia's driveway, having passed Gabriel's house a quarter mile back. Lydia didn't want him to walk her up to the house. It was too risky. Although she didn't tell him this.

She was still hoping he would give her a reason for what the group was planning to do. Because it didn't make any sense to her. She had more or less decided to go along but try to stay on the sidelines, as she had the night they trashed the train station. She didn't want to destroy anything. Yet, as perverse as it sounded, she didn't want to miss the excitement, the spectacle, either. But most of all, she wanted to be with Gabriel.

Lydia stared down at the ground and pushed her hair behind her ears, embarrassed. All she could think about was Gabriel kissing her goodnight. When she looked up she saw he was staring over her head, not even looking at her. She didn't want to make a move toward him if that wasn't what he had in mind, especially since he hadn't made a single attempt to kiss her since the night they'd trashed the train station.

Gabriel turned to leave. "Well . . . see you in English Monday."

She needed to come up with something fast. "Remember that night at the camp, I said I didn't have a car?" she blurted out. "Then you said, 'You've got friends with cars, don't you?' "

"Yeah, so?"

"Well, I never answered you because the truth is no, I don't." She paused, waiting. When he didn't respond, she added, "Except for you."

Lydia took a step closer to him.

"I know this probably sounds weird, but my dad won't let me take driver's ed at school. He doesn't want me to get my driver's license. So I was wondering—I need someone who's got a car, someone to teach me how to drive."

"And that someone you've got in mind is me, right?"

Lydia felt her face flush and was glad it was dark out. "I don't know a lot of people. Not well, I mean."

Gabriel knew this was true. He'd never seen Lydia with anyone in the halls at school. No one ever hung around her locker or walked to classes with her. She had to be the most alone person he'd ever met. And now she was telling him her old man wouldn't even let her drive. What kind of father would do that? Driving was a right, wasn't it?

"Sure, why not. But you need to get your learner's permit first."

Lydia was beside herself with excitement. "Really, you'd do that?"

"I said I would, didn't I?" Gabriel was starting to wish he hadn't been so hasty.

"I've got the book to study for the written test. I just need someone to drive me to the DMV to take it. Then I'll have my permit."

She was standing so close to him she could smell the wood smoke from the fireplace on his jacket. Before she realized she'd done it, she slipped her arms around his chest and hugged him. "Thanks." She turned her face up to him. Gabriel didn't seem to know what to do, so before he could back away, Lydia pressed her lips against his mouth. This time she felt his arms going around her. And miracle of miracles, he was kissing her back. But the kiss was brief, more friendly than passionate, and a moment later his arms dropped away. He took a step back.

"Thanks for walking me home," she said. Her voice was barely a whisper, husky with longing.

Gabriel nodded. "Sure." Then he turned to go, leaving her standing in the shimmering frost-crusted grass by the roadside.

Lydia filled one third of her glass with vodka, then added orange juice. It was two-thirty in the morning and she couldn't sleep. She hoped the vodka would help.

For the past hour she had lain awake thinking about Gabriel. She wondered why he hardly ever talked to her in school, except to say hi. They never hung out together. And he'd never once offered her a ride home. She wondered if he knew she still took the bus. Well, after tonight, he had to know, since she'd all but begged him to give her driving lessons. Still, he'd said yes, and that was something.

So why didn't he ever call her or ask her out? It was as if only some small part of who they were—the part connected to the group—acknowledged the existence of the other. When they were apart from the others, from Alec and Hollis, away from their hangout, they acted as if that secret part of themselves didn't exist.

Okay, so maybe they purposely ignored each other at school, and maybe it made sense. But that didn't keep her from fantasizing about herself and Gabriel as a couple. And at least now she had a plan. Two plans, really. One involved Gabriel, the other her escape. Up until now, she had thought the only way she'd ever be able to leave this place would be to walk the five miles to Knollwood and get on a bus. As long as her father refused to let her get her driver's license or learn how to drive, there was no other way out. No trains came through here, and it would cost a fortune to take a cab to the nearest airport, which was in Pennsylvania and well over an hour away.

Once she had even been desperate enough to walk down to Route 80, determined to hitch a ride, but had talked herself out of it. All she had to do was remember the body that had been found not far from the Knollwood exit off Route 80 a few years back—a headless, handless, footless corpse that no one could identify, a body that had been dumped, like so much garbage, by someone traveling through.

Now, since Gabriel had agreed to give her driving lessons, she'd be able to get her license and maybe drive away from this place someday. Even better, she'd be spending more time alone with him. In some ways, that was the best part of the plan.

Lydia climbed back into bed, setting the glass of orange juice on her nightstand, and pulled her comforter up to her chin. Her room was cold, but there was nothing she could do about it. Her father controlled the thermostat. During the day it stayed at sixty-five degrees. At night, sixty. All through the fall and winter.

All she could think of was that there would be no refuge for an entire week. No sanctuary and no being alone with Gabriel on walks home late at night. Hollis had forbidden any of them to go to the camp. And he was right, of course. It would be risky. But Lydia couldn't imagine how she was going to survive this week.

She just might have to break Hollis's rule, either that or go crazy. And really, which would be worse?

fifteen

On Tuesday night Gabriel showed up at Gem's house to watch *Hamlet* on video. Gem met him at the door wearing jeans slung low on her hips, flower print socks but no shoes, and a tight, long-sleeved purple tee with a V neck that plunged so low Gabriel almost forgot how to breathe when he first saw her. She led him into a small family room at the back of the house. All the furniture was large and overstuffed.

Suddenly Gabriel felt edgy. He didn't want to be here. He didn't want cozy or comfortable, or even sexy. He wanted the raw, decaying, mildewy old camp building. That was where he felt most at home these days.

When he sank down into the plush sofa cushions, he had the disconcerting sense that his whole body was being swallowed up. If Gem hadn't been standing two feet in front of him, he might have bolted right out the door.

She held up two different videos, one in each hand. "I found two versions. The one with Mel Gibson and the one with Kenneth Branagh. The Branagh version is a lot longer because it's the entire play, uncut."

Gabriel didn't even have to think about this one. It was a no-brainer. Short was definitely better. "The Gibson version's okay." He'd already spent weeks reading the play, talking about it in class, and was now trying to write a paper on it. And the truth was, the last thing he felt like doing was watching the movie. He was here because Gem had invited him and at the time he couldn't think of a good excuse. He had liked being with her. But that was before the LDs, before their plans to blow up the tool and die plant. Now he felt uneasy around Gem. He didn't belong here, in her world, and he wished like crazy he'd never agreed to come.

Gem put the video in the VCR, left the room, and showed up a few minutes later with a bag of tortilla chips, a bowl of salsa, and two cans of soda. For the first half of the movie neither of them talked.

Every so often, Gabriel stole a sidelong glance at Gem. Her profile was delicate, the full mouth, the small nose, thick long lashes. The only light in the room came from the TV screen, which flickered and kept changing the colors that illuminated her soft skin. He was only half watching the movie and had lost track of the scene. So when Gem suddenly said, in a low thoughtful voice, "It's incredible, isn't it? Hamlet spends all his time ranting and raving about how insidious his uncle is, how he's going to make him pay for killing his father, but then he plays right into his uncle's hands at the end."

Gabriel wasn't sure if she was looking for an answer from him, or if she was just thinking out loud, not until she turned her dark eyes on him, looking puzzled.

He dipped a tortilla chip into the salsa, stalling. "I don't know. I guess he didn't see it coming."

"How could he not?" Gem leaned toward him, shaking her head. "He knows how dangerous his uncle is. Claudius even tries to have him killed when Hamlet goes to England. Only, Hamlet intercepts the letter and discovers the plan. He knows his uncle's out to get him. So why does he agree to the duel with Laertes? It's like he totally underestimates the evil in his uncle, his deviousness, his ability to manipulate others."

"I don't know," Gabriel said irritably. "Why do they always have these old guys playing Hamlet?" He was growing annoyed. He had no idea where any of this was going, or why Gem had even brought it up, so changing the subject seemed the only reasonable course of action.

Gem blinked a few times. "What?"

"Well, he's a university student, right? He can't be more than nineteen or twenty."

Gem dipped a chip into the salsa, cupping her hand beneath it as she brought it to her mouth.

Gabriel thought the conversation had ended, and that

was fine with him. But then Gem said, "Yeah, it's pretty obvious by his behavior he's all raging hormones and teen angst." She stuffed the rest of the chip in her mouth, chewing thoughtfully. "Maybe that explains it. He was too busy screaming at his mother and stepfather—uncle, whatever—stabbing anything that moved behind a curtain, and humiliating poor Ophelia, to really think through how he was going to carry out an intelligent plan to avenge his father's death. I mean, even when he gets his chance to kill Claudius, he backs off with some lame excuse about not killing him while he's praying because then his uncle might go to heaven. God forbid. So that leaves his uncle alive to plot Hamlet's death. Face it. He's not exactly the sharpest tool in the shed."

"Okay. So Hamlet didn't see it coming. He screwed up. Can we maybe just watch the movie?" Gabriel tried to keep his voice even and normal. He turned his attention back to the TV screen. He couldn't figure out why there was this sudden tension between him and Gem. *It's just a stupid movie,* he thought. What was he getting so bent out of shape for?

Gem tucked herself into the corner of the couch, knees against her chest. She had no idea why Gabriel had gotten so defensive. They'd hardly said a word to each other since he'd arrived. All she was trying to do was get a conversation going, get him to talk about the play, maybe bounce some ideas off him. What was his problem?

When the movie finally ended, neither of them seemed to know what to do next. Gem asked Gabriel if he wanted another soda and he accepted, even though he didn't want anything to drink.

A few minutes later she returned with their sodas, but she didn't bother to sit down. "We could go for a walk if you want. Or watch another video."

They'd been sitting for over two hours. Suddenly the idea of taking a walk sounded pretty good. Gabriel reached for his sweatshirt jacket and pulled it on. "You could show me the camp."

"It's a little hard to see in the dark," she told him. "This time of year, anyway. In the summer, when the camp's full, everyone's got lights on, lights in their trailers, sometimes colored lights strung between the outlets on the trees and the trailers." Gem pulled on her hiking boots, laced them up, then slipped on her fleece jacket. She tucked her can of soda into the pocket. "It's kind of fun around here then. I mean, some people would think it was sort of, I don't know, tacky, I guess. But I've always liked all those lights. It's like one big ongoing party all summer long. People sitting in folding chairs outside their trailers, playing cards, telling jokes, visiting with each other. Kids running all over the place."

"Sounds great." Gabriel couldn't imagine any of it. But he liked the way Gem's face softened into a gentle smile when she talked about the lights and the campers. He thought that was how her face might look if she were in love.

Outside, Gem said, "Sorry about that whole Hamlet

thing. I guess I was trying to brainstorm ideas for my paper. And here you were trying to watch the movie. God, I'm such an idiot!" She shook her head.

"It's no big deal." At least now he knew why she'd brought up the subject. What he still couldn't figure out was why it had bothered him so much.

They walked down the driveway and through a gate. "Okay. Now we're in the campgrounds," Gem explained. "Our house is off limits to campers."

They sat on a wooden bench by the sandy beach of the manmade lake. Gabriel reached for a long stick on the ground and began sketching shapes in the sand. He had no idea what to say next. Why hadn't he just left after the movie? Why had he agreed to take a walk, for Pete's sake? He looked over at Gem. She was studying the design he was making in the sand. What was it about her, anyway? One minute he wanted to feel his arms around her, his mouth on hers, and the next, he wanted to bolt for the woods. She kept getting him all confused.

He felt as if he was living a kind of Jekyll and Hyde existence. In school he sometimes felt like the old Gabriel, the person he'd always been, or thought he was. And that was how he felt when he was with Gem.

Here, sitting beside her, their breaths forming one soft white cloud on the frosty air, he felt real. Not alive in the way he felt when he was smashing windows or pounding his fists through Sheetrock. This was different. Gem always seemed so calm, so grounded. And when he was with her, he could almost make himself believe he had some control over his own life. Almost.

When the silence became too uncomfortable, Gem got up and walked over to the edge of the lake. She was really blowing this evening. All that stuff about *Hamlet*. She could tell it had bothered Gabriel, but she'd kept right on talking. What was wrong with her? Couldn't she just come up with some normal safe topic for them to talk about?

Why did she care, anyway? So he was good-looking. Big deal. So were a lot of guys at school. But it was more than that, and she knew it. She was drawn to his sensitivity. He seemed so raw sometimes, like an open wound. She could sense that he was troubled but had no idea how to help him.

She stared up at the star-filled sky and then into the water. After a while she glanced over her shoulder and smiled at Gabriel. "If it was thirty degrees warmer, we could go skinny-dipping." Maybe that would get his attention.

For one chilling moment, Gabriel thought his heart might have stopped altogether. Did she know? Was she aware he'd been watching her swim on that warm September night?

Gem was laughing at his expression. He must look like a naïve jerk.

"Not here," she said, walking back to him. "I've got this other, secret place."

His lips almost formed the words "I know," but he swallowed them back. Then, before he realized what he was doing, he went to her, circled his arms around her waist, and pulled her to him. Her mouth was soft and warm. And she didn't even try to step back when he slid his hands beneath her jacket, gently outlining the V of her shirt with his fingers. They were so entangled in each other that neither heard the footsteps coming along the dirt road by the lake. They were wrapped up in their own world, hearing only each other's breathing and the pounding of their hearts. They didn't hear the owls hooting their warnings, or the distant barking of Sam and Sadie, Kate Hennessey's two Irish setters.

They heard nothing until Alec Stryker suddenly announced, "PG-13 maybe. Definitely wouldn't get an R rating. And you can forget X-rated." He screwed up his face. "Actually, now that I've gotten a better look, I'd have to say G. Yeah, G-rated. Maybe Disney could use you." He shifted his gaze to Gabriel. "Jeez, man, you can do better than that. You the Hart Man, right? Yeah, you the man—the Hart Man."

There was something ugly about the expression on Alec's face. Instinctively Gabriel's arms dropped to his sides. He and Gem took a step away from each other.

For a few seconds Gabriel had trouble getting his bearings. His two worlds had suddenly collided and he was reeling. He knew Alec worked part-time for Gem's aunt, but for some reason, he'd completely forgotten Alec also lived on the campgrounds, that he had his own trailer.

Except there he was, standing feet wide apart, in jeans and a leather jacket, with a shotgun leaning against one shoulder, looking for all the world as if he'd like nothing better than to fire a round of buckshot right into Gabriel's chest.

The small electric heater in the trailer had shorted out. Frost had begun to form on the inside of the windows. Alec threw the shotgun on the bed and grabbed a can of beer from the refrigerator.

He slumped into the yellow beanbag chair, attempting to roll a joint between chugs of beer. If he didn't get himself calmed down soon, he'd do something crazy. He was sure of it.

His hands shook so badly, half the marijuana spilled off the paper into his lap. He pinched up what he could of the pot that had landed on his jeans and dropped it back on the paper, rolled it, and ran the tip of his tongue along the edge.

Alec took a long toke from the joint, held the smoke in his lungs, and waited for his muscles to relax—especially his hands, which at the moment were clenched into tight fists. Since when had Gabe Hart started seeing Gem? He'd never even mentioned Gem before. Not that Alec could remember anyway. Then suddenly there was Gabe, putting his dirty rotten hands all over her. It sucked, man. The Hart Man sucked. Gem sucked. The whole thing sucked.

The marijuana had begun to roll through his body like

a soft, warm inner cloud. Alec took another long toke, squinting with pleasure. This was good stuff. Then he chugged half the can of beer. He hadn't bothered to take his sweatshirt or leather jacket off. The trailer was like a refrigerator. The lights still worked, so he knew he hadn't lost power. But he couldn't be bothered trying to figure out how to fix the damn heater right now. It was just a cheap plug-in job. He'd get another one tomorrow.

He took another beer from the fridge and flopped down on the single unmade bed, not bothering to take off his boots. It didn't much matter. The sheets were a dingy gray and hadn't been washed in weeks anyway. He punched the two pillows up against the wall and leaned back.

The beer and marijuana had begun to mellow him to a dull indifference. By now he'd figured out Gem and Gabriel obviously knew each other from school. They were in the same grade, probably even in a few classes together. So what did he expect? As far as he was concerned, Gem was the most beautiful girl he'd ever set eyes on. Why wouldn't the Hart Man think so too? And, shit, it wasn't like he knew Alec was hot for her or anything. It wasn't like Alec had ever told him how he felt.

Alec plunged the last of the joint into the empty beer can, listening to the hiss as it hit bottom, before he realized he'd wasted what was left of the roach. It didn't matter. He was feeling pleased with himself, with how reasonable he was being about all this. Besides, he doubted Gabriel and Gem were serious. There hadn't been enough time for that. He doubted the Hart Man moved that fast. It wasn't like he couldn't still squash this thing between them before it got too far along. And if there was one thing he was good at, it was screwing up people's lives. He'd had plenty of practice on his own.

sixteen

Sunday afternoon Gabriel sat in the great room in front of the computer struggling to write his paper on *Hamlet*. It had been due on Friday, but he'd made up some lame excuse about the hard drive crashing and bought himself the weekend. He could tell Mr. Sorensen hadn't really believed him, but he couldn't worry about that now. He had other things on his mind. Gem Hennessey for one. He hadn't been able to stop thinking about her since the night they'd watched the *Hamlet* video.

Thinking about Gem started him wondering again about Alec Stryker and the way he'd behaved when he came across Gabriel and Gem Tuesday night. Every time Gabriel played this scene over in his head—something he'd done at least a hundred times since it happened—a deep sense of dread engulfed him. He'd tried to shake it off, telling himself Alec was just busting his chops with that G-rated remark, trying to rattle his cage a little. That was the kind of thing Alec did. But it was more than that. Whenever Gabriel remembered the look on Alec's face, he felt apprehensive. He still couldn't shake the terrifying feeling that Alec had been looking for the slightest excuse to pull the trigger of the shotgun he had with him, and that he, Gabriel, had been the target.

Why? That was the part that didn't make sense. He'd never felt uneasy any of those other times he'd been around Alec. So why that night? The only thing different was that he was on Alec's turf, sort of. That, and something else: Gem. But that couldn't be it. All the time he'd known Alec, neither of them had ever mentioned Gem Hennessey. Not once.

Dark clouds rolled across the sky, colliding overhead. The air had a stillness that was almost suffocating. Outside, the few brown leaves left on the trees hung on the branches like sleeping brown bats. It was the first day of November, but the air was so warm Gabriel wore an old pair of cutoffs and a T-shirt.

A rumble of thunder echoed through the forest. The sky flashed white. The second flash sent the lights in the house flickering. He watched in frustrated horror as the computer screen went black. Maybe he just wasn't meant to finish this paper.

He stepped out on the deck just as the sky opened. Within seconds he was soaked to the skin.

For a short time he stood in the middle of the deck, his

face turned upward, letting the rain wash over him. The water felt cool on his body.

When he went back into the house, his sneakers made squishing, sucking sounds and his dripping clothes left a small stream of water as he walked across the oak floor. His mother would have a fit if she saw him walking through the house like this. Except his mother hadn't even come home this weekend. She was in Connecticut going over a manuscript with one of her bestselling authors. For the first time Gabriel had to admit to himself that he hated not having her there. Hated that she had chosen to spend most of her time in the city rather than be with her family.

Gabriel changed into a dry pair of jeans, T-shirt, and socks. His sneakers were soaked, so he didn't bother with shoes. Later he would put on his hiking boots, before he headed down to the camp. Outside, the temperature had plummeted almost twenty degrees. Already he could feel the change inside the house and pulled on a long-sleeved denim shirt.

Rain gushed from the leaf-clogged gutters, drilling small trenches in the soil around the house. Gabriel wondered if the water would flood the basement. They'd never had to worry about stuff like that in the city.

He wondered if his father had noticed the waterfall running off their roof. Probably not. So no one was more surprised than Gabriel when the rain stopped and he suddenly became aware of footsteps crossing from one end of the roof to the other and back. Someone was up there taking stock of the situation. He put on his hiking boots and went outside to check it out. The sun had burned through the storm clouds, and Gabriel had to shade his eyes to look up. What he saw, to his amazement, was his father, stuffing handfuls of soggy mulch into a huge black plastic leaf bag.

A shiny new aluminum ladder stood on the deck outside the great room, leaning against the side of the house. Gabriel's thoughts knotted into a tangle. One part of him was irked because his father was actually taking care of the gutter problem, which meant he had—to Gabriel's way of thinking—gone native. His dad was becoming one of them. But part of him was also feeling something else, something that surprised him: pride. He was actually proud of his father, an emotion he hadn't experienced in a long time. He wasn't sure exactly why he was proud. Maybe it had something to do with his dad's ability to adapt, something he would never have expected. The man knew art and that was about it. He hid himself in a studio all day, shutting out the world, and presumably all its pain, and he painted. What did he care about clogged gutters? But there he was, up to his elbows in leaf muck.

Gabriel didn't know what to make of it, but he needed to find out. Seconds later he found himself precariously balanced at the top of the ladder, trying to climb onto the slick shingles.

His father, dressed in his usual paint-spattered jeans and sweatshirt, was watching him. When, Gabriel wondered, had his dad's thick brown hair and beard gotten so gray?

He didn't say anything or try to help Gabriel onto the roof. He just waited. Gabriel's boots were clumsy and awkward, but he managed a lopsided gait to keep his balance once he was up there.

When he reached his father, Robert Hart handed him an empty trash bag. Gabriel could tell by the look on his father's face that he was both surprised and pleased. Usually his parents had to constantly stay on his case to get him to do anything they asked. And even then, most of the time, he could get out of whatever chore they had in mind if he played his cards right.

Gabriel went to work on the front gutter while his father cleaned the back.

"Where'd the ladder come from?" Gabriel called over to him.

"Bought it this morning." Robert Hart dug out another muddy handful of leaves and plunged it into the bag. "With all these trees around the house, I figured we'd have a real mess on our hands. I was hoping to beat that storm this afternoon, but it didn't work out." He pulled a twist-tie from his pocket, twisted it around the full bag, and dropped the whole thing over the edge to the yard below. "Once we get them cleaned out, I'll put up the gutter guards."

Gutter guards? His father had even thought of that. Despite himself, Gabriel was impressed.

At first neither of them said much. But then his father surprised him by asking what he thought of Shelby's hair.

Gabriel took a few minutes before he answered. He

had to be careful what he said. The wrong thing might worry his dad. Finally he opted for "Pretty creative."

He father shook his head and laughed. "Yeah, I'd say so. I guess the apple doesn't fall far from the tree."

If his father hadn't had a lot of artist friends who were themselves "pretty creative" when it came to how they dressed and wore their hair, Gabriel might not have found the question about Shelby all that disconcerting. But it wasn't like his dad to ask something like this, not even about his own daughter. He was a firm believer in free creative expression.

"Why? I mean, why'd you want to know what I thought about her hair?"

His father, who'd been kneeling, sat back on his heels and stared down at his muddy hands. "Do you think she's okay?" he asked, his voice so low Gabriel could barely make out the question.

He swallowed hard. "I don't know, Dad. Maybe not. It could be some weird phase. Maybe she's acting out."

Gabriel waited, although he wasn't at all sure what he was waiting for. But his father only nodded and went back to scooping out the leaves.

They worked until the gutters were clean. Then his father brought up the vinyl mesh and together they bent and positioned the wire, forming tunnels over the gutters.

A strong wind had come up and with the lower temperature, Gabriel felt the cold biting right through his denim shirt. Up until a few minutes ago, the sun reflecting on the roof had been warm. But now the sun had dipped behind the mountains. It was as if someone had lowered the shades, plunging a room into a gray dimness.

"Let's pack it in for today," his father said. "There's only one small section left. I'll take care of it tomorrow." He closed the top of the last plastic bag full of leaves and circled it with a twist-tie. "Why don't you call for a pizza?"

The nearest pizza place was seven miles away, and they had no delivery service, something that had bugged Gabriel since they'd moved here, and he always made sure everyone in his family knew it. But tonight he didn't seem to mind. He even told his dad he would go pick it up. He was actually looking forward to sitting down with his father and Shelby over a pizza. It was almost as if they were a family again. Almost.

And there was something else. For the first time that evening, he realized he hadn't once thought about the Lords of Destruction since he'd gone up on the roof, had forgotten, for a brief time, all about their meeting later that night.

Alec was the first one at the camp. He was edgy, spoiling for a fight. When Lydia showed up, he barely spoke to her. He was waiting for Gabriel. And the minute he saw him in the doorway, he said, "So where's your girlfriend?"

That got Lydia's attention. Up until then she had been occupying herself with stacking wood in the fireplace and stuffing kindling around it.

Gabriel knew Alec was talking about Gem, but he played dumb. "And that would be . . . ?"

Alec wasn't buying it. "So what's it like, doing it with the Snow Queen?"

At first Gabriel was stunned. He hadn't expected that from Alec, couldn't for the life of him figure out where the guy was coming from. His instinct was to smash his fist into Alec's mouth. Instead he could only stare in disbelief.

"Gem's a friend," Gabriel told him, taking a step closer to Alec. Gabriel was almost a full head taller, but not nearly as muscular. Still, Alec took a step back when he saw the look in Gabriel's eyes.

Lydia was kneeling in front of the fire, holding a log in both arms as if it was an infant. At the mention of Gem Hennessey's name, the air had gone right out of her lungs. "Are you talking about the Camp Tramp?" she said, looking up at Gabriel. She knew this was a rotten thing to say, knew it was only a cruel nickname kids had given Gem back in freshman year, knew too that there wasn't an ounce of truth in it. Still, Lydia couldn't seem to help herself. It didn't matter that she'd never actually gone out with Gabriel. What mattered was that she'd broken Hollis's rule about not coming to the camp over the weekend because of Gabriel. For two nights she'd sat alone in the dark, hoping Gabriel wouldn't give a damn what Hollis had ordered, hoping he would show up, as she had. Because then it would have been only the two of them. Now she understood why he hadn't come. It had *nothing* to do with Hollis or his stupid rule, and *everything* to do with Gem Hennessey. The betrayal Lydia felt flared into anger. "I can't believe you're actually getting it on with *her*."

Alec and Gabriel were both staring at Lydia. The silence that followed was more toxic than the stinging scent of burning wood from the fire. None of them seemed to know where to go with this. So they were relieved to hear the knob turn and the irritating screech of the hinges as the front door opened.

The three looked up when Hollis stepped into the room. He could tell from the expressions on their faces that something was wrong. But he didn't want to get into it. They had more important things to talk about tonight.

Lately Hollis had been showing up at the camp alone, without Alec. In fact, ever since they'd all begun hanging out at the camp, he rarely came by the trailer anymore, or followed Alec into the woods to hunt late at night. Not that Alec cared. But he did miss Hollis's interest in him. And although he didn't like to admit it, he also missed those occasional looks of admiration that used to flicker across Hollis's face when Alec would bring down a raccoon from a tree with a single illegal rifle shot. Or get a clean shot at a wild turkey, right through the head.

Hollis closed the door and stood there slapping a manila folder against the palm of one hand. "I've got it figured out," he told them, tossing the folder on the table. "Piece of cake."

Lydia, who was still sitting on the floor near the fireplace, trying to keep warm, began to twist the ends of her hair. Ever since the night Hollis proposed destroying the tool and die plant, she had been thinking about what she could say to talk the others out of going through with this insane scheme. Then this morning, quite by accident, she had found what she needed.

Fate, in the form of a small article in the local paper, which she hardly ever read, had handed her a bit of information none of them had known before. Ordinarily Lydia wouldn't have bothered to even glance at the newspaper. But there it was, right on the kitchen counter, next to the Mr. Coffee, right there on the front page of *The Knollwood Press,* an article about the town council and the old tool and die plant on Route 48.

One name caught her eye: Gerald Feeney. He was the owner of the plant and lived in Bergen County, clear on the other side of the state. There was no other mention of him in the article. But goose bumps danced up and down her arms at the sight of the name. There had to be some connection between this person and Hollis. And she wasn't about to let him manipulate all of them into some crazy scheme for his own personal reasons. Tonight she had come fully armed with this latest information.

She waited until Hollis began dealing out copies of his plan like so many playing cards. Then, looking up from her place on the floor and forcing herself to sound nonchalant, she said, "Who is Gerald Feeney?"

Hollis's hand, still holding one of the papers, froze in midair. Slowly he walked over to where she sat and attempted to hand it to her. "I want these copies of the plan back after we go over them. Nobody leaves here until I have all the copies. Understood?"

Lydia made no move to take the paper in his hand, wouldn't even look at it. "You didn't answer my question."

"I'm not sure why you're asking it."

"Because I happen to know Gerald Feeney owns the plant you want to blow up."

A slow, calculated grin spread across Hollis's face. Lydia had surprised him, caught him off guard. Not many people were able to do that. "So you read the local papers after all."

"Who is he?"

"My father." Hollis's voice was bland and emotionless.

But Lydia wasn't fooled. She could tell he was working hard to keep it that way. Splotches of pink were spreading across his cheeks. She had struck a nerve.

Gabriel, who had been reading through Hollis's notes, glanced over at him. "Why would you want to destroy a building owned by your own father?"

Hollis, his back still to Gabriel, said simply, "I have my reasons."

"Personal reasons," Lydia said. "And it doesn't bother you in the least that you might be setting us all up?"

Alec was standing right behind Hollis. His face was dark. He grabbed Hollis by the shoulder and spun him around, leaning into his face. "Let me get this straight. When I wanted to set that creep Lukowski's house on fire for all the shit he did to me, that was 'petty stuff.' Not big enough for you."

"I never said revenge wasn't a good motive," Hollis reminded him. "I wanted us to have a bigger target, that's all. Something to get people's attention. I want them to know there's a powerful force living right here among them, one that can blow them into oblivion anytime it chooses."

"And in the process you get even for what?" Gabriel said. "I'm not about to be a part of this till I know what it's really about." In fact, until Hollis had come through the door with his stack of "plans," Gabriel had been secretly hoping they would just drop this whole crazy idea about blowing up the old plant. A little vandalism to get his blood pumping, that was one thing—this was something else. Hollis's scheme could land them in prison, maybe even get them blown up.

Lydia moved closer to the fireplace. "I agree with Gabe. Why should we risk getting arrested, maybe sent to prison, just for some stupid revenge thing you've got going with your father?" But even as she said this, Lydia felt a pang of envy. What she wouldn't give to be able to get back at the nutcase like that, punish him for everything he'd done to her, to his family.

Hollis moved back to the table and stood at the end of it. The light from the candle flickered across his face. Quietly, reasonably, he told them how his old man had left him and his mom when Hollis was barely six, and had never looked back. How his father had moved his tool and die company to Bergen County, clear across the state. How he'd never paid child support, which meant Hollis's mother had to spend hours on her feet behind the Revlon cosmetics counter at JCPenneys, then drag herself to her telemarketer job in the evenings. And how, in all those years, his father had never once bothered to send them so much as a Christmas card.

When Hollis was finished, he waited, looking from Gabriel, to Alec, and over to Lydia, slowly gauging their reactions. So far none of them had said a word.

Then Alec pounded his fist on the table. "That sucks, man. We gotta nail that bastard."

Hollis had to struggle to keep his expression deadly serious. He couldn't afford to let out the smallest smile, let alone the bubble of laugher stuck in his throat. Alec was so easy. You pushed a few buttons, and he did exactly what you wanted. The others took a little more work.

Hollis stared down at the candle. "I knew you'd understand," he said.

Gabriel was impressed by Hollis's scheme of revenge, and that surprised him. Unlike Hamlet, Hollis would let nothing stand in his way. Hollis didn't have a wishy-washy bone in his body. Why hadn't he noticed that before? And there was something else, a small kernel of a plan had begun to form in his own mind. Another plan of revenge with Hollis at the helm.

Lydia had joined them at the table. She couldn't believe what she was about to say, but it had been creeping into her mind ever since Hollis had begun talking about his father. As far as she could tell, Hollis was the only one who stood to gain anything from destroying the plant. "If we do this," she told him, "then we should all get something out of it."

He gave her a patient look. "You are, Lydia. You're getting back at *them*."

"I don't give a rat's ass about *them*. I don't care about your father or the town council. So if I do this, I need to have a reason. And doing it out of the goodness of my heart to help you get back at your father isn't enough."

She sat on her log stump. Hollis sat too.

"What is it you want?" Hollis asked.

Without so much as a second's hesitation, Lydia answered, "Money." She didn't bother to explain why, in three months when she turned eighteen and left this place for good, she would need money. And a car, if she ever got her license. If Hollis could get the LDs psyched up enough to blow away a huge building, then surely she could get them to commit a few robberies.

"You want me to pay you to help us blow up a building?" Hollis laughed right out loud. "Lydia. You overestimate your part in all this. We don't even need you."

"You need my silence."

Hollis blinked, then shook his head. "Lydia, Lydia, Lydia. You'd resort to blackmailing your friends?"

"I'm not blackmailing you, you geek." She looked at Alec, then across the table at Gabriel, who, for once, didn't seem to know what to do with his hands. He kept folding and unfolding the piece of paper Hollis had given him. "Aren't we supposed to be in this together?" she asked them, waiting, praying Gabriel would look over at her and agree. "I mean, we made a pact. I'm not about to break it. All I'm saying is, if we do this for Hollis, then we should do something for Gabe and for Alec—"

"And for you, of course," Hollis added. But he was actually smiling at her with a newfound respect.

"Yes. For me, too. It's only fair."

"Fair? Well, of course." Hollis waved his hand in dismissal, as if this was already understood, and he wasn't at all sure why she'd even brought it up.

"I got a whole list of people that deserve payback," Alec said. "Enough to keep the LDs in business for years."

No one paid any attention to him.

Lydia leaned in closer to the candle. She reminded the others of the night she and Gabriel had copped stuff in the 7-Eleven. "I mean stealing junk food, what was that about? If we can do that, we can just as easily go for the money. Maybe hit a few gas stations or something."

Alec folded his arms in front of him and nodded his approval. "I could use some coin." He looked over at Hollis. "So, what about it? Lydia here wants money, I say we go for it."

Hollis could tell that if he balked, if he didn't go along with this, which he definitely didn't want to, the others might back out on his own plan. He needed them. He couldn't do it himself, especially without a driver's license or wheels.

For a while, before Lydia got into the act, he'd thought

he had them. But except for Alec, he'd miscalculated their willingness to help him carry out his plan. Or, more accurately, perhaps he had miscalculated their level of anger and their need to vent it. They weren't about to do it because he was their friend. He'd known that all along. None of them were friends. That wasn't what the LDs were about. They were each here to take care of personal business. And sometimes that meant negotiating.

So while the others sat, waiting for his decision, Hollis weighed the potential risks. If nothing else, he could buy time until he could come up with a more ingenious way to get Lydia money, using his computer. He lifted the sheet of paper with his plan neatly printed out in ten steps. A list of what they would need, of who would handle what, and how they would go about carrying out their—his—act of revenge.

"Only if I plan the robberies," Hollis told them. "And only after we take care of the plant."

Three heads nodded in unison.

By the time they left the camp, they each had their assigned tasks. The plan was simple. They would break into the True Value hardware store around midnight a few days before the actual planned explosion. They would steal an igniter, a wireless remote-control system, several empty five-gallon gasoline cans, and three or four full bottles of propane. Then Gabriel and Alec would each get the five-gallon gasoline cans filled at different stations in nearby towns over two or three days, so as not to raise any suspicions. They would hide everything in the old shed behind their hangout, what Hollis now referred to as head-quarters.

NOVEMBER 2 . . . EARLY MORNING

The cool glare of the computer monitor was the only light in Hollis's sparse bedroom. The silvery glow made his face and hands look cold as death as his fingers danced back and forth over the keyboard. Occasionally he took a break to grab a handful of M&M's from the supersized bag sitting on his desk.

It was after two in the morning, but even though he had school the next day, and an exam in physics class, Hollis couldn't bring himself to go to bed. Not yet. Not when he was so close to completing his Web site. *Web*. A crooked smile flickered across his face. After all, wasn't that what he was designing? An elaborate web to catch potential recruits—unsuspecting flies. That was how he imagined them. Once trapped, they would be stuck for life.

The site, www.netserv.com/angermanagement.html, set up through his local provider, offered tips to help peo-ple whose quick tempers got in the way of a healthy life. Along with snippets from trendy articles culled from pop psychology publications, there was space for people to anonymously write in their comments or share their sto-ries with others who were trying to "kick the hot temper habit."

But the promise of anonymity was false. Of all the computer programs Hollis had written, he was proudest of this one. It was ingenious. The split second someone logged on to his site, Hollis's program retrieved their e-mail address. It didn't matter if the person logged on as an anonymous user or not.

When the Web site was ready, in a day or two, he would begin collecting the e-mail addresses, putting them into a database. He would create a list of hundreds, maybe thousands, of angry people, people to whom the Lords of Destruction, under the guise of a more benevolent name, could send their literature: pamphlets for the purpose of recruiting new members. People who would welcome an outlet for their rage.

Hollis closed his eyes and leaned back in his swivel chair, imagining the years to come, imagining his place in the scheme of things. His destiny was to lead. He'd known this almost from the first day he'd set foot in school. Because there was only one thing worth having in this world: power.

Over the years he had carefully observed how people's minds worked. He'd learned how easy it was to get them to do whatever you wanted, whether it was collecting quarters from kids willing to pay half their lunch money to keep Ace Mahoney from beating the crap out of them—most of the profits went to Hollis, the brains behind the scheme—or whether it was manipulating a bunch of loners into blowing up your father's tool and die plant. It didn't matter. In the end it was all the same.

Because the most valuable thing he had come to understand was that people did not want the burden, the responsibility, of thinking for themselves. Although he wasn't sure why that was.

That was why the LDs had so much potential. It was becoming more obvious to him with each meeting. They were each smart in their own way. But easily manipulated. And that was what counted. Lydia had cunning. Gabriel had imagination. He needed people like that. As for Alec—Alec was a thug, pure and simple. One of life's unpleasant necessities. Without him, Hollis would have had to do his own dirty work. Such behavior was beneath him. He was their leader, the intelligence behind something larger and far more powerful, far more destructive, than any of his LD robots—his newly programmed Gabriel, Lydia, and Alec—could ever begin to imagine.

seventeen

On Thursday night, walking back to his trailer after taking the trash cans out to the road for the haulers, Alec spotted Gabriel's silver Toyota parked in the driveway by Gem's house. He was disappointed that Lydia's snide remark about the Camp Tramp—for which Alec had been unexpectedly grateful—hadn't dissuaded Gabriel. Lydia had it bad for the Hart Man. It was pathetic how obvious she was. Ever since the night of the 7-Eleven incident, Alec had assumed Gabriel and Lydia would hook up. Except now it didn't look like that was going to happen.

In his gut Alec knew it was only a matter of time before Gabriel stopped showing up at the Boy Scout camp on weekends. That was what happened when you got yourself mixed up with a girl. She expected you to be with her all the time. Which wasn't to say he didn't want such a relationship for himself. It just made sense not to dwell on it.

Instead Alec had been trying to convince himself he was better off alone. Except the longing—his desire for Gem—wouldn't go away. It was with him all the time now. And to make things worse, he found he couldn't even complete a sentence around her anymore. Every time he opened his mouth he ended up feeling stupid.

Whenever he stopped by the house to pick up his mail—since the camp store was now closed until April—he barely grunted at her when she came to the door, even though the whole time he couldn't keep his eyes off her full mouth, the mouth he had seen pressed to Gabriel's a few weeks back. It had made him sick with jealousy, the sight of them together. And there wasn't a damn thing he could do about it. At least not yet.

When he reached his trailer, he saw that a light was on. A strange chill slithered up his spine. Someone was inside.

There were people—people he'd dealt with over the years—his supplier, and others he owed, and not just money but favors. Now he worried that one of them had tracked him down. Or worse, maybe it was the cops. Maybe they had new evidence about the train station trashing, evidence that had led them right to his door.

He flung the door of his trailer open and stepped quickly to the side out of line of any potential fire. From somewhere inside he heard Hollis's voice.

"Call 911. They're holding me hostage. *Hurry.*" Then he laughed.

Alec couldn't believe the little geek had tried to make a fool of him. He stormed into the trailer. "If I'd had my shotgun, asshole, you'd look like a pincushion about now. Don't ever, *ever*—get it?—try that shit on me again."

Hollis looked up at him from the beanbag chair, where he sat leafing through a *Guns* magazine he'd found lying on the floor. "Then I guess I'm lucky you didn't have your shotgun with you."

The sight of Hollis sitting there looking through pages of a firearms magazine was disconcerting. Alec didn't know what to make of it. "What the hell are you doing here, anyway? How'd you get in?"

"Spare key, the ledge above the door." Hollis gave Alec a disapproving frown. "Not very original of you."

"That answers how," Alec said, ignoring Hollis's remark. "What about why?" Since Hollis rarely came around anymore, Alec's instincts told him this wasn't just some social call.

"Isn't that Gabe's car parked in the Hennesseys' driveway?" Hollis tossed the magazine aside.

Alec shrugged and threw his jacket on the bed. He grabbed a beer from the fridge and leaned back against the counter. "Yeah, he and Gem got a thing going." He didn't bother to offer Hollis a beer. He knew he wouldn't take it anyway.

"A thing?"

"Come on, man. Yeah, a *thing*. He's probably screwing her right now." He yanked the tab with so much force it popped off in his hand.

Hollis seemed to be considering this new information. "You don't think he'd be stupid enough to tell her anything, do you?"

"Who knows? Right now the guy's thinking with his dick, not his brain." Alec was suddenly encouraged by the worried look on Hollis's doughy face. He chugged the last of the beer, stuffed his arms back into his leather jacket, pulled his shotgun from the box under the bed, and jammed a few rounds of shells in his pockets.

A slow smile spread across Hollis's face. He was just beginning to understand that Alec wanted Gem for himself. And he was mad as hell at Gabriel. "Feel like killing something tonight?"

Alec ignored him. He took a step toward the door. He still wasn't clear on why Hollis was there, but he didn't much care right then.

Hollis rolled his bulk out of the beanbag chair and followed him. He expected there would be a lot of dead deer and raccoons by morning, and he didn't want to miss a single shot.

NOVEMBER 6 . . . EARLY MORNING

It had been less than an hour since Gabriel had left Gem's house. Exhausted, he'd tried to get some of his homework done, but he'd finally given in and gone to bed, setting the alarm for five so he could finish studying for a math quiz.

Sometime around one, he awoke. Cold white moonlight streaked through the open blinds. He had forgotten to close them. And he had been so careful lately, careful to make sure his door was closed so the hall light didn't slip into his room, careful to close the blinds each night. Except tonight. Now it was too late. The Shadow People stood by the side of his bed, the moonlight behind them.

He was getting tired of this. Tired of hiding his head beneath his pillow, waiting for them to disappear. Tired of his racing heart, the pain in his lungs when he tried to take a normal breath, the sweat-soaked sheets. Why wouldn't they leave him alone? What did they want from him?

Well, he wasn't going to let them get to him this time. He'd had it. Taking a deep breath, he propelled himself out of bed so fast he almost lost his balance. Then he lunged for the door. Let them follow him if they wanted. He wasn't about to hang around, giving them the satisfaction of seeing him cower under the pillow.

A few minutes later he stood in front of the microwave, wearing only his boxers and a T-shirt, waiting for a bag of popcorn to puff up. At the sound of bare feet padding across the cold tile floor, he glanced over his shoulder.

Shelby stood in the middle of the kitchen in her plaid flannel pajama bottoms and a Chicago Bulls T-shirt. Her uncombed hair, with its Pepto-Bismol pink streaks, stuck out in all directions, stiff with styling gel.

The last few kernels popped and Gabriel hit the Stop button. He knew better than to leave the popcorn in for the specified time. If you did, it burned. He had the timing down perfectly so he didn't blacken one single piece.

He filled a large metal bowl and set it on the table, nodding to Shelby, who helped herself to a handful of popcorn as she sat down.

"How's it going?" Gabriel wasn't sure what Shelby was doing down here in the kitchen. But he was pretty certain she had something on her mind.

She shrugged for an answer, dropped her fistful of popcorn on the table, and began arranging the pieces in straight little rows. "Why doesn't anybody in this house ever talk about Ben?"

He hadn't been expecting that. "I don't know, Shel." He got up to get them sodas, even though she hadn't asked for one. He was stalling for time, trying to find an honest answer for her, not just some stupid cliché people say when they don't know how to comfort someone. He opened two root beers, set a can in front of her, then slumped back into his chair. "I think it's too painful for them. For Mom and Dad. Maybe they think by looking like they're getting on with their lives—you know, toughing it out—they're setting a good example for us. Maybe they think we'll do the same."

"Their example sucks," Shelby said, squeezing a piece of popcorn between her thumb and forefinger.

Gabriel nodded. "Yeah, you're right. It does."

Shelby selected another piece of popcorn from the end of the second row and popped it in her mouth. "They talked about him once, at least."

"Yeah? When?"

"A few days after the funeral. They thought I was asleep, but I wasn't. They were in the kitchen. It was like, I don't know, four in the morning or something. And they were yelling. Well, Mom was, anyway."

"How come I didn't hear it?"

"You weren't home. You were staying over at Danny's."

Gabriel remembered that night all too well. He'd gone to an all-night party at Danny Perillo's with his girlfriend, Celia, and a bunch of their friends. He'd been trying to pretend his life was normal, pretend they hadn't buried his brother two days before. He'd spent the night feeling guilty and drinking too much beer. But he didn't want to think about that now. "So what was she yelling about?" He reached into the bowl for another fistful of popcorn.

"She was screaming at Dad for letting Ben go to that party, for letting him wander around the city at all hours of the morning. She said he always let Ben do whatever he wanted. She said since the day Ben was born Dad had completely . . . undersomething—I can't remember the word. You know, like got in the way whenever she'd tried to discipline Ben."

"Undermined?"

Shelby nodded. "Yeah, something like that."

"What'd Dad say?"

"He said Ben was over eighteen. He had a right to come and go as he pleased. And it wasn't anybody's fault. It just happened."

"So what? Like Mom was blaming Dad?"

Shelby swept all the popcorn into a pile. She nodded.

"Jesus. What was she thinking?"

Shelby slid the palm of her hand across one damp eye. "I miss Ben. I want to talk about the stupid stuff he used to do. He'd like that, us telling stories about him. But we don't."

Gabriel spun the lightweight aluminum bowl a few times before grabbing another handful of popcorn. "Remember the time Ben and Danny Perillo put Kool-Aid in the steam irons at school because they were mad about having to take a sewing class?"

"It's called consumer science," Shelby reminded him, tossing a piece of popcorn into her mouth. A wistful smile spread across her face. "The coach made them take it because they got into this shredding match in the locker room."

Gabriel laughed. "Yeah, Coach Willis. He was mad as hell when he saw half the basketball team had torn up each other's T-shirts after they'd won that big game against Briarwood. He said if they could rip 'em apart, they could damn well learn how to sew them back together."

"What a bunch of morons." Shelby laughed along with

him. It was the kind of prank Ben and his friends had pulled all the time when they were in high school. "I don't think Ms. Lehman ever did find out who put the Kool-Aid in her steam irons."

Gabriel shook his head, smiling at the memory. For a brief moment it felt as if Ben were still alive, as if he might walk into the kitchen any minute, grab a fistful of popcorn, and throw it at them for their irreverence.

And so they stayed there, at the kitchen table, telling funny Ben stories to each other for comfort until the popcorn was gone and the grandfather clock in the front hall chimed two.

They looked across the table at each other on the second chime. "Guess we'd better get some sleep," Gabriel told her.

Shelby trailed after him. He heard her whisper behind him in the upstairs hallway, "Doesn't it feel like Ben's here? Just a little?"

They stopped outside her bedroom door. "Yeah, it does."

She fidgeted with the doorknob, not looking at him. "They're going to get divorced, aren't they?"

"Maybe not." He knew he'd just admitted he'd been worrying about their parents too. But he couldn't pretend he didn't know what Shelby was talking about. He was only sorry he couldn't offer her more hope. Because right now he suspected his sister needed hope more than anything else. But before he could say another word, she slipped silently into her room, leaving him alone in the dimly lit hallway with his memories of Ben and his fears for their future.

Gabriel lay awake most of the night, staring up at the ceiling. He couldn't stop thinking about Ben. Every time he was about to doze off, another memory crept into his thoughts, forcing him to relive both the good and bad times he'd had with his brother. If only he didn't miss him so much.

Okay, so maybe he couldn't make the pain of Ben's death go away, but he could make the bastards who'd killed him pay for what they'd done. And they *would* pay. Because ever since the night Hollis had told them his reason for wanting to blow up the plant, Gabriel had been forming a new plan to avenge Ben's death. And he owed it all to Lydia. From the first moment she'd crossed Hollis, while he'd been telling them about his father, from the first moment she'd asked flat-out what was in it for all of them, from the moment she'd laid her cards on the table, Gabriel knew what he wanted from these people. Especially from Hollis, for whom he had a newfound respect.

If they could blow up a building to get back at Gerald Feeney for what he had done to Hollis and his mother, then they sure as hell could track down and destroy the thugs who had murdered Ben. And they would do it with impunity. Because Hollis was brilliant. More than brilliant. He was a genius. Fifteen years old and applying to M.I.T. for early acceptance. With brains like that, and his knowledge of computers, Hollis could probably hack his way into the computer files at NYPD's central headquarters at One Police Plaza.

Hollis would get all the information they needed, all the case evidence to date; then he'd come up with an ingenious plan of revenge, and not one of them would ever get caught. Gabriel felt certain of it. As certain as he did about his plans—the ones he would never tell Dr. Cortes—for Ben's killers. Sometimes, when justice wasn't being served, you had to take the law into your own hands.

When the digital alarm buzzed its shrill warning, Gabriel slapped the button on top with a vengeance. He'd gotten two hours sleep, if that. Forget studying for the math quiz. Maybe he'd tell his dad he was sick. Spend the day catching up on his sleep. He fell back to sleep and woke an hour later to the sounds of Shelby padding down the hall and the bathroom door closing behind her. If she could drag herself out of bed, so could he.

By the time he got to school, his first class had already started. He stumbled through the early part of the morning in a fog, sure he had blown the quiz. Not until Gem smiled up at him as he slid into his seat in English did it suddenly occur to him that he hadn't thought about her once since he'd come home last night. Yet only a few hours ago they had been making out on the couch in her family room. It was that double-life thing again—Jekyll and Hyde. It gave him the creeps.

And here was Gem, looking beautiful as always, in a snug-fitting sage-colored top that barely came to her waist and revealed two inches of bare midriff when she sat back in her seat, stretching her arms above her head. Her dark eyes crinkled slightly at the corners as her smile silently asked, "Remember last night? I do."

The last thing he expected at that moment was to see a dark shadow cross his desk and to look up into the expressionless face of Lydia Misurella, who said simply but firmly, "We need to talk. Meet me out by your car after last period," then headed up the aisle to her desk, hips swaying gently in her short, clinging skirt, and slipped into her seat, not once turning to look back at him through the whole period.

If Gem was surprised or curious it showed only in the slight flush of pink on her cheeks. She opened her textbook and flipped through the pages as if she hadn't been paying the least bit of attention to what was going on next to her.

But in truth, she was dying inside.

Lydia stood inside one of the stalls in the girls' room, finishing off her vodka and cranberry juice instead of going to her last class. She still couldn't believe she'd waltzed right up to Gabriel in English and told him to meet her after school. She wondered if maybe she'd lost her mind. Then she decided yes, she had. And it was all Gabriel's fault. He'd made her fall in love with him.

If she hadn't wanted to believe it Sunday night when

Alec had started busting Gabriel's chops about Gem, then she had no choice but to believe it now. She had seen the way Gabriel looked at Gem in class a few hours ago, and it had made her crazy.

What was she supposed to do when she saw him smile at Gem Hennessey that way? Sit quietly in her seat pretending she'd never felt Gabriel's sweet mouth on hers? Never felt his arms around her, and their hearts racing so fast in unison she'd been afraid she might actually die from all that pleasure?

Was it any wonder that the other night at the camp she had almost forgotten about her plan to talk the others out of blowing up the plant? Finding out about Gem and Gabriel had made her angry enough to set off the whole explosion herself, single-handedly. All she had been able to think of while the others had gone on planning, while Hollis had blurted out that lame story about his dad, was how much she wanted to get away from this place. That was when it came to her. If they could all do this revenge thing for Hollis, then they could damn well help each other carry out their own plans. For Lydia, the plan meant getting money. Money was her only means of escape. Without it, she wouldn't get very far. And she wanted to put plenty of distance between her and everybody else around here. The distance of a whole continent, if she could. She had even begun to toy with the idea of leaving the country, going to Canada or Mexico maybe. So she had dared to ask Hollis flat-out what was in it for the rest of them. Her brazenness had paid off.

Only now, standing in the rest room stall, she was feeling anything but brassy. She'd put herself in a ridiculous situation. She had no idea what she would say to Gabriel in the parking lot.

She peeked beneath the door of the stall. No one was in the rest room. She opened the door, tossed the empty cranberry juice bottle in the trash, and inspected her face in the mirror. Her cheeks were flushed from the vodka. She held her hand in front of her mouth and breathed into it, then pulled a stick of gum from her backpack. Better to play it safe.

Her hair was tangled in a few places, but instead of digging in her backpack for a comb, she simply raked her fingers through the ends a few times and pulled a few loose blond strands from her purple top. She opened the door of the rest room and looked out. The dismissal bell rang as she stepped into the hall. Perfect timing.

By the time she saw Gabriel walking across the parking lot, Lydia had already decided what this *meeting* would be about. If nothing else, she might be able to discover how serious Gem and Gabriel really were.

The wind was so strong, it lifted tiny stones from the asphalt and flung them at Lydia's legs. The short skirt left her legs vulnerable, and the stones felt as if they were taking little bites out of her skin. Gabriel's jacket was unbuttoned, and the wind caught the flaps, ballooning the material like a sail. As soon as he reached the car, Lydia asked if he'd mind giving her a ride home.

Gabriel, looking puzzled, unlocked the door for her,

then climbed into the driver's seat, but not before Lydia saw him glance nervously around the parking lot. He was probably searching for Gem and hoping she hadn't seen them together, which only made Lydia more determined than ever to spend this time alone with him.

The ride from the school to their road was only about fifteen minutes. Lydia knew she couldn't waste any time. But before she said anything, Gabriel announced unceremoniously to forget about him teaching her to drive.

Lydia assumed he was backing out because of Gem. But then he added, "You have to have someone twenty-one or older in the car with you." He glanced over at her. "I don't know what I was thinking, when you asked me. I mean, I forgot all about that."

When Lydia began to breathe again, she managed an indifferent shrug, although it was far from what she was feeling. "Well, that's one of the things I was going to tell you. You need a parent's or guardian's consent to get a learner's permit if you're under eighteen. I called the DMV to find out if I had to sign up for the written test ahead of time. They told me when I came in for the test and eye exam I needed a parent with me, or a signature on some form. Yeah, right. Like my dad's going to sign it." Actually, she hadn't planned to tell him any of this, especially since she'd already decided to forge her father's signature.

"What about your mom?"

"She wouldn't go against anything Dad said. He's turned her into some sort of Stepford wife. She's not even—" Lydia suddenly realized she was telling Gabriel far more about her family than she wanted him or anyone else to know. "Anyway, that's not why I asked for a ride home. It's not about me; it's about Alec."

"Alec?"

"I think you should know he's got it pretty bad for Gem Hennessey." Lydia was pleased with her delivery. She hoped it made her sound like she was just a friend who had Gabriel's best interest at heart. Her short skirt had slid up to the tops of her thighs, but she didn't bother to adjust it. She waited to see if Gabriel noticed.

"I sort of figured that out Sunday night." Gabriel kept his eyes on the road, didn't so much as shift his glance her way.

When he didn't say anything more, Lydia added, "He's not somebody you want to cross."

"What's between Gem and me is none of his business. If she wanted to go out with Alec, she would have."

There it was. Gabriel had practically said flat-out something was going on between him and Gem. Lydia's mouth felt so dry, she could barely swallow. A little cranberry juice and vodka would be nice right about now. "How much do you know about Alec Stryker?"

Gabriel shrugged. "How much do any of us know about each other?" He finally glanced her way, not at her legs but at her eyes. "Okay, I'll bite. What about him?"

Lydia took a deep breath and began to tell him Alec's history, or as much as she knew of it, which was part truth, part rumors, as much as anyone in town knew. Still, it was a disturbing picture, and she could tell Gabriel was surprised, even a little worried. Good. That was the plan. "He's dangerous. I just thought you should know."

Gabriel recalled the look on Alec's face the night he'd come upon Gabriel and Gem kissing. "What are you saying? That he'd try to kill me? That's nuts."

Lydia shrugged. "Who knows what he's capable of?" When Gabriel didn't answer, Lydia said, "Well, he does have guns." She leaned the side of her head against the window and closed her eyes.

As Gabriel turned the car onto Thorn Hill Road, he wondered what Lydia was thinking behind those closed lids, eyelids that had a slight purplish tinge to them, wondered why she'd told him all those things about Alec. Was she warning him because he was a friend, or was it something more? He'd already begun to suspect Lydia had feelings for him that he didn't share. And he'd been trying hard not to send her the wrong signals.

They were almost to the top of the winding mountain road. A few hundred yards from her driveway, Lydia made him stop the car. She opened the door and began to slip out, her skirt riding even higher, her long legs lingering in front of her. Over her shoulder, she said, "I'll walk from here. It's better that way." She got out and closed the door before Gabriel could respond. But she didn't miss the look on his face. It was surprisingly sympathetic.

The Toyota lurched forward. Gabriel lifted his hand in a brief gesture resembling a wave but without looking her way.

She watched him head up the road, glad she hadn't given in to the temptation to stay in his car and talk a little longer. It had been on the tip of her tongue to ask him to give her driving lessons anyway, on some of the back roads or in a vacant parking lot where they weren't likely to get caught. The real reason she'd asked him in the first place was because she wanted to be alone in the car with him. The more time they spent together, the better her chances with him.

But she'd chickened out. It didn't seem right, asking him to break the law for her. *With* her, though—now, that was another story. She smiled. There was still hope. There was still Hollis's plan. She thought about the night they had copped the food at the 7-Eleven and the night at the train station. There was a chance—just a small chance—that on the night they all came together to carry out Hollis's scheme, those feelings between her and Gabriel, which had seemed to come from out of nowhere those other times, might surface again. That was something Gem Hennessey could never give him. And that was when any last lingering thoughts of dissuading the others from their course of destruction went smack out of her head. She wasn't about to miss the plant explosion for anything in the world.

eighteen

On Saturday night when Gabriel arrived at the camp, the cynical smirk of surprise on Alec's face told him Alec probably hadn't expected him to show, had expected him to have a date with Gem. But Alec had called it wrong.

Not that Gabriel hadn't wanted to call Gem for a date. That had been the worst part. He kept finding himself in front of the phone, his hand only inches away from dialing her number. But each time he fought down the urge. How could he ask her out for Saturday night when he knew the LDs planned to hit the local True Value for supplies? He couldn't. They would be counting on him. Besides, if he didn't follow through, he'd never get them to go along with his own plan.

They waited until after midnight before breaking into the hardware store. Alec disconnected the alarm system and got them in the back door without a single glitch. Hollis picked out the wireless remote-control system he wanted; Lydia grabbed plastic five-gallon cans for the gasoline, and Gabriel and Alec loaded the back of the pickup with twenty-gallon propane tanks. Then they got back in Alec's truck and drove to the camp, where they unloaded the goods, hiding them in the shed out back. It was, as Hollis had foretold, a piece of cake.

Over the next few days Alec and Gabriel came and went, each taking one gas can at a time, getting them filled at different stations and returning them to the shed.

On Wednesday, a story referring briefly to what "appeared to be a break-in at the local True Value" showed up in *The Knollwood Press*. According to the article, the owner hadn't been able to determine what had been taken. More information would follow a full inventory. There was no evidence of vandalism. The alarm system was on but had probably malfunctioned. Alec had gotten a good laugh over that, since he'd stopped to reconnect the system before they drove off.

The night of the True Value break-in, Gabriel's adrenaline had been at peak. He was feeling so high, he actually took Hollis aside while they were storing the stolen goods in the shed and asked him how he felt about hacking his way into the NYPD computer system.

Hollis had been interested. But he wanted more details

first. Gabriel thought that was fair. Sooner or later he'd have to tell Hollis his motive, tell him the whole story. But for now it was enough Hollis hadn't flat-out said no.

NOVEMBER 11

The Lords of Destruction went over the plan until all of them knew exactly what they had to do and how they would carry out the act. By eleven-thirty they were ready.

Sitting on Gabriel's lap in Alec's truck, Lydia thought the smell in the cab that night was different, as if their cumulative adrenaline was sending out a peculiar but distinguishable scent. Something pungent but electrifying at the same time. Hollis's face had gone from its usual pasty white to a blotchy pink. It was the only outward sign of his intense excitement.

Alec was something else. He pounded his palms on the steering wheel in a frantic, frenzied effort to match the beat on his heavy metal tape, and sang disturbing lyrics at the top of his lungs. He was driving way too fast, weaving slightly, until Hollis, his voice low and controlled, said, "If you keep this up, the cops will pull us over before we ever get to the plant. Do you want them to see what we've got in the back of your truck?"

The speedometer dropped from eighty-five to fifty-five within seconds.

Ten minutes later Alec pulled the pickup into the parking lot of the abandoned plant and drove over the weeds growing through the cracks in the asphalt until he reached an area behind the building out of sight of any cars driving by. Not that there would be much traffic. By now it was well past midnight.

Lydia still wasn't sure how Hollis intended to cause the explosion, even though he'd explained it to them in great detail only an hour before. But at the time her mind had been focused on Gabriel and what might happen between them after the explosion. She didn't want to hear how Hollis was going to pull off the destruction, because then it would become too real to her. Better if she had only a vague idea.

The plan required electricity. That much she knew. If the power was off, so were all bets, unless Hollis had something else up his sleeve he hadn't told them about. But he had assured them the power was on because he had seen construction workers there during the day. They had already begun the renovation. They would need power for most of their tools. As it turned out, he was right. The place was littered with power saws, electric drills, sawhorses, drywall, and metal beams.

"We need to make sure nobody's in there, no homeless person looking for someplace to sleep," Gabriel said after Alec had gotten them through the back door.

Hollis turned to Lydia. "That's your job," he told her. "But you'll have to do it without a flashlight. We can't risk someone seeing a light in here. Gabe, Alec, and I will unload the truck."

Lydia didn't much like the thought of sneaking through the huge empty building alone in the dark.

Carefully she made her way up a flight of stairs to a completely gutted open space. She stood on the top step for a few minutes squinting into the dark. At the far end were what appeared to be wooden crates. As it was downstairs, construction equipment lay all over the room. Trying to maneuver her way through this mess in the dark would be crazy. Besides, the doors had been locked, right? Alec had had to break in. No one else could possibly be in the building.

She remained where she was for what seemed like a reasonable amount of time to have scouted out the top floor, then made her way back downstairs and checked out a few rooms off the large main floor. As far as she could tell, the place was empty, except for the four LDs.

When she came back to the main room, Hollis handed her one of the four gas masks Lydia had brought from home and a can of gasoline.

Gabriel put on his mask, then stared in amusement at the others. He wondered if he looked as ridiculous as everyone else. Of course he did. They resembled a bunch of two-legged anteaters, for God's sake. He laughed inside the mask, but the sound came out muffled and hollow.

They each carried a can of gasoline to one of the four corners of the main room, then began pouring it over the floor, working their way toward the back door. After they'd covered the floor with gasoline, they brought in the propane tanks.

While the others set the tanks up in different parts of the room and opened them up, letting the propane gas into the air, Hollis plugged in an old lamp he'd found at the local flea market. It had no lampshade or bulb.

"Make sure that thing is turned off," Alec called to him from across the room.

"It's off," Hollis assured him. Then he went out to the truck and came back with a lightbulb. He smacked it against the concrete floor, shattering it just enough to break the outside glass but not damage the filament, then screwed it into the socket.

"It's done," he called to the others in a husky whisper. "Let's get out of here."

They headed for the truck, slipping off the gas masks as they ran.

Lydia trailed behind the others like a sleepwalker, wondering if maybe the gas had somehow affected her mind, had somehow penetrated the gas mask. Because she felt suddenly light-headed, unable to sustain a single thought. Fragments of words floated in and out of her head, but she couldn't seem to seize on any of them. If she hadn't known better, she would have thought someone had slipped her some kind of weird drug. Here she was, climbing into the truck, sitting on Gabriel's lap, like those other times, only nothing felt real. Not even Gabriel.

Unlike Lydia's, Gabriel's heart was pounding so fast he was sure he would die before this night was over. Well, so what if he did? At least it would be on the most intense, exciting night of his life. He put his arms around Lydia and pulled her close, felt her heat in a way he'd never experienced it before. He knew he was sending her the wrong message, knew he'd have to deal with it later, but right now none of that seemed to matter.

Alec drove the truck out of the parking lot and over to the other side of the road, several hundred yards from the plant. "You don't want to be sitting in the truck when this thing blows," Hollis said. "You won't get a good view. This is something you don't want to miss." He looked at the others and grinned, showing all his crooked teeth. "You're going to remember this for the rest of your lives."

They climbed out of the pickup and stood on the shoulder. Lydia thought Hollis seemed almost gleeful. Not a word she would have ever associated with Hollis Feeney.

"Come on," Hollis said, leading them up a wooded slope. "You'll want a better view than this."

When they were all positioned at the top of the hill, Hollis pulled the remote control from his pocket. "It's time," he said, his voice shifting from glee to a kind of awed reverence. He imagined his father inside the building, feet and hands tied to two sawhorses, his body sagging between them like an old hammock. It made the moment all the sweeter as Hollis pressed his finger—hard—on the button that turned on the lamp. He could almost see the single spark from the filament of the broken bulb shooting into the room full of fumes, the gas fumes hovering above the floor, the lighter propane fumes, which had by now reached the ceiling, all of it, igniting in a split second. Then suddenly a deafening roar, like the rumble of an exploding volcano, filled his ears.

Flames blasted through dozens of windows all at once, leaping wildly into the black sky.

The four watched the roaring fire engulf the entire building. No one spoke, until finally Hollis threw his arms forward in a grand gesture and shouted, "Magnificent!"

"Fucking awesome!" Alec yelled, punching the air with his fist.

"Jesus," Gabriel whispered.

Lydia said nothing, only looked on in horror at what they had done, thinking how lucky they were that no houses were nearby.

When she could collect her thoughts, she said, "We'd better get out of here. People will have heard the explosion; they'll be able to see the sky lit up miles from here. The fire department's probably already on its way."

The four of them headed down the hill to the truck. But Gabriel didn't get in the cab. Instead he grabbed Lydia, swung her up in the air, and lifted her into the back of Alec's pickup. Then he climbed in beside her. From there they watched the stars swallowed by the thick black smoke that ballooned above the wreckage. He knew Lydia would get the wrong idea, but he couldn't seem to help himself.

Hollis lingered a few minutes more, barely moving, keeping his eyes on his creation, until Alec finally had to grab him by the arm and pull him toward the pickup.

"You owe us big-time," Lydia called to Hollis, just as Gabriel reached over and pulled her down beside him, silencing her with his mouth. And Lydia, sensing that everything she had dreamed about herself and Gabriel was about to come true, let herself fall into the dream utterly and completely.

But Hollis never heard her ultimatum. He rolled down the window as Alec pulled away from the shoulder, peeling off down the road, and stuck his head out so he could watch the flames shooting into the night sky until the very last second when they turned off the main road.

nineteen

When Gabriel got to homeroom on Thursday morning, everyone was talking about the plant explosion. It had made the front page of the largest paper in New Jersey.

He was still feeling so high he could barely contain himself. It was almost impossible to maintain a serious expression while everyone around him speculated on how the explosion had come about. But somehow he managed.

Only a few times, as he passed Hollis or Lydia in the hall, did he shift his eyes their way and share a tiny smile. They would have high-fived each other if they'd dared. Later in the day, he allowed himself to almost imperceptibly rap his knuckles on Lydia's desk as he passed by her in English. Lydia's heart fluttered in response, secure in the knowledge—after what they'd shared the previous night—that he was now hers.

It wasn't until he sat down at his desk and caught the puzzled look on Gem's face that he became uncomfortable. But he'd been cruising on high ever since the explosion, and he wasn't about to lose the rush. So he gave her a grin and a nod, then started cracking jokes and talking incessantly in class until Mr. Sorensen suggested he might want to spend some time in detention, thinking about "the value of silence." Gabriel didn't care. He planned to ride this wild wave until it finally crashed on shore. And crash it did.

On Friday morning the headlines told a grimmer tale. During the investigation the police had found the body of a man in the charred rubble of the tool and die plant. According to the reporter, people who lived in the area not far from the plant claimed vagrants sometimes slept in the abandoned building. They were pretty certain it was another homeless person, probably passed out on drugs or alcohol. Otherwise he would have heard the perpetrators in the building. But now, since the plant was under renovation, and the doors locked, no one could figure out how the man had gotten in.

The article concluded by saying the body of the victim was too badly burned to make an immediate identification, but the investigation would continue.

Victim? Gabriel sat in homeroom staring at the headlines of one of several copies of the paper circulating among the students. He shook his head in disbelief. There wasn't supposed to be any victim. Unless you counted Hollis's father, who lost out on a deal with Digitech. But even he wasn't really a victim, Gabriel decided, because he'd probably collect a bundle from his insurance company.

Sweat stung his face and neck like prickly pins. How could this have happened? Lydia had checked the building, hadn't she? She'd said it was empty. He sat, almost motionless, until the bell rang. But he never went to his next class. Instead he headed for the parking lot and his car. If he stayed in school, he would see Hollis and Lydia. It was unavoidable. And right now he didn't think he could bear to look at their faces.

He did not go to the camp that night. He doubted he would ever be able to go to the camp again, or even pass by it. But it was equally difficult spending the night alone in his room. He tried going down to the great room and watching TV. When that didn't distract him, he surfed the Net for a while, not paying much attention to where each click of the mouse took him. He skipped dinner, certain he wouldn't be able to eat anything anyway.

All evening he'd been fighting back the urge to call Gem, knowing that if she ever learned the truth about him, about the LDs, she would turn away from him in disgust. But some instinct, some deep need to be with her, continued to gnaw at him until he could no longer stand it. And when he thought about spending another torturous night like this one on the following evening, he gave in and called her.

A week earlier, after Lydia had come up to Gabriel's

desk and asked him to meet her in the parking lot, Gem had decided to stay after school to work in the chem lab on a project that wasn't due for three more weeks. From the window she had a perfect view of the parking lot. The last thing she had wanted to do was head for her truck while Lydia and Gabriel were still out there talking. So she turned on the Bunsen burner and waited.

What she hadn't been expecting was for Gabriel to unlock his car door and for Lydia to climb into the passenger seat. If they'd exchanged any words at all, it couldn't have been more than a sentence or two. As they drove off, Gem had slid off the stool and walked over to the window, watching the dried leaves whip around the tires as the car tore down the driveway and onto the main road. It was crazy, she knew, but she was afraid that once the car was out of sight, she might never see Gabriel again.

So no one was more surprised than Gem when Gabriel called her a week later to ask her to a movie Saturday night. As if nothing had changed, as if Lydia hadn't entered the picture.

NOVEMBER 14

Even with Gabriel's arm around her shoulder, as they sat in the back row of the movie theater, Gem knew something wasn't right. He was a million miles away.

When she reached for a handful of popcorn from the large tub sitting on Gabriel's lap, she realized he wasn't even watching the movie but was staring at the back of the seat in front of him. She leaned into him, her mouth warm on his ear. "Is something wrong?"

Her question caught him off guard. He thought she was totally into the movie. But Gem had pretty much nailed it. Something *was* wrong. Terribly, horribly wrong. He couldn't get the LDs out of his head. It was Saturday night. They would be at the camp, wondering where he was. Maybe they would think he'd dropped out. He began to worry about what they would do if he tried to leave the group. Because he'd been thinking of doing just that from the first moment he'd learned about the man who died in the explosion.

He shook his head and lifted Gem's hand. "Not a thing," he said.

He hadn't been paying attention to the movie. But now, suddenly, buildings were exploding all over the place. Gabriel stopped breathing. What the hell kind of movie was this anyway? He stared in horror at the screen. Somehow the scene in front of him seemed more real than what had happened on Wednesday night.

Gabriel stabbed his thumb and forefinger into his eyes, pressing hard. The flashing explosions, the bright light, made his eyes burn. They felt hot and dry. The soundtrack pounded in his head. His heart was racing full speed. And then it was over. The houselights came on, and Gem was standing over him, watching. She couldn't step into the aisle until he either stood up or moved his legs.

As he rose from his seat, Gabriel was momentarily shaken by how wobbly his legs felt. It was as if he'd been the one up there on the screen sweating out whether his plan would work or whether thousands of lives would be lost. And now that the movie was over, the relief had made him weak, unsteady on his feet.

When they reached the lobby, Gem gently ran her hand along his arm. "If you're not feeling well, we can call it a night. It's okay."

Gabriel leaned back against the edge of the concession stand. "So I guess you're not up for pizza then?"

Gem blinked a few times, confused. "Sure, if you want. I just thought—"

"Don't think. Forget the thinking." He kissed her lightly on the mouth, then put his arm around her waist and propelled her through the door.

They stopped at the Pizza Hut down the road. Gabriel ordered a large pie with everything but anchovies on one half and plain cheese—at Gem's request—on the other.

The place was mobbed after the movie, and it took forever for their waitress, in her tidy black and white uniform, hair caught up in a large claw clip, to bring them their sodas. Gem had been working up her courage, and when the sodas finally came, she asked Gabriel, as she had the first day he walked into the camp store, why his family had moved to Knollwood Township. She was hoping by now he trusted her enough to tell her.

Gabriel stared out the window at the cars coming and going in the parking lot. He'd never talked about Ben or about his family with Gem or anyone else since he'd moved here, and wasn't sure he wanted to. He was afraid of how she might judge them. In his old school there had actually been kids he'd hung around with who started making themselves scarce after Ben was murdered. Like they thought some of the Harts' bad luck might rub off on them or something. Or maybe they were embarrassed because they didn't know how to act around him, what to say. He had no idea what their problem was. But he knew they saw him differently, even if he never fully understood why. He didn't want Gem to see him the way those other kids had, whatever it was they saw.

Still, he needed to talk about what had happened to him, to his whole family. He missed his sessions with Dr. Cortes. And Gem looked so open, so willing to deal with whatever he told her.

"It's not easy for me to talk about," he said.

Gem stripped the paper from her straw and slipped the straw into her soda. "I just wondered, that's all. You don't have to tell me."

"It's not that I don't want to."

"Did something happen to your family? Back in New York?"

"Yes." He paused and drew a deep breath. "Something . . . really terrible. I had a brother. Ben. He was murdered."

Gem's eyes grew large, then softened. She looked around the crowded restaurant. "I know a place where we can go to talk." She stood up, taking her soda with her. "Let's get the pizza to go, okay?"

Without another word, Gabriel followed her up to the checkout counter.

A few minutes later they were heading east on Route 80, the smell of the pizza filling the car from the backseat.

Gem gave him directions to a scenic overlook that was closed to the public after dark. But they didn't let that stop them. First they ignored the No U-turn sign, cutting across a dirt road through the median and pulling onto the westbound lane; then they ignored the Closed sign at the scenic overlook, driving straight up to the parking lot. Not another car was in sight.

Gem pointed to the stone-based picnic tables on the lawn. The lawn sloped downward toward the scenic view, barely visible in the dark. "We could sit at one of those."

"It's warmer in the car," Gabriel said. "Let's stay here."

Gem turned toward him, leaning the back of her head against the window. What little moonlight there was poured through the windshield, illuminating one side of her face. "Do you want to tell me what happened?"

And he did. He told her about the call from the police, and how the family had raced down to the hospital only to discover it was too late. How he'd never had a chance to say goodbye to his brother. And how the stupid cops still hadn't found the scumbags who'd done it. He told her about his father, and how he'd wanted to get them all out of the city, as if it was the only place in the world where people got murdered. He told her about his mother, and how she hardly came to the house anymore even on weekends, and how he was pretty sure his parents were going to get divorced. He told her about Dr. Cortes, and how he missed talking to her. He told her everything. Everything, that is, except about the LDs. And by the time he was finished, their pizza was ice cold and their sodas were warm.

The first thing Lydia noticed was that the lawn had been mowed. All around the abandoned building the wild raspberry brambles and the sumac shrubs had been hacked away, exposing the mildewed latticework around the porch. The shrubs circling the pond were also gone. Only some of the larger cedar trees remained. The tall brown grass was neat and trimmed. She saw all this before the moonlight, glinting off the white paint of the For Sale sign, caught her attention, sending her heart into a tailspin.

Someone, Kate Hennessey probably, was selling the Boy Scout camp. Lydia's refuge. Lydia thought she might just sit right down in the middle of the road and cry. And if a car came along and didn't see her there, if it ran right over her, all the better. This was the last place left to her on earth. And even though it had already been invaded by the others, she had learned to adjust; she'd had to.

But this—she rested her hand on the For Sale sign as if the sheer force of her will could make it vanish—this would mean the end of everything. If someone bought the place and moved in, it would be over. But maybe that was how it should end, she thought. Maybe this was justice of sorts. She had come here tonight, hoping to find

Gabriel alone, hoping he would pull her into his lap and tell her the nightmare they were caught up in wasn't real at all. That no one had died in the explosion Wednesday night. It was all a mistake.

But when she opened the door, she found only Hollis and Alec inside.

"She's selling our place right out from under us," Alec shouted at her as Lydia lowered herself onto the mildewed couch and let her head flop against the back.

"It's hardly *our* place," Hollis reminded him. He was sitting in the Adirondack chair eating french fries. An open bag from McDonald's sat on the arm of the chair. "Not legally, anyway."

Lydia wondered how he had the stomach for food. She hadn't eaten a thing for two days. Not since she'd read about the death of the homeless man. "What about squatters' rights?" she said, wondering why they were talking about something so inane. Shouldn't they be talking about what they'd do, what they'd say to the police, if they were caught?

Hollis pinned a french fry between his crooked teeth and snickered. "That only works with public land. Kate Hennessey *owns* this place. We're trespassers. Remember?" He looked down at his watch. "Where's Gabe? It's after ten."

"Maybe he decided not to come." Lydia stared into the fire. If this was true, she thought, if Gabriel was dropping out, then maybe he had decided to end things with her, too. And the thought of losing Gabriel might have brought her to her knees right that moment, right in front of the others, if a dull thud hadn't startled her. Hollis's McDonald's bag was lying on the floor; a half-eaten hamburger poked out of the top. He snapped up the bag and set it in his lap. The look on his face shocked Lydia. There was something hard and cold about the thin set of his lips. She had never seen Hollis angry before.

"Gabe belongs here with us." Hollis got to his feet and tossed the McDonald's bag into the fireplace. Frantic embers flew into the air.

"You want to know where the Hart Man is?" Alec looked straight at Lydia, ignoring Hollis. "He's with Gem." The expression on Lydia's face was so pitiful, Alec almost felt bad about breaking the news to her. Except that his own pain overshadowed any sympathy he might have had.

"How do you know that?" she said.

"Because I saw them driving out of the campgrounds together."

Alec Stryker was the biggest loser Lydia knew. He made her skin crawl at times. So it seemed odd they should suddenly have something in common: their smashed hopes for love, and the two people responsible— Gem and Gabriel.

Alec narrowed his eyes and bared his teeth. He swung around to face Hollis. "What do you want to bet the Hart Man told Gem about us hanging out here? That's why

Kate Hennessey's decided to sell the place. To get rid of us."

"I warned you about this," Hollis said to Alec. "We need to know how much he's told her about us."

"Maybe he hasn't told her anything," Lydia said, coming to Gabriel's defense. "I don't think he'd do that. And besides, there are less drastic ways to keep us off her property. All Kate Hennessey has to do is alert the police to trespassers. Obviously she hasn't done that."

"Let's hope you're right," Hollis said to Lydia.

"And if she's not?" Alec looked over at Hollis, his expression daring Hollis to name Gabriel's fate.

But Hollis wasn't playing. "Let's wait and see. We've got more important things to worry about right now. We'll see what he does, see if he's with us or not. Then we'll decide what to do."

Hollis and Alec left early. Lydia had tried to get them to talk about the dead man, but Alec kept changing the subject. Even worse, Hollis had acted as if it was no big deal. "He was a nobody," he told Lydia.

For a while, after the others had gone, Lydia sat in the Adirondack chair watching the dying embers, drinking vodka, and thinking about Gabriel and Gem until she couldn't stand it for another second.

Ten minutes later she was headed up the road toward the Stony Brook Campgrounds. The road was barely visible, and it was almost impossible to see beyond a few feet into the woods on either side. They were that thick with hemlocks and cedars.

Lydia stuffed her hands into the pockets of her peacoat, wishing she'd brought gloves. The wind had picked up and the temperature had dropped to almost freezing.

Standing in front of the campgrounds store a short time later, Lydia knew exactly why she had come here. She needed to see for herself, to see if Gabriel's car was parked by Gem's house. It wasn't. At least as far as she could tell, standing there by the store. Maybe they weren't back yet.

She thought about waiting awhile longer and was looking for someplace to sit, someplace where she wouldn't be noticed, when she spotted the Lakota Wolf sign and remembered the preserve. It had been here almost two years, but she'd never visited it. Now she felt a strong desire to see the animals, although it was obvious everything was closed. Probably for the whole winter season.

By now the tips of her ears burned with the cold. It would be a long walk back home. But she had come this far. And the wolves had to be around here somewhere. She noticed a dirt road at the end of the parking lot that led into the woods and began walking toward it.

She half expected the wolves to begin howling as she approached, setting off all kinds of alarms, warning Kate Hennessey a prowler was on her turf. So Lydia was startled when she found herself only a few feet away from an eight-foot chain-link fence with nothing but the sound of owls hooting in the distance.

Inside the fenced area it was wooded and dark. Lydia squinted through the links, trying to see movement, any movement that might indicate the wolves were nearby. She'd read somewhere that the preserve was twenty acres. Twenty acres was a lot of space. The pack might be all the way at the other end, sleeping. Did wolves sleep at night, she wondered, or did they run?

She was still standing there, deciding whether to walk along the fenced-in area, looking for them, when the dim light from a banana-shaped moon suddenly glinted off two large yellow eyes. There, beneath a large oak, stood an enormous wolf, its dark gray fur shimmering silver on the tips. It was watching her. Lydia's heart began to race. She looked away, knowing if she looked it in the eye, it would think she was challenging it.

Then slowly, in the most nonthreatening way she could manage, she lowered herself to the ground and sat cross-legged, facing slightly away from the animal. Every so often she shifted her eyes enough to catch a glimpse of it. It was sitting now, its jaw partly open, its tongue hanging like a limp sock over huge pointed teeth.

And there they stayed, Lydia on one side of the fence, the wolf on the other, until Lydia couldn't be sure which of them was caged in. "You must hate it in there," she whispered. "Why don't you just jump the fence? Why don't you escape?" Maybe the wolf didn't realize it could lunge for the top and probably pull itself over.

After a while the wolf lay down, but it kept its head up, still watching Lydia. That was how they stayed until frost began to form on the ground around her and her legs started to feel numb. She rose slowly, not wanting to startle the wolf. But it wasn't necessary, because the wolf never made the slightest sound to give her away.

twenty

Ever since the plant explosion, the Shadow People had haunted Gabriel without mercy. No matter how many times during the night he awoke, they were always there beside his bed. Watching. Waiting.

Sometimes he lay trembling, his sheets soaked with sweat, trying to force himself fully awake. It was the only way to make them disappear. Other times he hid his face in his pillow.

Tonight he wondered if maybe the dark shadowy forms weren't manifestations of his nightmares after all. Maybe they were the spirits of people who were sleeping, spirits that left the body and traveled in the night, returning right before dawn. People in some cultures believed that, believed the soul left the body at night to wander the earth. He'd read about it somewhere.

A sudden wave of fear, so powerful it made him nauseous, washed over him. He rolled on his side, pulling his pillow over his head. What if these were the dark souls of the four teens who had killed Ben? What if now they had come for him?

Gabriel spent Monday trying to dodge Hollis and Lydia, although with Lydia in his English class, that wasn't easy. But it turned out he didn't have to worry because she never even looked his way as he passed her desk to get to his seat. It was Hollis who finally caught up with him in the boys' room. He checked the stalls to make sure the two of them were alone. Then he turned to Gabriel. "Where were you Saturday night?"

"That's my business."

"Is it?" Hollis kept his cold gray eyes leveled at Gabriel. "I'd say in light of recent developments, it's *our* business, wouldn't you? Whatever any of us says or does could have major repercussions for the others."

Gabriel's throat was so tight he wasn't sure he could speak. But he finally managed to say, "You know what, Hollis? I don't owe you any explanations. Think what you want." He turned to leave.

"We're meeting Friday night," Hollis said as Gabriel slammed the door open with the side of his fist. "I'd be there if I was you."

Ever since he'd learned about the body found in the charred ruins of the plant, Gabriel had been trying to figure a way out of this whole mess, short of going to the police. If he did, he would have to own up to his part in all of it, including the break-in at True Value, the plant explosion, and the death of the homeless man. All he had to do was imagine the look on his father's face—a look that said for the thousandth time the wrong son had been murdered—and any thought he had of going to the cops went right out the window. His parents had been through enough. One son murdered, the other a criminal. It would be too much for them.

He tried to think of ways he could get out of going to the camp. But if Hollis and Alec thought he was backing out, there was no telling what they'd do. That much he'd understood from the menacing tone in Hollis's voice in the boys' room on Monday. Until that moment, Gabriel had been living with the illusion he could walk away from the LDs whenever he wanted. Now he saw that wasn't going to happen, because they would never let it happen. So he braced himself for the worst and headed down to the camp.

He stood outside staring at the For Sale sign for a full five minutes after he arrived. At first he was relieved. If Kate Hennessey sold this place, then it was over. The LDs had nowhere to go, no other hangout, nothing to keep them together. For those first few minutes, before he stepped inside the building, Gabriel was actually hopeful.

Hollis and Alec sat hunched over the table whispering when Gabriel came through the door. They turned to look at him. Alec was wearing his snide grin. "I think what we need to do is see if Gabe and Lydia are willing to pass the final part of the initiation." Alec glanced over at Hollis, who was sitting across from him, then turned his attention to Lydia to see if she was paying attention.

Lydia sat in the Adirondack chair, her feet propped up on the milk crate, legs crossed at the ankles. She stared at the ceiling, her eyes on the patterns of flickering light from the candle and the fireplace. They waited for her response.

When she didn't so much as blink in their direction, Hollis said, "I think you'll like this"—he paused for emphasis—"assignment, Lydia. Alec and I have decided we should pay the Hennesseys a little visit."

Gabriel frowned. "The Hennesseys? Why?" He pulled out a log stump and sat down with the others.

"Because," Hollis said, "this last part of the initiation is a test. It's a test of loyalty."

Gabriel felt as if he was being sealed up inside a small brick room, chained to the wall, watching Hollis and Alec laying brick upon brick, cutting off his air. "You don't need to test my loyalty," he told Hollis. "I think I've already done enough to prove myself."

"It's not up to you," Hollis said. "Haven't you figured that out yet?"

Alec let loose a laugh that sounded almost like a growl. Even Hollis gave him a strange look.

"I'm not asking you to do anything big," Hollis said. "Nothing you haven't already done. Just some more of your mindless vandalism."

"I thought that sort of stuff insulted your superior intelligence," Gabriel said.

"This is different. First, we have a plan. It's been well thought out. Second, we have a motive. We want to send a message to someone."

Gabriel's blood turned to ice. If Hollis's plan involved the Hennesseys, he wanted no part of it. And he said as much.

"So you've decided to side with the enemy," Hollis said. His voice was flat and even. The statement carried no emotion, just observation. As if it didn't matter to him one way or the other what Gabriel chose to do.

"I just don't see the purpose in it. Kate Hennessey doesn't even know we hang out here." He jerked his thumb over his shoulder in the direction of the door. "I saw the sign out front. She's not selling the place to spite us, if that's what this is all about. She probably needs the money."

"Man, are you dense or what?" Alec raked the fingers of both hands through his hair as if he was going to tear it out by the roots. "Don't you get it? Hollis wants you to *choose*."

Gabriel shook his head. He was totally confused. "Choose what?"

"Not what," Lydia said from across the room. "Who. He wants you to choose between the Lords of Destruction and Gem Hennessey."

The wood smoke from the fireplace stung Gabriel's eyes and nose. He rubbed them, stalling. He couldn't believe what he was hearing. These people were supposed to be his friends, weren't they? They'd been hanging out together for two and a half months. How could they even ask something like this of him? Gem was another part of his life, a different part. She had nothing to do with these people. He thought about the time they'd spent together on Saturday night, how she'd listened to him for hours in the cold car, and how he'd felt so close to her, so close he'd almost whispered between kisses that as soon as the weather was warm again, he wanted to go skinny-dipping in the pond with her. And that was when Gabriel finally understood the "someone" the LDs were sending the message to wasn't Kate Hennessey at all. The message was for him.

"Look," he said. "I told you, Gem doesn't even know about us. You think I'm going to tell her? I'm not stupid, for Christ's sake. She's a separate part of my life. Leave her out of this."

"You don't have a life apart from us," Hollis informed him. It was a simple statement of fact. There was no malice in it.

Gabriel stared over at Alec's black T-shirt with a skull and crossbones on the front as Alec reached inside his leather jacket and pulled something shiny from the inside pocket. It took Gabriel a few seconds to realize Alec was holding a small .22-caliber semiautomatic. "Well, hey, if that's how you feel about Gem, then you probably don't want anything to happen to her," he said.

Gabriel's legs felt as if they'd turned to water. He wasn't sure he could stand up even if he wanted to. He knew Alec had no problem killing animals just for the hell of it. Now he wondered if it was possible for him to kill a person. Of course it was. They'd already done it, hadn't they? Images of the charred corpse of some poor homeless man flooded his mind.

He needed to get out of there. He needed to be able to think straight. And he couldn't do that with Alec sitting there tossing that stupid gun from one hand to the other like some baseball.

"How many more people are you planning to kill?" Gabriel asked, looking from Hollis to Alec.

"More?" Hollis pretended to be genuinely puzzled.

"The homeless man? Or maybe you don't read the newspapers," Gabriel said.

"That disgusting bum? You're not serious? You can't possibly consider that a crime." Hollis let out a quick snort, which barely resembled a laugh. "To my way of thinking, we've done the world a service. Cleaned up some of its trash."

Gabriel looked over at Alec's grinning face and felt a wave of nausea wash over him. Neither Alec nor Hollis had so much as an ounce of remorse for what they'd done. That much was obvious from the looks on their faces.

"He was a human being," Lydia said. Three heads turned to her in surprise. They'd more or less forgotten she was there. She looked straight at Gabriel. "And it's my fault he's dead. It was too dark to see anything, and the whole upstairs was a mess of construction stuff." Tears glistened on the tips of her lashes. "I thought nobody could possibly be up there, since the doors had been locked." She briskly swatted her hand across her cheek. "It was too dark . . . the place was a mess . . . I . . ."

"So you didn't bother to check it out, right?" Hollis nodded at her like a parent who had managed to worm the truth out of a lying child. Then he looked over at Gabriel. "You see, it isn't even our fault. It's Lydia's."

"Bullshit." Gabriel was on his feet, bending over so that his face was only inches from Hollis's. "We all set the explosion that killed that guy." He heard a loud *click-click* and turned his head to face the barrel of a gun.

"Down, boy," Alec told him.

Slowly Gabriel lowered himself back onto the tree stump. He had only now begun to realize with horror that Alec and Hollis had already decided what would happen if he and Lydia didn't play their game. Obviously they saw no other recourse. Gabriel and Lydia knew too much. They were wild cards. Either they went along, or Alec would do more than threaten to pull the trigger.

Gabriel couldn't bring himself to look at the other two.

He stared across the room at Lydia instead. But she turned away, staring into the fire. He wondered how they had managed to get her to buy into their latest plan. Because it was obvious she wasn't making waves. Had they pulled the gun on her before he'd gotten there? Or was she going along with it because she wanted to? Did she know he'd gone out with Gem? Was she angry with him? He hadn't even considered that possibility until now. He thought about the night of the explosion, the two of them in the back of Alec's truck. Maybe this was payback. Maybe the three of them had cooked up this whole scheme. Or worse, maybe it was all Lydia's idea. He didn't want to believe she would do such a thing. No. She wouldn't. They would have had to coerce her, just as they were doing to him. "If I do this, whatever you've got planned, you'll leave Gem alone?"

"Absolutely," Hollis said. "Once you've proved your loyalty to the Lords of Destruction, passed the final step of initiation, then you're home free."

Gabriel wanted to believe Hollis, but he didn't miss the twitch at the corner of Alec's mouth, as if he was fighting back a grin. "What's the plan?"

"Like Hollis said, nothing big." Alec slipped the gun back into his jacket pocket. "Kate Hennessey told me she and Gem were going down to Virginia this weekend. For some funeral. Kate's cousin or something. They won't be back until late Sunday night. She's put me in charge. All we're going to do is mess up the camp store a little. Kind of like leaving a calling card. Except I'm also going to be your witness. After you guys are gone, I'll call the police. I'm going to say I heard all this racket and found this gang of kids breaking into the store, and I'll say I went after them, but they got away. When Kate Hennessey gets back, I'll give her the same bullshit story. Me and Hollis figured the whole thing out. It's ironclad."

The smirk on Hollis's face when he looked over at Alec told Gabriel that Alec hadn't figured anything out. This was Hollis's plan.

Gabriel was trying to remember what Gem had told him earlier that day in English. His head had been so messed up over the death of the homeless man and with trying to avoid Hollis and Lydia that he hadn't paid much attention to anything else. He seemed to recall her saying something about not being able to see him this weekend, something about leaving tonight to go somewhere with her aunt. He'd forgotten he'd even asked her out for Saturday night. It was just as well she couldn't go. At least Gem and her aunt wouldn't be around when the LDs trashed the store. He wondered what Gem would think if she knew he was about to trash the store to save her life. She'd probably expect him to come up with an alternative plan that didn't involve either her life or the store. He wished like hell he could do that, and maybe—if there was enough time—he would. But right now the LDs were waiting for his answer.

"When?" Gabriel could barely get the word out of his mouth.

"Saturday night," Hollis said. "We'll meet here at ten."

Alec had been walking in the woods for over an hour. After the others had left the camp, he couldn't bring himself to go back to his trailer, although he wasn't sure why. Instead he had left his truck in the cinder-block garage, taken two cans of beer from the cooler in the back, stuffed them in the pockets of his jacket, and climbed the trail behind the garage leading up past crumbling outhouses and beyond, into the deep recesses of the forest. It did not matter if the sliver of a waxing moon barely lit the trail, he knew these woods better than the inside of his trailer.

Every so often he slipped his fingers into the inside pocket of his jacket, running them gently over the handgun. He felt exposed, almost naked out here without either a shotgun or rifle. Handguns didn't belong here. But this was all he had with him, and he wasn't about to go back to the trailer to exchange it for a rifle.

The last time he'd felt this restless was the night before the plant explosion. Every nerve in his body had felt raw and vulnerable, just as they did now. And that was when he realized it was the waiting, the knowing, the anticipation that was doing this to him. He wasn't used to doing things that had been carefully planned out. All of his criminal offenses over the years had been spontaneous acts, like the night he and Gabe and Lydia had trashed the train station.

But the plan to blow up the plant, and now to break into Kate Hennessey's store, that was something else. Alec thought about the store trashing as he wandered along the trail, finally coming to the deer stand he liked to sit in. Frost stung his fingers as he climbed up to the platform, opened a beer, and leaned back against the tree.

Old Lady Hennessey had been decent to him. So why, when Hollis decided to use her and Gem as part of this stupid initiation thing, had Alec agreed? Never even thought twice about it. And tonight he'd played right along with Hollis, enjoying the smell of Gabriel's mounting fear. He never once questioned it earlier when Hollis told him to bring the .22 with him. But he'd known instinctively just the right time to reveal it. Hollis had been counting on that. Alec could see that now. Not that it hadn't been worth it to see Gabriel squirm as Alec swung the gun from hand to hand a few inches from his face.

Still, some small part of him wished he hadn't mentioned to Hollis about Kate Hennessey and Gem heading down to Virginia for the weekend. It had given Hollis ideas. Alec knew this whole initiation thing wasn't really about the Hennesseys. It was about Hollis making sure he could control Gabriel. He was a loose cannon as long as Gem was in his life, and they all knew it.

The boards beneath his backside were cold. He could feel the chill right through his jeans. He drained the last of the beer, then pulled the other can from his pocket.

And there was something else bothering him: the dead man. Alec couldn't seem to get this crazy image out of his head. A picture of some poor out-of-work sap, wearing everything he owned, curled up in some cluttered corner of the plant trying to sleep it off—the booze, whatever.

What disturbed him most was the man's face. Whenever he imagined it, it resembled an older, unshaven version of his own.

What had Hollis said? That they'd done the world a favor? Cleaned up some of its trash? He realized now how much it bothered him that Hollis never so much as winced when he learned what they had all done, never showed any signs that he even gave a damn.

Alec stared down at the can of beer in his hand. Maybe the bum wasn't God's gift to humanity, but hell, just because you screwed up, just because you never figured out how to get it right, you didn't deserve to die like that, did you? Jeez, he himself was only one seedy trailer and a part-time job away from being on the streets. And the truth was, he couldn't shake the chilling thought that he could just as easily have been the man sleeping in the plant the night of the explosion—the man Hollis called trash.

Lydia moved up closer to the metal fence and leaned her shoulder against it. The largest of the wolves, the one with the darkest coat, the one Gem had named Dark Cloud—although Lydia had no idea the wolves even had names—came up to the other side of the fence and lay down only inches away. They were that close.

Two of the other wolves joined the large one, lying near him. Several feet away, the others maintained a respectful distance. Lydia felt their presence in a way she had never experienced human contact and pressed her side nearer to the fence, leaning her head against the cold metal, trying to get closer to the wolves. She had come to visit them every night that week.

Tonight, after she'd left the Boy Scout camp, after she had watched Alec and Hollis threaten Gabriel with that stupid gun, she'd thought of heading out to Route 80 and taking her chances. She'd hitch a ride. Get as far away from this place as she could. Instead she had come here.

Now, in the quiet of the preserve, her mind began to grow calm. That was what happened when she came to this place. And each time she left feeling just a little stronger, with a better sense of who she was, although she had no idea why that should be.

Sometimes surprising thoughts came as she sat with the wolves. Tonight, for the first time, she realized that for all her desire to leave home, for all the plans she'd been making, she didn't really want to go at all. What she really wanted was for her family to be *different*. Or at least the way they had been before they'd moved to this place. She needed them, wanted to be a part of them, but not as they were now. It was too difficult, too painful. Like living with strangers.

All this time she had been kidding herself about leaving home. Just the thought of it sent her heart pounding with anxiety. She wasn't ready to be on her own, and she knew it. All this time she had believed she was waiting for her eighteenth birthday, because then her father couldn't send the cops after her, couldn't force her to come back home. She didn't doubt for a minute he would do just that. But that wasn't the reason she had waited. It was because she was scared. And here, with the soft contented breathing of the wolves only inches away, she could finally admit that to herself. In the wild these wolves could have run twenty miles every night if they chose. Now they had only twenty small acres. Yet they didn't seem to mind.

But tonight she thought of more than her family, she thought of Gem and her aunt, and the homeless man she'd killed. She thought of Gabriel and the LDs, and grew sickened at the thought of all they had done. This was not who she was or who she wanted to be. And yet she had just sat back and let everything unfold as if it was the most natural course in the world for her. Now she had no idea how to stop the rush of events that had been set in motion over the past two months. The situation had taken on a life of its own. She knew only that she had to find a way out, a way to sever ties with all of them, even Gabriel.

twenty-one

In the predawn hours of Saturday, Gem Hennessey dreamed that thin slivers of glass were embedded in her tongue. They rose from the fleshy surface like crystal stalagmites. Gabriel was there. He was trying to gently remove one of the delicate shards, but the pain was unbearable and Gem shoved him away from her. When he put his hand on her arm to comfort her, she realized with acute agony that her skin—every inch of her body—was covered with tiny fragments of glass. The slightest touch from Gabriel sent her into a kind of dizzying whirlwind of excruciating pain.

When she finally opened her eyes and realized it was almost dawn, realized with relief the nightmare was behind her, she was surprised to find she could still feel the sting—like dozens of paper cuts—on her tongue and marveled at how she could feel such intense physical pain—pain that was not even real—in a dream.

A few hours later Gem was loading the back of the pickup with meat for the wolves when Alec Stryker showed up. He stood a few feet from the truck, his mouth gaping in surprise, before blurting out, "You're supposed to be in Virginia."

Gem gasped, stunned by Alec's sudden appearance. Her breath came in short, sharp spurts, small white clouds on the frosty morning air. It took her a few minutes to realize Alec was here because Aunt Kate had asked him to look after the wolves.

"I didn't go. I have a major history test on Monday, so Aunt Kate said I didn't have to." As soon as the words left her mouth, she regretted them. Now he knew she was here alone. A tremor of fear traveled through her, and she tightened her grip on the side of the truck. The last thing she needed was for Alec to see she was afraid of him. She would have to take precautions later, be especially careful to lock doors and windows, keep the cordless phone with her, ready to dial 911 if it came to that. She hoped it wouldn't. But at least she had the presence of mind to recognize she could be in danger. Better to be ready for it than to let it catch you off guard.

Once she'd worked through her own fear, she noticed Alec seemed confused, even a little upset. He wasn't his usual obnoxious, swaggering self. Instead, he took a step back and said, "So, I guess you can handle the wolves, right?"

Gem gave him a curt nod. "I can take care of them.

And myself." She had no idea why she'd added that, but the moment she said those two words, Alec's whole expression changed. She should have known better, known he would take those words as a challenge.

"Sure you can," he said, a sneer sliding across his face. "You think you got it all under control." He slid his hands into the pockets of his leather jacket and moved toward her with slow calculated steps, until there was less than two feet between them. "I suppose you think you got Gabe Hart under control too."

Gem swallowed hard. "What's that supposed to mean?"

"It means you better keep your eye on the Hart Man. He's not exactly your one-woman sort of guy."

"Why should I believe anything you tell me?" Gem said. She could feel the cold metal of the truck through her hooded sweater as she pressed her body closer to it.

"Yeah, you're right. Why should you?" Alec squinted up at the trees where the morning sun had just begun to spread over the tops of the bare branches like melted butter. "Okay, so don't believe me. Ask Lydia Misurella."

Gem surprised them both by throwing the full weight of her body forward and shoving Alec out of the way with both hands. Stunned, he stood watching as she climbed into the driver's seat and slammed the door.

"You're a real jerk, you know that? A real loser," she shouted down at him before heading the truck toward the preserve.

Alec stood there in the driveway, listening to the sound of his father's voice, yelling *Colonel Shitforbrains* over and over and over. "You're dead," he shouted after the receding pickup. "You hear me! *Dead*."

The first thing Gem did when she got back to the house was call Gabriel to tell him there had been a change of plans. He'd asked her out for Saturday night before he found out she was going to Virginia, and now she wanted him to know she could go after all. That was, if he still wanted to go out. And if he couldn't? Her fingers stumbled on the pushbuttons, forcing her to redial his number. Maybe he'd made other plans. Plans with Lydia Misurella. Either way she was determined to call.

She couldn't bring herself to believe there was someone else. Especially after the night he'd told her about his family. About Ben. They'd been so close that night.

The phone rang four times before the answering machine clicked on. Gem was caught off guard. She had expected to find someone at home. It was only nine-thirty.

For a few awkward seconds she stumbled through a brief message, hoping like crazy he'd call her back.

If Gabriel hadn't left the house early that morning, determined not to come back until it was time to head down to the camp, he might have gotten Gem's message. But that never happened.

The night before, his mother had surprised them all by showing up at the door, briefcase in hand. It was the first weekend she'd been home in almost a month.

"She wants us to go out for breakfast at the Knollwood

Inn tomorrow," Shelby told him. "Like a family. Then we're supposed to go for a hike up in Worthington State Forest or something." She snickered. Her breath floated in white clouds on the night air. "Boy, that's rich. Do you believe her? We don't see her for almost a month, and she thinks she can waltz in here and whip us all into the Brady Bunch or something."

Shelby had her arms perched on the partially open window of Gabriel's car, staring in at him from the outside.

Gabriel had escaped to his car less than fifteen minutes after his mother came through the front door. He was still reeling from the shock. If he didn't get his head clear, he wouldn't be able to behave like his old self around her. Because right now he was so far from the Gabriel Hart who used to live on West 86th Street, he was sure his own mother wouldn't recognize him.

Desperate, he'd left the house, climbed into his car, and rolled down the window to let in the frosty night air. A few minutes later Shelby showed up.

"What the hell's she doing here?" Gabriel said, more to himself than his sister.

But Shelby answered anyway. "They're worried about me."

"What?" He turned to look at her. She was grinning, obviously pleased.

"Yeah, first Dad tried to have this talk with me about what was going on in my life. I think the hair and nose ring freaked him out."

"And?"

She shrugged. "And what? You think I'm going to tell him stuff? About my friends?" Shelby grabbed the edge of the rolled-down window with both hands and rocked herself back and forth. "I told him I was fine. School was fine. My friends were fine. We were *all* fine. Just fine."

"Obviously he didn't believe you." Gabriel stared through the windshield at the closed garage door. The automatic light at the end of the roof shone down on the two of them like a spotlight.

"I think Mom came home to rescue me. If I play this right, maybe I can get her to stay around for a while. Maybe even work things out with Dad."

Gabriel had to laugh at that. Shelby the optimist. She just never gave up.

The next morning he left the house before anyone was out of bed. He couldn't bear spending the whole day with his family. It was too hard right now. His life was too messed up. Instead he left a note on the kitchen table.

I think you should spend the day alone with Shelby. She's the one who needs help. I'm fine. See you later.

Gabe

"Gem didn't go with her aunt," Alec said. "We'll have to call it off."

Hollis shifted his stocky bulk. The sides of his buttocks

hung over the edge of the small chair next to the foldout Formica-top table. They were in Alec's trailer. It was almost time to head down to the Boy Scout camp.

"There's no reason to call it off. She'll be up at the house."

"If she catches us, she'll call the cops."

"She won't know about any of this till it's over and we're long gone," Hollis assured him.

"If the Hart Man finds out, he won't go along with it." Alec was already on his third beer. He had laid out four lines of white powder on the Formica table top and snorted two of them. Then he held out another rolled piece of paper to Hollis, who screwed up his face in a disgusted grimace.

"Keep that up and you'll pass out before we even get into the store."

"I can handle it," Alec told him. The truth was, he was hoping to get to that blissful moment when he wouldn't care what they did. Once he was there, none of this would matter. All he had to make sure of was not to get caught, which meant he had to pace himself, be careful not to go over the edge. The cocaine would keep him running on autopilot. He'd need to be wired up but alert. Because if they caught him this time, they would probably put him in the state prison for the next twenty years, maybe longer if they figured in a manslaughter charge.

After the third line disappeared into his nose, he didn't even blink when Hollis said, "I hope you don't think this is just another train station trashing."

Alec sat across from him, staring. He had no idea what Hollis was talking about.

"Gabe and Lydia think that's what this is about. Petty vandalism."

"It's not?"

"Of course not. It's another dress rehearsal."

Alec reached for his can of beer and took a long swallow. "Dress rehearsal? For what? You're full of shit, Hollis, you know that?"

"For our next project," Hollis said, ignoring Alec's last statement. "We need more practice working as a team. Not that the four of us didn't pull off a masterpiece at the tool and die plant." He shifted his weight, trying to fit on the chair. "But we'll be taking on bigger, more dangerous jobs. We need to set an example for the others. We'll need to impress them with our skills if we expect to win them over."

"What others?" Alec shook his head. His nose was running, a thick white paste, but he didn't seem to notice.

Hollis looked away, trying to stifle a gag. He ignored Alec's question.

"You'll never get them to go along with another of your schemes," Alec told him. "Especially not the Hart Man. A little vandalism maybe, but nothing else. That's why he didn't show up at the camp the weekend after he found out about that bum. He doesn't have the stomach for it."

"Fine. We don't need them. There will be others. There will *always* be others."

"Man, I don't know what you're talking about."

"Then lay off the beer," Hollis warned. "Because I'll be giving orders. If you don't understand enough to follow them, you could screw this whole thing up." He had already decided there were some things it was best not to share with Alec. Alec was a loose cannon tonight. Anyone could see that.

Hollis got up from the small chair and pulled the box of guns from beneath Alec's bed. "I'll take care of the important things, like making sure we don't leave behind any evidence. You just need to keep an eye on the others, see that they're outside when I give the signal."

He grabbed the .22 semiautomatic handgun from the box under the bed and handed it to a bewildered Alec. "This is your department," he said.

Alec opened his mouth to ask what he was talking about, but Hollis was already out the door.

Lydia waited at the end of Gabriel's driveway. They were supposed to be at the camp in twenty minutes. She had never walked there with him before. Everyone had always shown up whenever they felt like it. Tonight she didn't want to go alone; she didn't want to be alone at all.

She sat down on a decaying log from a fallen oak tree. Gabriel's car wasn't in the driveway, and it occurred to her he might have already driven down to the camp. But she doubted it. He never took his car.

Ever since they had found out about the homeless man dying in the explosion, Gabriel had barely spoken to her.

It was as if he wanted to put that night and everything associated with it out of his mind. And that would include those passionate few moments he'd spent with Lydia in the back of Alec's truck.

It was over. Lydia could see that now. She had lost him. He would never be able to look at her without knowing she could have prevented that poor man's death if she'd done what she was told. Followed orders. And maybe she deserved to lose him. It was her punishment. Still, she wanted to be alone with him one last time. Even if he didn't say a single word to her. So she waited.

Just as she was about to give up and head to the camp alone, Gabriel's Toyota came around the curve in the road. The headlights flashed in Lydia's face and she put her hand up to cover her eyes. When she looked again, she saw the car parked at the end of the driveway in front of her and Gabriel heading in her direction.

"I thought we could walk to the camp together." She said this before Gabriel had a chance to ask what she was doing there.

Gabriel stood awkwardly shifting his weight from one foot to the other. He glanced down at his watch, squinting in the dark. He felt drained. He wasn't at all sure what to do next. He wondered if he should say something to her about the night of the explosion when he'd lifted her into the back of Alec's truck. Except, it wasn't like it was anything serious. They'd been having a little fun, that was all, working off some of that adrenaline high. He wondered if he owed her an explanation, wondered if he should tell her about Gem. And if he did, what would he say? That they'd gone out? Would probably continue going out? He didn't know himself what the future held for him and Gem, for any of them. So in the end, it was easier to explain nothing. "Yeah, I guess we'd better go."

He left the car where it was and began walking. Lydia fell into line beside him. If he was glad of her company, he didn't show it.

As they approached the camp, Lydia stared up at the front porch wishing she had a brick with her. This place had been her refuge for four years. Yet in that moment she would have gladly shattered every window in the place. And she might have done just that if they hadn't been boarded up.

Suddenly she was reminded of the night they trashed the train station, Gabriel gleefully hurling rocks through the windows. She looked over at him now. He was staring down at his hiking boots, lost in thought. Hardly some hardened criminal. Certainly not somebody who should be hanging out with the likes of Alec Stryker. She had an uncontrollable urge to put her hand on his, to say, "We don't have to do this. Let's run away. Put a whole continent between us and the Lords of Destruction, between us and our crazy families."

But she said none of this. She knew they were in danger, especially Gabriel. And since she was planning to tell the LDs she was leaving them after tonight, wanted no part of them anymore, she knew her own life was equally in danger. If she had ever had any doubts about what Alec

and Hollis were capable of, they had been laid to rest the
night before when Alec had pulled the .22 from inside his
jacket and put it to Gabriel's head.

NOVEMBER 21 . . . 10:19 P.M.

The four of them piled into the front seat of Alec's
truck, just as they had done on so many other nights.
Lydia sat on Gabriel's lap, as always. Her longing for him
was as intense as ever, and there wasn't one single thing
she could do about it. Gabriel's mind was light-years
away. Only the husk of his body sat beneath her.

Over and over, as the truck bumped into the potholes
on the narrow road to the Stony Brook Campgrounds,
she told herself all she had to do was not get caught. Then
just stay away from Hollis and Alec from now on. She
would tell them on the way back she was getting out, that
she'd left a letter behind telling everything. If they hurt
her, the letter, which she'd locked away in a metal box in
her closet—although she would never tell them this—
would be found and opened. It would be over for all of
them.

Hollis shifted his weight and Gabriel felt himself
squeezed up against the door. The three boys were shoulder to shoulder. There was no room to breathe.

He was glad Hollis had spent only a few minutes brief-
ing them, telling them to smash and destroy anything they
found in the store, but not to take anything with them
because it could be discovered later and used as evidence.

As soon as they were done, Alec would call the police from the pay phone, which stood partially enclosed in a metal box on a post outside the barn, and report he'd just chased off a bunch of kids he'd caught trashing the camp store. By then the other three would be long gone. That was more or less the gist of it.

At least that was the plan as Alec, Gabriel, and Lydia understood it. None of them had seen Hollis come up behind the pickup and slip a large red plastic can beneath the tarp in the back of the truck before climbing into the cab with the others.

Alec pulled up next to his trailer and parked in the empty campsite next to his. He was pumped. He wanted to hurt someone. No. Not *someone*. Gem Hennessey. He hadn't been able to think about anything else since their encounter that morning. He hopped down from the driver's seat and came around to the passenger side. "Let's do some major damage," he told the others.

Neither Gabriel nor Lydia so much as glanced his way. They were standing beside the front of the pickup waiting for Hollis, who unzipped his jacket and stepped onto the running board but didn't climb down. For a few minutes he stood there gazing in the direction of the store. From here they could see only the back of the building.

Lydia noticed that beneath his unzipped jacket Hollis wore his ridiculous Darth Vader T-shirt. She remembered the first night he had come to the Boy Scout camp, dressed in that same shirt, and how hard she'd had to work to keep from laughing right in his face. Only now she knew better, knew Hollis was more than just some computer geek, some boy genius. Something was seriously wrong with him. Which was why she couldn't even muster up a cynical smile when she spotted the ominous black helmet mask on his shirt.

Gabriel narrowed his eyes, trying to see in the dark. The sliver of moon offered barely a hint of light. The others looked like dark figures against a fuzzy gray background. For one terrifying moment he thought the Shadow People had stepped right out of his dream into the night. Or maybe he and the other LDs were really home sleeping soundly in their beds, maybe these were their souls, wandering the earth at night. The thought sent icy waves washing over him. He began to shiver in the frosty air. He couldn't seem to make his teeth stop chattering.

Hollis, who had been watching him, cleared his throat to get everyone's attention, then swept his arms outward in the grand gesture of a head ringmaster. "It's show time," he announced, then leaped from the running board and led the others toward their appointed destination.

. . . 11:03 P.M.

Gabriel, his body numb with cold and fear, stood across from the store. He still couldn't believe Hollis had actually set fire to the place. But there was no other way this could have happened. He could smell the gasoline. This was no accident. And the look on Hollis's face confirmed Gabriel's worst fears.

Gabriel looked up at the dark sky and clenched his fists. His eyes burned from the smoke; tears cut streaks through the soot on his face. How could he have been so stupid? How could he have ever listened to Hollis? How could he have not seen this coming?

Lydia grabbed him by the arm, tugging frantically. "The wolves," she shouted. "I have to do something. I can't let the fire get to them."

Before he could stop her, she took off through the woods in the direction of the preserve, where a few minutes later the police would find her furiously trying to smash the padlock of the main gate with a large rock.

Alec stood a few feet away, swaying slightly, unsteady on his feet. Hollis never ceased to amaze him. Here he'd thought tonight was going to be just another routine trashing. He should have known Hollis would never settle for something so ordinary, so unimaginative, not after the tool and die plant. He looked over at Hollis, who was standing almost shoulder to shoulder with him. He didn't know whether to salute him or bolt for the woods and never look back.

Gem, who had been running toward them, suddenly stopped halfway across the dirt road. Her arms dropped to her sides. Until that moment she had thought Gabriel and the others were there to help, believed Gabriel had gotten the phone message she'd left him that morning and was coming to see her, believed Alec had come running from his trailer at the first sign of smoke, believed Hollis, who was always hanging around Alec, had simply followed him. And that was when she saw Lydia Misurella, spotted her just as she turned and ran down the road toward the preserve.

With a jolt of horror, Gem realized Lydia was with Gabriel, realized these were the people responsible for the fire. She could see it in Alec's guilty expression and in Hollis's delighted one. When she turned to Gabriel, the pain on his face terrified her.

The fire behind Gem was moving closer to the propane tank by the minute. The flames cast her in shadow. They played tricks with Gabriel's eyes, because the next time he looked at her face, it was no longer Gem he saw, but Ben. Ben, staring back at him in alarm. Gabriel's blood turned to ice, goose bumps ran along his arms and legs. "Ben," he whispered.

In that moment he understood. Somehow he had become one of *them,* one of the thugs on the subway. He saw himself standing in front of Ben, watching as the others plunged their knives into his ribs, his stomach, his heart. Watching as Ben, terrified for his life, gasped in outrage and fury.

He had to stop this. He couldn't let them kill Ben. Only, as he took a step forward, it was once again Gem's face looking back at him.

Somewhere in the distance sirens screamed into the night. Fire trucks? Gem must have called them as soon as she spotted the flames. He hoped so. They had to put the fire out before it reached the propane tank and spread to the barn, and to the house, before it spread to the wolf preserve, before it destroyed everything in sight.

Hollis grabbed Alec by the arm. "Kill her," he ordered, jerking his double chin toward Gem. "Now." His voice was without emotion. Cold and even. As if he were asking Alec to do something reasonable, like turn right at the stop sign.

Gabriel stared at them in disbelief.

Alec froze. He wanted to kill her. Didn't he? Kill her for the pain she'd caused him. Kill her for not wanting him, for calling him a loser. So why couldn't he move?

"She's a witness," Hollis reminded him. "Kill her or we all end up in prison."

But Alec just stood there. And in that split second, Hollis jammed his hand inside Alec's jacket and grabbed the .22 just as Gabriel lunged toward Gem, just as Hollis aimed straight for her heart, just as Alec reached for the gun, just as Hollis pulled the trigger.

Gabriel saw only Gem's face, never felt the bullet enter his body, wasn't aware he'd been shot until his knees suddenly collapsed under him and he found himself lying on the ground as an unbearable searing pain tore through his back.

The sirens were screaming in his head now. A blur of people circled above him, like large whirling insects, shouting orders and spinning in all directions. But he couldn't make out a word anyone said. He couldn't seem to make his eyes focus. There was only the burning pain, and finally, the plunge into darkness.

When Gabriel opened his eyes again, he was in the hospital in a tangle of IV lines. Shelby stood next to his bed wearing her Chicago Bulls T-shirt. Gabriel had no idea what day it was.

The minute he blinked and Shelby was sure he was awake, she said, "You just couldn't stand that I was getting all the attention, could you!"

In that moment he didn't know whether to laugh or cry, so he did both. The voice was the old Shelby, his annoying kid sister from West 86th Street. And for just the tiniest flicker of time, he was back home again.

EPILOGUE

In mid-February, when everyone on Thorn Hill Road had hunkered down for the winter and snow had completely buried the smaller azalea bushes, the trial of the four Lords of Destruction was just getting under way at the county courthouse. Gem Hennessey shoveled snow from the front steps and sidewalk, making a path to the barn to get the truck so she could plow her way down to the preserve to feed the wolves. She refused to show up at the courthouse until the day she was needed to testify. She hated that she would have to testify against someone who had come between her and a bullet, who had saved her life, and whom in spite of everything, she still loved.

Gabriel Hart was the first to stand trial. Like Alec Stryker and Lydia Misurella, he would be tried as an adult. Robert and Margaret Hart did not miss a single day of the proceedings. They sat in the second row. Gabriel was glad his back was to them most of the time. He couldn't bear the look in their eyes. They forgave him. He could see it in their faces. And he didn't deserve it. Even worse, they blamed themselves. He could see that, too. He wished they'd just stay home and stop trying to be so supportive.

Lydia was more fortunate. Although some might have thought otherwise. She wouldn't have to feel her parents' eyes on her back all through her trial. Arthur Misurella had put his house up for sale three days after his daughter's arrest and moved what remained of his family to a remote area of Montana where flocks of unruly reporters couldn't swoop down on them every time they tried to set foot outside the front door, where they could hide with their stockpiled supplies, their gas masks, their guns, ready for whatever disaster struck, where, with any luck at all, no one—especially the press—would ever find them.

All four of the LDs faced charges of vandalism, breaking and entering, theft, arson, conspiracy to destroy the tool and die plant, and manslaughter. Alec Stryker, who already had an extensive juvenile record, also faced charges of weapons and drug possession after the police searched his trailer, and the additional charge of possession of a weapon with intent to kill.

Only Hollis Feeney, age fifteen, would be tried as a juvenile. The people of Knollwood knew of his remarkable intelligence, knew he had already been accepted at M.I.T.